Confessions of a
Virgin
Sex Columnist!

Confessions of a Virgin Sex Columnist!

KAY MARIE

All Works By Kay Marie

Confessions
Confessions of a Virgin Sex Columnist!
Confessions of an Undercover Girlfriend!

All Works Writing As Kaitlyn Davis

Midnight Fire (4 Books)
A YA Paranormal Romance

Once Upon A Curse (2+ Books)
A YA Dystopian Fairy Tale

A Dance of Dragons (3 Books, 4 Novellas)
A YA Epic Fantasy

To my family for their unconditional love,
my friends for their overwhelming support,
and my fans for their incredible enthusiasm.
Thank you from the bottom of my heart.

Confession 1

I'm a sex columnist. Okay, well, that's not really the confession. I'm sort of, kind of—I'm a virgin…sex columnist.

I'm having a panic attack.

Well, at least I think I'm having a panic attack. Rapidly beating heart that shows no sign of slowing? Yes. Inability to breathe resulting in the strangest sounds known to man escaping my lips? Yes. Fingers shaking so badly that it took three attempts to press my button on the elevator? Yup. Feeling totally and completely detached from my surroundings? Um, well, I'm standing in front of my apartment door with no recollection of the subway ride and ten minute walk that brought me here…so, yeah, that too.

Crap.

Definitely a panic attack.

"Bridget!" I call through the front door. She's my roommate, my best friend, and in this moment, my hopeful savior. But there's no answer.

"Bridget!" I call again, flinching at the high-pitched shriek.

Is that my voice?

Oh god, my throat is tightening. I can hardly breathe. Is my vision going too? I cannot pass out in the hallway with my keys still in my hands. What would my neighbors think? What if someone robs me? I'd be prime bait. What if—?

I shake my head. So not the time for that. I need to breathe. Just breathe and get the door open. Easy, right? I force my hand to still long enough to shove the key in the lock and jiggle the knob until finally it clicks. With one hard shove, the door swings open and I jump inside, falling back against the wood just as it slams shut.

I close my eyes.

I breathe.

I'm home, finally.

"Bridge, are you here?" My voice already sounds smoother, calmer. But my heart is still thumping painfully in my chest—this isn't over, not until I tell her the truth, not until I tell someone the truth.

I'm a farce.

A complete and utter farce.

An answering grunt comes from the kitchen. She must be eating, but that's okay because that means she won't be able to say anything until I'm done. Or she'll spit her food out all over the floor that I washed yesterday.

Worth the risk.

"Bridge, I need to tell you something and I don't want you to say anything until I'm done because I'm freaking out and if I don't say it now I'm not sure I ever will. Okay?"

Silence. Good, she agrees.

Opening my eyes, I push off the door and spare a glance at our galley kitchen as I make my way to our small living room. The fridge is open, and she must be behind it because I hear someone rummaging through the food. But that's good, because it'll be easier to say this without having to look at her. After all, I've been lying to her for the better part of three years. Lying—to my best friend!

And here comes the hyperventilating again.

"Okay, so," I start as I fall onto the couch and bury my head between my knees. I read somewhere that it's calming, but it doesn't seem to be doing much now. Maybe I'm supposed to close my eyes? But all that does is start a somewhat nauseating dizzy spell. Open, definitely keeping them open. I start to count the lines in the hardwood floor below my feet—why haven't we bought a carpet yet? We've lived here for three months already.

I shake my head—so not the point.

Just spit it out.

"Okay, Bridge, well the thing is, I told you something a few years ago because I was embarrassed and at the time it seemed like no big deal, like something I would fib about for a little while, but soon enough it would be true and it wouldn't really be a fib anymore. Anyway something happened today and I need your help, but in order to get your help, I need to tell you the truth about this fib, that grew into a lie, that exploded into this constant gnawing at the back of my mind because I was keeping a secret from my best friend. Does that make sense?"

I shake my head miserably.

Of course it doesn't. I don't even understand myself.

I take a deep breath and try again.

"Okay, never mind. Don't answer that. The thing is, do you remember that first weekend home after freshman year? We were at that party—I think Stephanie hosted it? Doesn't matter, but we were at that party and no one had hung out since Christmas, and someone suggested we play that game, *Never Have I Ever.* You know, the one where you start with five fingers up and if you've done whatever someone says they never have, you need to put one finger down, and the first person who's done five of the things loses? Well, do you remember we were playing and at some point I was the only one with all five fingers up because obviously I was the mega-prude of the group? And then someone gave me this challenging stare and they said, 'never have I ever been a virgin?' And everyone looked at me, and everyone put down a finger, and everyone was waiting, and judging, and wondering if I really truly got through freshman year at college without having sex? And I was a little drunk, so I gave into peer pressure and put my finger down? And then I looked at you and your eyes were about as wide as dinner plates and you grabbed my arm and hauled me away demanding all of the details, and then I gave you all of those details? Well...what I'm trying to say is none of those details were true. Are true. Have ever been true."

Spit. It. Out.

Now.

I take a deep breath and pick my head back up from between my knees, talking to the room now instead of the

4

floor, feeling more than a little lightheaded. The rummaging in the kitchen has gone utterly silent. I have Bridget's full attention.

"So, the thing is, Bridge…I'm, well…" I take a deep breath. "I'm a virgin."

As soon as I say the word, all breath leaves my body and I collapse against the cushions.

Virgin.

I'm a twenty-two year old virgin.

The word fills the air around me. Expanding. Growing. Suddenly, I can't see anything else in our tiny Manhattan apartment except the word *virgin* in big, Broadway-sized flashing lights. That song from *Les Misérables* starts playing in the back of my mind—how does it go again? On my own… something, something… all alone. And in each flicker of those flashing lights is a snapshot of my past self, asking how in the world I ended up here, confessing to my best friend that I've lied to her for years.

When male ballerinas start leaping across my mental stage production in black leotards, I close my eyes, shaking my head and expelling the picture to force my mind back to the reality of the situation.

"Bridge?" I ask, sighing. "Please say something. I think I'm losing my mind."

Still nothing. I lick my lips. Might as well just get it all out of the way now.

"And the whole virgin thing isn't everything, it's not even what I'm freaking out about. I got a job, finally. After three months of interning for the newspaper, they offered me a job. Only, it's not for the arts and literature section where I've been working—it's for the lifestyle section. Me—the one with no fashion sense, limited social skills, and a T-shirt that reads 'books 4 life.' And that's not even the best part—they want me, the virgin English major, to write a column. A dating column. Okay, a sex column..."

My throat is starting to close, and it's highly possible that hives are breaking out along my neck. I can't help but reach a few fingers up to rub at my skin as I try to swallow, fighting the chalky feeling on my tongue.

"And, I sort of said yes."

Well, there it is. I said it. Now do you see?

I'm a farce. A fake. In my utter desperation to land a job with a full-time salary (and benefits!), I created the worst situation any hopeful journalist could ever be in. I'm going to be a reporter who can't report the truth. A liar. A sham. They'll run me out of the city before my first column is ever printed. I'll never work in newsprint again. I'll be forced to return home a failure, begging to oversee the editing of my high school gazette, surrounded by stories about football games and science projects for my entire life, praying for a student-teacher affair or drinking scandal to liven things up. I'll—

"Um, Skye?"

Did I say any of that tirade out loud?

"Yeah?" I call back, pulled from my paranoia.

But then my heart stops.

I stop.

Time stops.

Even my brain stops...for a second anyway.

The full sound of that voice carries to my ears and it's not Bridget's. It's not even a woman's. And I recognize it.

I'd recognize it anywhere.

"Ollie?" I squeak.

"Skye…" he answers. Is it possible for someone's voice to be smiling?

But I don't believe it—I don't want to believe it. I ask again, hoping for a different answer. "Oliver McDonough?"

"Skylar Quinn?" he asks, and I actually hear a snicker this time.

I stand up and run to the kitchen, tripping over my own feet and throwing my arms against the wall to keep from falling over as I soar through the opening.

And there he is.

Six foot two. Sinfully dark brown hair. Brilliantly turquoise eyes.

Oliver McDonough.

Bridget's older brother.

And the last person I ever wanted to see in the world.

Confession 2

I am sort of in love with Oliver McDonough—no wait, I was! No, I am. No, I was. Am? Was? Crap!

I haven't seen him in four years. In fact, I've actively been avoiding him for four years. And now he's here. In my kitchen. Drinking my milk—from the gallon no less! Did I mention he looks completely and utterly gorgeous? Maybe even hotter than I remembered…if that's even possible…

Okay, I'm veering off track.

"Ollie?" I gasp. "What are? Why are? When?" Great reporting, Skye… I swallow, stilling my racing words and form an actual sentence. "What are you doing here?"

"Here in New York or here in your kitchen?"

Here pretending to be your sister while I confess my deepest secrets? Here looking at me with that infuriating half-smirk smile thing you do? Here pretending like the last time we saw each other wasn't the most horrifying moment in my entire life?

I don't say any of that, of course. Instead, I shrug. "Um, both? Either?"

He puts the milk back in the fridge and closes the door. I can't help but notice a toned bicep below the sleeve of his white T-shirt—the same bicep I used to fantasize about during chemistry class, the bicep of the most popular guy in the school, the bicep of the quarterback. Six years since he stopped playing football, and crap, he still looks good.

"I'm guessing Bridget forgot to mention that I got offered a job at a new steakhouse opening on Fifth Ave? As a sous-chef?"

I shake my head. "Nope, she didn't mention anything."

He licks his lips, biting back a wider grin. "So she probably also didn't tell you I accepted the offer and just moved to New York?"

"I don't recall ever hearing about that…" I trail off as my palms begin to sweat. I have a very, very bad idea where this is going.

Astronomically bad.

Iceberg straight ahead bad.

Ollie's eyes brighten a shade, crystal aqua, clearer than any Caribbean water I've ever seen. He leans against the wall, crossing his arms, looking at me through a side-glance, the hint of a dimple on his cheek. My rapid heartbeat has nothing to do with my panic attack anymore.

Oh yeah, this is bad.

"So," he says, lifting his brows and looking at me apologetically, "she probably also didn't tell you that I'm moving in for a few weeks until I can find my own place?"

"You're the new roommate?" I shout and then clamp my hands over my lips. I've said enough to him tonight—too much. In fact, all of that information is crashing back down around me.

Ollie is my new roommate.

Ollie knows I'm a virgin.

Ollie knows I'm a sex columnist.

And right now, Ollie is looking at me like he can read every panicked thought racing through my mind, like he's thinking about the same thing I'm thinking about—the night that we are to never ever speak of. The reason I've been avoiding him. The thing I never want to even think about again.

He reaches out his hand, fingers an inch from mine, but I step back, crossing my arms and cocking my hip, pretending to be cool, to be unfazed. I've gotten really great at pretending not to care about him.

"Awesome," I murmur, trying to smother the crack in my voice.

Where is Bridget? Because I am going to kill her.

Ollie opens his mouth, looking at me with distinctly downcast eyes, and I know what's coming next. The apology—the one I don't want to hear. The one he never said then, and the one I won't let him say now.

But I'm saved by the sound of jingling keys right outside our door. Bridget's home.

I glance back at Ollie, but his eyes aren't on me anymore. They've retreated.

"Skye, are you okay? The doorman was worried, he said—Ollie!" Bridget cries. All I see is the bright red blur of her hair as she rushes past me and flings herself into his open arms. "You're here! Why didn't you tell me you were coming today?"

Ollie wraps his arms around her waist, picking his little sister up in a bear hug. "I wanted to surprise you."

He holds her for a second longer, but Bridget squirms to get out of his arms and turns to me, eyes wide, mouth open in horror. "I forgot to tell you Ollie was moving in. Shit. I'm so sorry, Skye. But it's perfect, right? Just like old times, the three amigos together again."

Before you ask, no, Bridget has no idea what happened with Ollie. And yes, I'm the worst friend ever. But she can never—and I mean never—find out. So I force a smile and lighten my tone, panic attack completely forgotten. "Just like old times."

Bridget looks at me, then looks at Ollie, and back to me—grin growing wider with each glance. Her excitement is palpable, and the last thing I want to do is ruin it. "This is going to be perfect," she finally says and leans against the counter.

"Perfect." Ollie grins.

"Perfect." I grimace.

"Good, we all agree. Now I can get out of these shoes," Bridget says, reaching down to rip off her high heels, and I can't help but smile. My best friend, the one I saw only in paint-stain-covered outfits for the majority of my life, has become posh. Black heels. Stockings. Tight-fitting dress. A blazer. Her hair is even pulled back in a not-at-all messy bun. Well, at least it was until she just started ripping out the bobby pins, letting her curls fly free.

11

"We just got a new artist at the gallery," Bridget continues, still removing pins from her hair, "and you would love her, Skye. The opening is next week, and I want both of you to come."

"Okay." I shrug, trying to ignore the fact that Ollie is looking at me. Staring at me. A flush warms my cheeks and suddenly I'm hot. Like, burning hot. Sweating. Pull it together, Skye. I squirm. It's not like he has freaking laser beams in his eyes! But he might as well...

My eyes start to shift closer and closer to meeting his gaze. But at the exact moment I almost break and sneak a peek, his eyes shift and I can breathe again.

"Sorry, sis, I'm guessing the opening will be during prime dinner hours. But I can meet you out after for celebratory drinks?"

"Okay." Bridge sighs and opens the fridge, grabbing a bag of carrots to munch on.

"So, Skye had something she wanted to tell you before," Ollie drawls.

This time I can't help it, my eyes immediately find his, narrowing in the best angry look I can muster. All it does is deepen the humor in his expression. And in that moment, I know he knows—knows that I've completely lost my nerve. Now that I made the confession once—you know, the virgin sex columnist thing—I'm not sure I can do it again. Especially with Bridget so happy, and so excited. I really don't think I can handle her being mad at me, not now, not while I'm emotionally traumatized by Ollie's surprise return to my life. Now more than ever, I need my best friend.

Alarm bells go off in my head.

Retreat!

Retreat!

I step back, swallowing. "No, it's nothing we can't talk about later. I'll, um, just let you guys catch up. I'm wiped anyway."

Ollie won't release me so easily though—of that I'm sure. Ever since we were kids, he's never let me get away with anything. Ever. One time I stole three of Bridget's peanut butter cups on Halloween night—I mean, they're the best candy, let's be real here—but anyway, he saw me take them. And the whole night, he kept thinking of ways to bring peanut butter into the conversation, grinning at my every flinch, laughing at how much it ate me up inside. Until finally, I confessed, practically shrieking and crying to Bridget. Her response? She gave me three more. But still, Ollie's always loved to push my buttons.

But not this time, buddy. Not this time.

So I'm not at all surprised when he casually says, "Not so fast, Skye."

"Yeah, come on. Hang out," Bridget joins in, pouting.

"No really, I—"

"Come on, Skye, weren't you just saying that you needed to tell Bridget something?"

I stare at him pointedly. "No."

"Oh, wait," Bridget says, turning to me with a curious gaze. "Yeah, the doorman was worried about you, he said you looked really panicked when you came home. I totally forgot about it when I saw Ollie here."

My avenue of escape is getting narrower by the second. In fact, I think the doorway behind me is literally shrinking. Does the room feel more cramped to anyone else? I swallow, heart pounding again. I'm too young to experience so much anxiety in one night.

Bridge sees the impending panic, but all it does is make her narrow her gaze, zeroing in on me. I need new friends—these people know me too well.

"I just had a bad day at work," I mumble and then look at the floor.

But crap, no! Why did I look at the floor? That's like the most obvious clue that someone is lying ever. Stupid, stupid mistake. Quickly I fix my gaze, throwing my head back up, but it's too late.

They saw.

"Well, it's really great actually," I say, mouth dry, pitch way too squeaky. "I got offered a full-time position working for the newspaper. They even want to give me my own little weekly column, nothing huge, but still, it's pretty exciting."

Before I even get the words out, Bridget is squealing and running to throw her arms around me. "I'm so happy for you, Skye! What are you writing about?"

"Um, nothing really, just same old, same old," I murmur into her hair, hoping Ollie won't hear. But over Bridget's shoulder, I meet his stare.

Big mistake. He's a balloon about to pop, his cheeks are so full with held in laughter.

I shake my head, motioning no.

He crosses his arms, shrugging just slightly.

I widen my gaze, pleading.

And then I wait.

And wait.

And—

"She's the new sex columnist," he says.

Jerk.

"What!" Bridget pulls back, blocking my view of her brother as shock fills the space between us. "I thought you were working in the arts and literature section, for the book review editors?"

"I was, but a new position opened up in the lifestyle section and they wanted me, so..."

"Hey," she chastises, sensing my self-conscious tone. "It's a real job as a real reporter in a real newspaper. You have your own column! This is amazing—we need to celebrate!"

Bridget releases me to rummage through the cabinets. I refuse to look anywhere but the floor. Is that a dust-bunny in the corner? I just cleaned. How is that even possible?

"Aha!" Bridget cries. "Tequila. Mix. We're making margaritas."

"You know," Ollie says in a hesitant voice, stretching his arms over his head. Terror floods my system as I wait for his next words. "I have to stop by the restaurant tomorrow morning."

I breathe a sigh of relief.

"So?" Bridget asks.

"Better make mine," he pauses, letting the words hang there for a moment. But he wouldn't... He won't... Oh, but he would. And he will. "A virgin."

No. I will not let him do this to me again.

But then I feel the heat of his gaze from across our shrinking kitchen. "You know the plane I flew today was really amazing. Outstanding snacks. Great service. But I can't remember the name of the company. It was Atlantic…something Atlantic…"

"Virgin Atlantic?" Bridget supplies as she searches for the blender. My stomach leaps into my chest, flipping like a freaking Olympic gymnast. "Yeah, I heard they were great."

"Yeah, they were playing this special on that singer, Madonna—you know, *the* Madonna?"

I refuse to give in.

Refuse.

I won't do it.

"And—"

"Okay, okay!" I scream. "Bridget, I'm a virgin. I'm a virgin sex columnist. I'm a total professional sham. Are you happy now, Ollie?"

"Would it be wrong to say yes?" he asks.

But Bridget drowns him out by dropping the blender. "But you told me you and John, freshman year…"

"I know," I say and bite my lip, "I know I did, but it wasn't true."

"You guys were together for three and a half years in college, why not?"

"Well, he comes from a really Christian family and he wanted to wait until marriage, and that was fine with me, and—"

"Didn't you guys break up because he cheated on you?"

"Yeah, well…John said the whole waiting until marriage rule only applied to people he could see himself marrying. Apparently, band girls had a different set of rules."

Ollie is having a coughing fit in the corner. I want to punch him.

"But why did you lie?"

"We were at that party freshman year, and everyone had all these crazy stories, and we were playing that annoying game, and I just felt like such a loser—"

"Well, that's stupid," Bridget interrupts, cutting off my words. "It's nothing to be ashamed of. I mean, please, you know my first time was nothing special. I would totally take it back if I could."

"Your what?" Ollie bellows from the corner.

"Please, Oliver." Bridget rolls her eyes. "Control yourself."

"Who was he? Was it that asshole Jimmy, god what was his last name? Jimmy… Jimmy…"

"Ew, no, it wasn't Jimmy." Bridget and I make eye contact, biting our lips, holding in barely containable mirth. Jimmy was one of Ollie's football teammates in high school and Bridget dated him for this exact purpose—to annoy her brother.

"Andrew? That creepy artist guy from college?"

Bridget and I remain absolutely silent, because, obviously we both know that yes, it was Andrew, that creepy artist guy from college. Truth be told, he was a fantastically gorgeous brooding painter Bridget dated during her freshman year—and yes, he was ridiculously sexy, and yes, he was a bit creepy. Bridget still blames the paint fumes for taking away her sanity—I blame the brood. The brood does things to girls, makes them crazy.

I should know.

Ollie can do a mean brood when he wants to.

"It was Andrew." He fumes at the realization. "That guy? Really? I'm going to kill him. You cried over him for all of Christmas break—there were tear stains on my wrapping paper!"

"I'm an artist," Bridget says with a shrug. "I feel things very deeply. It's a blessing and a curse."

"But—"

"Okay," Bridget shouts over him, grabbing her brother by the arms and pushing him out of the kitchen. "That's enough sharing for one evening. Ollie, go unpack. Skye and I need to talk."

He protests for a few more minutes, but even though Bridget is smaller than him (and not by much), her will is iron. I learned a long time ago to never try to out argue her. It's exhausting and in the end, pointless.

Which is why when she finally pushes her brother from the room and I can breathe easily again, I tell her the honest truth when she asks, "So, are you okay?"

"I don't know." And I don't. "How in the world am I supposed to write a sex column?"

"You'll be fine. You're a writer, embellish. And I'll help you—if you need any sordid details, don't hesitate to ask."

"As if I have to ask." I nudge her and raise my eyebrows.

"See what I mean? I've probably already given you enough material for your first few months of columns anyway." That just might be accurate. Bridget has a long trail of broken male hearts behind her. "Be excited, it's a new challenge. It's your dream job, sort of. Close enough anyway."

And she's right.

I'm getting paid to write. I have benefits. I have an office I go to every day and coworkers and a boss I'm sure I'll hate soon enough.

"I'm a journalist," I say, suddenly realizing for the first time in all of the fear that my dream has sort of come true. "I'm a real journalist."

And we do in fact drink those margaritas. Lots of them. Too many of them. But in the slight tequila haze, my anxiety drains away.

Everything will be fine.

My job.

My life.

Living with Ollie.

Everything will be fine.

And I truly believe it as Bridget and I say goodnight, and I stumble into my tiny room with a twin bed that's lofted over my dresser drawers. I'm happy as I struggle to launch myself onto the mattress, using my corner desk as a prop for my foot. I'm excited as I lie down for sleep, ready to dream about my first real day of work tomorrow morning.

But then a gentle knock sounds against my door.

And there's only one person it could be.

"Skye?" he whispers into the dark.

I could pretend to be asleep, but the alcohol has drowned out my neuroses, replacing them with curiosity. "What do you want, Ollie?"

"I just..." He sighs. My eyes are closed but I can perfectly imagine the way he's running his hand through his hair, messing it up—an unconscious move he doesn't even realize makes my heart melt. Makes every girl's heart melt.

"Don't apologize," I say. It's the closest reference I've made to talking about what happened. And he understands immediately. Understands that I don't want to talk about it— but I doubt he understands why. It's not because I'm embarrassed or hurt or vulnerable. It's because I can't bear to hear the regret in his voice. Because before he did what he did, before that moment, I had the best few minutes of my life. And I don't want to hear that he wishes they never happened.

"Okay, can I say one thing then?"

"Sure." I rollover, finally sitting up. Even in the dark, his eyes shine, glowing blue. Or maybe that's just the alcohol talking.

"It's just, I can tell you're nervous about the new job, but you shouldn't be, Skye. You're a great writer, and well..." He shrugs, scanning the room for a moment. There's a note of honesty in his tone that I rarely ever hear, that I've learned to recognize over the years. "You don't have to have sex to be sexy, Skye. Some people do, maybe, but not you. Never you."

And then he's gone, leaving me alone in the dark with my racing heart.

Confession 3

I'm hungover for my first day of work. Hungover! I'm the girl who used to show up to class ten minutes early so I could organize my pens before the lecture began. The girl who color-coordinated her notes. How did I end up here?

My head is pounding and there is only one thing I can think about, my sweet release from this misery—coffee. I've spent the past hour in a no food, no drink new employee orientation, and as I make my way to the elevator with the rest of the horde, all I can think is that this city is truly out to get me.

I passed five coffee shops on my way to work. Five! Could I stop and buy anything? No, of course not. Why you ask? Let me explain.

The plan this morning? Wake up early. Take a shower. Eat a nutritious breakfast. Brew a cup of coffee to go. Pick out a fabulous outfit. Leave the apartment with twenty minutes to spare just in case my commute went awry.

The reality? Roll out of bed after pressing the snooze button three times. Chug a gallon of water. Realize you now feel bloated and your headache hasn't dissipated at all. Splash water on your face when you look at the time and realize you are already five minutes late. Throw on the first thing you find. Grab a handful of pretzels from the open bag on the counter, quickly realize they're stale…eat them anyway. Run down the streets like a maniac until you get on the subway. Notice you are sweating profusely. Cry inside because you can't do anything about it.

Yup. That about explains my morning.

And now, I'm waiting on the elevator, creepily stalking the wondrously delicious smelling cups in other people's hands. A gentle waft of mocha teases my nose. Then a hint of vanilla. Is that caramel? I lean in.

Oh god, yes it is.

I want one.

So much.

When the door opens, I flinch, pulled from my cravings just in time. It's my floor.

"Excuse me," I mumble as I squeeze through people, wincing when the full force of the newsroom's fluorescent lighting hits my fragile eyes.

It's going to be a very long day.

My gaze slides longingly to my former home—a cubicle in the far corner of the room, barely visible behind the mounds of books piled around it. The shelf against the wall is overflowing, and I itch to open the packages resting unopened on the floor, wondering what new books were sent in for review. The seat is open, waiting for me. And I almost give in, running as fast as my feet will take me to where I know I belong.

But I can't.

Instead, I tear my eyes away and look in the opposite direction to the lifestyle section. The wall is covered in fashion spreads, the latest looks from the runway. And next to them is *the* bright red door—the one the rest of the women in the office talk about only in hushed voices—the fashion closet. There are office legends about what sorts of designer items wait behind that door. And the closer and closer I walk, the more and more I feel as though I've stepped into some sort of alternate newsroom universe. Everyone here is a woman. Everyone is uniquely beautiful. Perfect hair. Perfect makeup. And the clothes…

My breath catches, looking around. There are no muted colors to be found. I could be naked and be less out of place here than I am now in my navy suit and white button down shirt. I see neon yellow pants, an evergreen jacket complete with magenta cuffs, a bright blue dress under an oversized cable-knit sweater—and is that a jumpsuit? Prints and bold colors surround me. One girl is wearing a bright red and pink polka-dotted blouse paired with an orange beaded necklace—and it actually looks good!

I stop in the middle of the hallway, unable to move any closer as my eyes sink lower and lower, dread mounting. And yes. There they are. Heels. A sea of them. And not comfortable heels, as if such a thing really exists, but four-inch stilettos that give me vertigo just looking at them. The longer I stare the dizzier I become.

Will I have to wear those?

My toes ache, crying out—no, no, don't do that to us!

I lean against the wall, off-balance in my plain nude flats. Suddenly the room is spinning. Or am I spinning?

I need coffee.

No, I need a brain-transplant.

Okay, that might be a little drastic, but I need something and fast, because there is no way I'll ever be able to fit in here. Ever.

"Skylar?" a voice calls.

I swallow my terror and turn toward the sound. An office door is open, and waiting just inside is the woman I can only assume is my new boss.

"Good morning," I manage to say in a surprisingly strong voice.

"Skylar, come in." She stands, walking over to greet me. "How was orientation? Let's talk before I show you where your desk is."

All I can do is nod dumbly as she leads me inside.

"I'm Victoria Neives," she says after sitting down and folding her hands on top of her amazingly neat desk. "I first want to apologize for how unorthodox this whole situation was. Normally, we would have met at the interview and you would have had a few days to adjust to the whole idea of working here, but you came so highly recommended that I decided to act fast."

Ooh, highly recommended? I like the sound of that, so I sit up a little higher and smile. "Thank you."

"Don't thank me yet," she replies, leaning back in her chair, looking at me with a somewhat sorry expression.

Oh god, am I getting fired? After only an hour? That's

got to be a record or something. But they wouldn't. Not yet. Not before I've even had a chance.

"You've probably noticed that you're not the typical girl we might hire for the style section…"

Crap! I *am* getting fired.

I nod politely, trying to keep my jaw from dropping too noticeably while I search for a solution. Is it the heels? I'll wear the heels, I swear. Or the color thing? I can buy a neon blouse. Okay, maybe not neon exactly, but something not black or tan or navy. I can be fun. I am fun.

"But that's the exact reason we hired you. You're a normal, everyday girl. Not a socialite. Not a model. Not a fashionista. Just an average girl."

Okay…so I'm not fired.

I'm average, normal, and not at all unique or special in any way, but I'm not fired. That's good…right? In a backhanded, no I'm not going to go cry in the bathroom I swear, sort of way?

"The newspaper thought that the lifestyle section was getting too lofty, too untouchable. Everything was celebrity parties, high society, couture fashion, and they don't want to change that. After all, people love to live vicariously. But market research showed that we were losing touch with younger demographics, women your age who have become used to finding all of this and more online. So they wanted us to bring something new to the mix, a human-interest angle that would hook a younger market and perhaps pull on the nostalgia of our older readers. And that's when we came up with the idea of your column—a small snippet each week about the sex and dating life of your everyday, college graduate. Something every woman could relate to. And we chose you because you were already working for the paper, the book editors couldn't stop raving about how wonderful your writing was, and the few pieces I did read were witty, funny, and the exact sort of thing our section needs."

Is it actually possible to be stunned speechless? Because I think I am. She likes my writing? She read my writing? She picked me because of my writing?

But Victoria presses on, unaware of my barely contained glee. "You'll have the normal duties of an assistant of course, copyediting, managing the databases, updating the calendars, filing event invitations, communicating with our freelancers, writing a few articles for the online site, but the other girls can help you get acquainted with that."

"Other girls?" I ask, finally finding my voice.

"Oh, silly me." Victoria stands, utterly graceful. "Let me introduce you to the other assistants."

I scramble to follow, the ugly duckling to her swan. I can't help but make the comparison—she's even wearing a cream suit, one that looks absolutely regal and stunning, especially against her dark skin. But it's more than just the clothes. It's everything. The tilt of her head—raised just enough to look down on everyone else. The curve of her spine—long and lean, especially on her five-foot-ten-size-zero frame. The bounce in her step, as though the entire world is her runway.

I, on the other hand, am hunched over, wide-eyed, hugging my purse for dear life as though I'm venturing into the wilds of the Amazon and not a corporate office. But really, it might as well be. Somehow, I just know I'm about to be fed to the sharks. Well, if it's the Amazon, more like being fed to the crocodiles, right? Or the…what do they have down there?

Stay focused.

I look up just in time to see three other girls lift their heads in unison, as though they have a sixth sense and know where Victoria is at all times. And maybe they do…there's a sort of superhuman air about them.

"Victoria."

"Victoria."

"Victoria."

They all chorus in the same high-pitched, pleasant voice that hovers somewhere between earnestness and insincerity. I need to learn that voice. It says, yes, you interrupted me and yes, I don't feel like speaking to you right now, but hello, good morning, you are fabulous, and I am your servant. And then they all dip their heads to the side and smile the same inquiring smile, waiting patiently for Victoria to keep speaking.

They can't be human can they? Highly advanced robots? Clones? Aliens who have snuck their way into society, waiting until the day the mother ship returns to finally take over the world?

The last one.

Definitely the last one.

I read too much.

"Ladies, this is the new assistant, Skylar Quinn," Victoria says, moving to the side so I'm no longer hidden behind her. I keep my feet in place, trying my best not to cower as their eyes dip to my completely unfashionable outfit and then lift to my almost makeup free face. At least I don't wear glasses. Then I really would be a walking cliché.

But to my amazement, their smiles don't waver. They don't even flinch. They hold still, steady, faces warm and inviting.

Robots…maybe they're robots.

"Hi, I'm Isabel." One girl steps forward and offers her hand, which I shake hesitantly, somewhat afraid to squeeze too hard and break the fragile bones in her fingers. Something about her seems familiar…and then I realize she looks just like Victoria. Same build, same deep brown eyes, same wavy brown hair.

"I'm Blythe," the next girl says. I shake her hand with a little more force and a little more fear. She's Upper East Side Barbie, with that same sort of air about her that the cheerleaders had in high school. What did it say again? Oh yeah—I remember now. I'm better than you, you are the dirt beneath my feet, worship me. And the longer I meet Blythe's eyes, the smaller I seem to feel.

So I look away, to the third and final girl.

"I'm Rebecca," she says, not offering her hand, but something about her seems a little more down to earth. I don't have time to figure out what that is though, because she turns away from me and looks at Victoria. "Are we still having the weekly meeting? It's almost ten. I'd be happy to print out the agenda."

"Yes, thank you, Rebecca. Please print an extra copy for Skylar. I'll take her to the conference room now."

And then we're off, walking the opposite direction back down the hall toward a glass-encased space at the other end of the newsroom. Finally somewhere familiar—somewhere I've been before.

The conference room.

And there's a coffee machine right outside.

Come to mama.

But as we approach, Victoria leans in, whispering to me. "Now do you see what I mean? We need you, the average girl, something this office is sorely lacking. Isabel, you probably noticed the resemblance, is my niece and her father is one of the wealthiest men in the Dominican. Have you ever heard of Casa de Campo? They own three waterfront homes there. She was a model for a while, but wanted a more stable life so I found her a position working for me. Blythe, on the other hand, grew up in a brownstone across from the Met. Her parents are big donors and she gets invitations to all of the major parties, the perfect socialite to keep us up-to-date with the Manhattan scene. And then, Rebecca, of course. Her father is a famous designer. She's the darling of New York Fashion Week."

Her next words remain unspoken, but I hear them anyway. And then there's me…totally normal, totally insignificant me.

Yeah, I'm starting to get the message.

But I just smile and nod, trying to copy the robotic movements of the assistants we left behind. I end up with a stiff neck and an uncontrollable twitch.

I'll work on it.

As we round the last corner of desks, I see it. The coffee machine—and not just any old machine, but the fancy one. I could get a vanilla latte. A mocha. A vanilla mocha. A double espresso with hazelnut. A cappuccino. A—

"Would you like some coffee before we head into the meeting?"

Oh god, was I salivating?

I swallow, licking my lips and feeling for drool. None. I breathe a sigh of complete relief.

Be cool…just be cool. "Yes, thank you."

"I'll meet you inside."

Nailed it.

And for a few minutes, I can actually breathe. Even just the smell of coffee has alleviated the pressure in my skull. Against the muffled roar of the newsroom, I experience a moment of complete peace, telling myself over and over—you have a job, a real job, as a real reporter. This is your dream and you have it.

But then the rest of the lifestyle team rounds the corner, a rainbow that's shockingly bright against the gentle storm cloud gray of the rest of the room, and my bubble shatters. I hastily click the button for a vanilla latte and follow the group inside. The click of a closing door has never sounded quite so ominous.

Victoria sits at the head of the table, queen of the court with her hands folded on the tabletop. There are about twelve other people in the room, the assistants I met as well as some editors I haven't been introduced to yet. And I realize I was wrong about one thing—there is one man on the style team, and I think he's wearing pants that are tighter than any article of clothing I own.

Just as I'm finally about to take a glorious sip of coffee, Victoria begins the meeting, and I know what's probably first on the agenda—me. The stranger in the corner hunched over her mug, completely out of place—the one getting baffled, curious looks from half the people in the room.

"Welcome, everyone. I have some really wonderful news today. We hired a new assistant. Skylar, introduce yourself to the group."

Eyes widen. Jaws minutely drop. And about a dozen gazes scan my body, judging the stuffy conservative suit, the button down, the barren face, the un-manicured nails, the barely brushed, let alone styled hair, the lack of jewelry—well, I have on gold studs, but that's practically nothing.

For a moment, I'm thrown into that nightmare every kid has growing up, that one where you show up to school and walk into class completely and utterly naked. Everyone is pointing and laughing, and you're horrified, unable to move, wondering how in the world did your mother let you out of the house nude? But then you wake up and relief washes over your body because, thank goodness, it was just a dream.

Yeah, I sort of feel like that. Except I'm awake. I think...

I pinch myself, hoping to come to in my tiny bedroom.

No such luck. Definitely awake.

I cough, clearing my throat and searching for my voice—which I'm pretty sure is burned out from screaming like a little girl in the back of my mind. "Hi, I'm Skylar Quinn, the new editorial assistant. I just graduated this past May, and I've been interning for the arts and literature team, specifically for the book review, for the past three months. And, um, today is my first day."

As soon as I say book review, they all knowingly nod. Not in an obvious way, but when twelve people do it, it's sort of easy to notice.

"And, tell them about your vision for the column," Victoria says encouragingly. "We spoke about it at some senior meetings, but I'd like the team to hear your plans."

I sort of want to hug her. But I won't. Especially because a tingle of jealousy has tightened the air, shifting the mood in the room. I look to my left at the three assistants now straining to hold their smiles in place.

"Um..." I trail off. I didn't even know about the column until yesterday—was I supposed to come up with a game plan overnight? Think, Skylar, think. Pulling crap out of thin air is what writers are born to do. "Well, as Victoria and I discussed, I want to make the column as approachable and entertaining as possible, to hopefully bring a new demographic and new readers to the newspaper, so I was thinking..." Come on! Words, say words. "Well, lots of girls my age," and by that I mean me, "don't actually feel that comfortable talking about sex, or reading about sex..." Or, you know, actually having sex... "So I thought this column could be more about the dating life of the average young professional woman. The trials and tribulations, various dating failures, the few successes, sort of entertaining experiences that every girl or woman can relate to."

Well, that actually sounded pretty great if I do say so myself. But there's stillness in the air, as though everyone is in on something I'm missing.

"But, there will be some sex, right?" one of the editors finally asks.

They're staring, so I try to play it cool, looking down at my notebook while I swallow my hysteria. "Oh, sure, I mean, what's the dating life of the average young professional without some sex?"

Not this average young professional, of course, the one you sort of hired to write about it. But lots of others I'm sure.

I chance a peek, scanning the group for a reaction.

They're nodding. They're smiling.

I might actually pull this off!

"And what's your idea for the first column. If you're ready, we'd like to go to print with the launch next week."

I say the first thing that comes to mind. "What to do if you're crushing on the guy you live with?"

Wait, what?

No!

No!

Abort.

I can't write about that. Bridget will read this. Ollie might even read this. Say something else, quick.

"Or, um," I press forward before they get too attached to the idea, "I mean, what to do if you're crushing on the guy who lives next door or in your building. Like me, for example, there's this guy who I see every morning, in the, um, elevator. Yeah, the elevator. I can experiment with flirting, trying to get him to ask me out, that sort of thing and then write about how it goes."

My first professional lie, and it's not even noon. That has to be a record.

"Well, that's not that difficult," Blythe chips in from the corner, smile way too kind to be sincere. "My neighbor asked me out on the elevator just this morning. I didn't even have to do anything."

Well, good for you.

"That is so funny. I just got asked out by a guy in my building too," Rebecca chimes in, but her tone actually does sound genuine. Aloof maybe, but genuine. "I was doing laundry over the weekend at the same time as this guy in my building, and when I went to get my clothes from the dryer, there was a Post-it note waiting with his phone number on it."

Who are these girls? I haven't been asked out since college. And really, that was only my ex John. And, well, if I'm being totally honest I wasn't so much asked out on a date. It was more of a drunken mutual attraction that happened to turn into a relationship that happened to last right until the end of my senior year.

Can I just bury myself now?

But Victoria leans in, excited. "I love it, Skylar. The idea is already resonating with girls your age. Go for it, and I expect a first draft on my desk by Friday. Now, Alexandra, where are we on the new designer previews?"

I'm dismissed. And I can't reach for my coffee fast enough.

Yum.

Still delicious.

I sink back in my chair as the meeting continues in what I can only describe as a foreign language. This—insert name I don't recognize—is a new—insert name I don't recognize. And she—insert name—is just like a new age—insert name—totally reminiscent of—insert name.

And so on, and so forth, until my hand cramps from taking so many notes on people I need to research just to be able to grasp a basic understanding of what is going on for next week's meeting. But it does give me another great idea for a column.

A new age love story—how the modern woman and her café latte defied the odds and managed to survive in the wilds of a hostile work environment.

They'll love it.

Not.

Confession 4

I'm an utterly terrible flirt. Really. I know some girls might say that just to hear their friends jump to their defense and shower them in compliments. Not me. Oh, I'm really great at coming up with something fabulous to say five minutes after the boy is already gone, but in the moment? I'm a deer caught in the headlights, then...bam!

I'm determined to hit this first column out of the park. So determined that when I arrive home after my first day, I dive full force into reporter mode, which in this case could loosely be defined as stalker mode. But I need to find a boy—not Ollie!—to harass—I mean flirt with—for research. So I wait, idling by the mailboxes, keeping an eye on the entrance.

He's too old.

He's with a girl.

He's too cute—I'd have no chance whatsoever.

He's not my type.

And then miraculously, a boy I've never noticed steps through the front door. Sandy blond hair. Gangly build that I secretly find sort of cute. Business casual. And as he walks by the doorman he nods in greeting—polite!

Okay, go time.

I pick up a discarded letter from the floor, pretending I actually have mail—which really, for the first time ever, the one time I really need mail, I have nothing, not even a *dear resident* marketing pamphlet. But the envelope I just grabbed from the floor will do.

Trying my best to look casual, I step next to the boy to wait for the elevator, peeking at him a few times, until there's a *ding* and the door slides open. He lets me in first—such a gentleman—and then steps in behind me.

The doors close.

Silence descends.

I lick my lips, turning my head to the side to take a full-on look at him. He senses the movement and reciprocates. I smile. He smiles. I coyly look away for a moment, and then glance back. He's still looking at me. Cue second smile, friendlier this time.

Wow. We're totally vibing. This never happens. Maybe this job was the good luck charm I needed.

"Hi," I murmur.

"Hey," he says.

"I'm Skye." I shrug.

"Neal." He shrugs.

A very long second of quiet passes.

"Hey—" I start, unsure of where I'm really going, but then the elevator swings open, cutting me off.

"Have a good night," he says over his shoulder.

"Yeah, you too," I call after his disappearing body just as the doors are closing.

But hey, I think that went well. I take it for a win. We had a conversation—sort of. Words were said. Introductions were made. That counts—I think.

"Bridge!" I shout when I walk into the apartment.

"On the couch!"

"Bridge," I say, turning the corner into the living room and dropping my bag on the coffee table. "I think the first day went really well."

"Awesome," she says, and then turns away from the TV, giving me her full attention. But she flinches when her eyes land on my face. The flinch turns to a bitten lip. Which then turns to a grin.

"What?"

Now she's shaking her head. God, she's just like her brother.

"What?"

"Nothing," she sputters. "Might want to check the mirror though."

I race to the bathroom, heart stopping as my eyes land on my reflection.

There's a freaking forest growing in my teeth. A forest!

"Crap!" I shout, digging for the spinach that's nestled in the gaps between my incisors. I ate that like two hours ago—why didn't anyone tell me?

And then I remember the elevator, the boy, the vibing... No wonder he was smiling!

And the rest of the week passes in pretty much the same fashion. Even though I've never seen Neal in my building before, he's miraculously on my elevator the next morning.

"Skye, right?" he says when he steps on. I smile politely. To which he exclaims, "Hey, you got it out. I wasn't sure if something was stuck or if it was just some weird medical thing. Didn't want to hurt your feelings."

Weird medical thing? Did he think I had fungus growing in my mouth? Ugh!

There are no words. I just nod and stare at the floor for the rest of the ride. That night I make sure to sneak onto the elevator when he's not around. Thankfully the next morning he's nowhere to be seen and I can rest easy. But that night, I time everything incorrectly and he sneaks onto the elevator at the last second.

"Skye," he says, smiling. But I can't tell if the smiling is cordial or if he's still laughing at the memory of my green, fungus-infested teeth.

"Neal," I force the words through closed lips. I'm too embarrassed to do or say anything else.

I hide in my room all night writing a column about how dating where you live is the worst idea possible. I've been reduced to a bundle of nerves, unsure where and when Neal might show up, heart pounding anytime I walk into a common space. I'm the opposite of a stalker—I'm an avoider. But I have to admit, writing about the experience is a little fun. With help from Bridget, I throw a few R-rated tidbits into the story, and voila—my first sex column.

Victoria loves it.

She makes me rewrite it five times—but she loves it.

And it's finally Friday, meaning I have two blissful days off from the stress. Or I would, except Bridget decided it was high time I learned to flirt, so she dragged me to a club downtown and now I'm leaning over a bar, trying to get the bartender to notice me long enough to order a drink. Looks like the key to my success would be to pull my shirt down by about three inches.

Yeah, not happening.

"Bridget, you try."

Ten seconds later, we have cocktails.

"So, what are we—holy crap, what did you just order?" My entire face spasms as I take a sip of whatever beverage Bridget just bought.

"Long Island Iced Teas," she says with a shrug, easily taking a sip of her drink.

I shake my head. Bridget and I are both creative types, but while studying for my art involved a lot of reading and even more writing—alone in my room I might add—studying for her art involved lots of experimentation—the typical college kind filled with boys and alcohol and things it might be incriminating for me to mention by name. "I thought the purpose of this evening was to teach me how to flirt, not to get me drunk."

Bridget slides her gaze away from the cute guy at the other end of the bar, meeting my eyes pointedly. "The purpose of tonight is to loosen you up in whatever way I can. We start with a little alcohol and then we move onto the rest. Come on."

She grabs my hand, pulling me away from the bar and into the throngs of people pressed up against each other on the dance floor. So not my scene. We weave in and out, pushing people around, being pushed around in return, making our way closer to the music. Finally, we find a small space to claim as our own and hold steady, rocking to the music as we sip our drinks, keeping our elbows out as defense against the dancers bumping into us from all sides. But the longer we drink and the longer we dance, the more relaxed I feel.

And I'll admit, it's fun. Especially when our favorite songs come on—mostly girl-power pop anthems—and we both belt out the words, totally and completely free in the moment because no matter how loudly we sing, no one will be able to hear us.

But then the inevitable happens.

"So," Bridget shouts, but I can still barely hear her. "Let's find some guys to dance with."

My heart sinks.

For a moment I wonder, why? Why can't we have fun with just the two of us, like we normally do when we go out? With Bridge, I know I can trust her. I know I can depend on her. I know we have a great time together. I know she's not a creepy a-hole who'll ditch me as soon as he realizes I won't go home with him. You know, the usual stuff.

But then I remember the column, the research, my desperate search for a topic to write about next week, and I relent.

"Okay!" I shout, nodding to emphasize the point in case she can't hear me.

We drop our elbows, no longer keeping the crowd at bay, and it's as sure a sign as any that we're open for business

Wait—not business.

Open for fun? For a good time? For... Okay, there's just no completely innocent way to say this, but you know what I mean! We're available to dance.

In less than ten seconds, a guy comes up to Bridget, grabbing her waist and pulling her close, and she accepts the offer, unsurprisingly. Shall I count the reasons why Bridget is a boy-magnet? I mean, aside, from her dazzling personality of course? Well, number one—red hair. Number two—tall and thin figure. Number three, at least tonight—ridiculously tight little black dress.

Shall I count the reasons why I am not? Well, you probably already know them. Neurotic. Shy. Book nerd. Oh, boys come up to me sometimes, sure, but my usual response is to run in the opposite direction rather than, you know, do something drastic and actually say hello.

Hmm.

I sigh, looking around, dancing by myself, trying to stay close to Bridget and her mystery man so I don't look completely pathetic. Soon enough, a boy takes pity.

Hands grip my waist, pulling me back into a waiting body. He starts gyrating against my hips, not really to any rhythm I can follow, but I try to just relax and let him take the lead. There's no greeting. No asking if I'd like to dance. No manners.

Is chivalry totally dead, people? Come on.

I turn, peeking over my shoulder, and yell, "Hi."

He doles a lazy smile in my direction, but doesn't bother to say anything back. His bloodshot eyes are still scanning the dance floor, checking out other girls.

Ick.

No, thank you.

Without so much as a goodbye, I shrug out of his embrace, trying to hold back a grimace. A few minutes later, another boy approaches. Pretty much the same thing happens. And two times after that, I'm done.

"I'm going to the bathroom," I shout in Bridget's direction.

She motions, using girl sign language to ask if I want her to come with me. But she's still dancing with the same boy—who is pretty cute, I'll admit—and I can tell she's having a good time, so I tell her to stay put.

A few minutes later, I'm free of the dance floor, standing close to the exit, reveling in the gusts of wind blasting in my direction every time the door opens.

Air.

Blissful, cool air.

I breathe in the sweat-free smell, closing my eyes for a moment as my entire body drops a few degrees. So much better. I can actually reach my arms to the side without touching another human being.

Being alone is wonderful.

"Skye!"

Well, it was fun while it lasted. My eyes shoot open, searching for the voice I could barely hear over the ringing of my own ears. "Ollie?"

And there he is, smiling at me with a questioning knot in his brows. "What are you doing? Where's Bridget? She told me to meet you guys here after the restaurant closed."

"What time is it?" I grab his arm, bringing the cell phone in his hand closer to read the clock. 1:37? How did it get so late so quickly?

But then I stop, realizing I'm touching Ollie's arm. Touching him. And his skin feels warm and soft, contoured with muscles, firm and strong. And my fingers tingle, too aware of the contact. My entire body goes still, frozen, as my mind focuses on the tiny little space between us.

Since that first night, I haven't seen Ollie the entire week. The restaurant life is work all afternoon, work all night, mornings off. He's usually asleep when I leave in the morning and working when I come home.

But now he's here. Inches away. And we're touching.

I look up.

Ollie is still watching me.

My heart leaps into my throat.

But then I remember, and I drop his arm. I remember that I already went down this road, already spent most of my life crushing on Ollie, and I won't do it again. "Bridge is dancing with someone," I say, and take a step back, licking my lips. "I just needed a break."

His ocean-hued eyes flick to the dance floor, darkening with a hint of overprotectiveness, but then they find their way back to me, filled with something I don't recognize. He blinks, and the storm clouds dissipate. "Do you want anything from the bar? I need a beer. The first Friday shift at a new restaurant is always tough."

"Water?"

He nods, disappearing. For a moment, I expect to see him walking to the dance floor with some girl. But he doesn't. He comes back. To me.

"So why did Bridget drag you down here? Doesn't seem like your usual scene."

I roll my eyes. "How'd you guess?"

"Well, the fact that you were standing alone in a dark corner was sort of a dead giveaway. But the look of general disdain on your face didn't hurt."

I try to hold back my grin, but from his self-satisfied expression I know it didn't quite work. I shrug. "She thinks I need to learn how to flirt."

"Do you?"

"I don't know."

"Want help?"

I start choking on my water. Nice—way to be cool. "From you?" I squeak when the fit subsides and I can finally speak again.

"What?" He shrugs, leaning against the spot beside me on the wall while he takes a long sip of his beer. I try not to notice the nicely chiseled shape of his jaw—and fail miserably. "We're…friends. I can help."

I'm not sure I like where this is going.

Scratch that—I one hundred percent, no doubt about it, do not like where this is going. And yet…

"Sure." The word just pops out of my mouth, from nowhere. Stupid voice with a stupid life of its own. But then, trying to draw some boundaries, I rush to add, "Strictly in the name of journalism of course."

Ollie grins, taking another sip from his bottle. "Of course."

"So, what's first, teacher?" I chug my water, mouth growing dryer by the second.

"You really want to know how to attract a guy?" Ollie glances at me, lips slightly pursed, turquoise eyes twinkling from the strobe light, a slight layer of stubble across his cheek. Does the room feel low on oxygen to anyone else? Because I suddenly feel unable to breathe.

He leans in closer.

Yeah, definitely can't breathe. It's a little painful actually. Constricting my chest.

"Just show him that you're interested," he whispers, holding my gaze. The rest of the room seems to fade away. The lights go dark. The sound mutes. All I can hear is the thud of my racing pulse.

I look away first, sucking in a long, slow breath. "And how do you suggest I do that?"

"Go and say hello, sometimes just a look will do." Ollie shrugs, pausing to scan the room. "Like that girl at the bar over there, that's the third time she's made eye contact with me."

I zone in on the girl he's talking about, standing at the bar with her friends, sipping on a cocktail, eyes still locked on Ollie. Short dress. Big hair. Suggestive grin. Heels that reach about as high as my thigh.

My stomach drops immediately, and then coils into a tight ball of anger. Okay, jealousy. No, anger. Well…ugh. Let's just stick with anger. "Oh my gosh, she sees us talking here and she's still ogling you so blatantly."

"What? It's not like we're dating," Ollie mutters.

"Yeah, but she doesn't know that. We could be. I just," I pause, stammering for a response that doesn't make me sound totally whiney and bitter. "I could never do that. If that's flirting, no wonder I'm horrible at it."

"Well, it's not all her fault."

I look at Ollie, aware of what's coming next and waiting for the appropriate time to release my eye roll.

"Women just can't help themselves around me."

Instead of the roll I expect, my gaze just sinks to the floor. I'm in no place to judge anyone—not for falling for his charms. "You should go talk to her," I find myself saying, eyes still on the stain-covered ground.

"Really?" He looks at me, but I refuse to reciprocate. The floor is much safer. Much easier to understand. Much less complicated. "I don't want to leave you here all by yourself."

And I suddenly realize what this entire conversation has been.

Pity.

Pity for his little sister's best friend alone in the club.

And now that I realize it, I can't bear to talk to him any longer. I can't bear to stand next to him. Can't bear to have him so close.

"Go, go," I say, swallowing back the pain and finally glancing up with a smile. "I'm fine, really. I just needed a break. I'm going to go find Bridget. You should talk to her."

"If you're sure…"

"I am," I say and nudge him with my shoulder. "Go."

"I'll see you at home," he says, then winks, "or not."

I don't watch him leave. I don't want to see him lead her to the dance floor, put his hands all over her body, and, ugh, kiss her.

A few minutes later, Bridget finds me. Her smile drops immediately when she sees my expression, eyes filling with concern. "Are you okay? What's wrong?"

"Nothing." I shake my head and shrug.

And though I know her boy is out there somewhere waiting for her, expecting her to come back, Bridget grabs my arm and says, "Come on, I'm so over this place. How about pizza on the way home?"

And that's just one of the reasons why I love her.

Confession 5

The best boyfriend I've ever had was a fictional character. After all, the only one I've really had was John, and after almost four years, that ended with him cheating and me ruing the day he was born. So, yeah, I'll stick with my books.

The past few weeks have passed in a blur of failed romantic attempts and columns chronicling my ineptitude in the dating world.

Leaving my number with the cute barista? Now I need to walk an extra five minutes out of the way each morning to buy a coffee. Well that, or face him again and ignore the fact that he never called me—even though he put a heart next to my name three mornings in a row! I thought we had something, nameless barista boy, I really thought we did. And it would have made such a cute story too.

Visiting the local sports bar during Monday Night Football? A twenty-dollar dry cleaning bill to wash out the beer stains on the jersey Bridget's work friend let me borrow. Well, that and the number of a man who's old enough to be my father—because he thought it was adorable that I called a touchdown a goal. Sorry, my time at high school football games involved drooling over the quarterback—yes, it was Ollie—staring at his butt in those tight pants—come on, we've all done it—and gossiping with Bridget.

Or how about the time Bridget thought going to the gym would be a great idea? After half an hour on the treadmill, I was red-faced, oozing sweat, and in absolutely no place to attract anyone.

Of course, we've gone to about a million clubs and even more bars, but I'm pretty sure I don't have the right pheromones to attract a guy in that situation—not drunk enough, not sexual enough, or if I'm telling the truth, too worried that every guy who approaches me is a sociopath. Okay, I'll admit I have an overactive imagination. Pair that with my addiction to crime shows and you might see where I'm coming from.

But after weeks of dead ends and fruitless attempts to get a boy's attention, you'll understand why I'm miserable when I come home and announce, "Victoria says I need to find a boyfriend."

Then I proceed to collapse on the couch, wallowing in a cocoon of my own despair. I sink further when Ollie walks out of his bedroom, grinning like a buffoon.

"Aren't you supposed to be at work?" I ask, too exhausted to move.

"Lucky you, it's my day off."

Bridget just rolls her eyes at the two of us, scooting over to give Ollie room on the couch—a couch that wasn't really made to fit three people despite our three bedroom apartment.

"So, what happened?" Bridget asks after tossing and turning for a few seconds. In the end, she leans against her brother and puts her feet on my lap so all three of us fit together in a discombobulated puzzle pieces sort of way.

I leave my head dropped against the back of the couch and stare at the ceiling while I recount my morning at the office. "Victoria called me in for a meeting to check in about the status of the column and how it's working out. She said the content is resonating well according to early research, and the online postings are getting a good amount of social media interaction."

"But?" Bridget asks.

"But." I sigh. "She's worried the content is becoming too stale and thinks we need an ongoing storyline to really pull people in—a Mr. Big to my totally unworthy Carrie. So, I need to get a boyfriend. By next week. Or at least go on a real date." I finally shift positions, burying my head in my hands. "What am I going to do?"

"Make something up?" Bridget says cautiously.

I slap her leg. "No! I'm not going to risk all of my journalistic integrity. We just need to think about what I haven't tried yet."

There's a pause.

A long pause.

Okay, a humiliatingly long pause.

I peek at Bridge, and I'm pretty sure there are daggers shooting out of my eyes.

"What?" she grumbles. "I'm thinking."

I refuse to look at Ollie—I don't need to actually see the

grin rapidly widening his annoyingly perfect lips. I can picture it just fine on my own.

"What about online dating?" Bridget asks, cringing in anticipation of my response.

"Aren't I too young for that? I thought online dating was for, like, single moms with kids in college. Widowers. You know, people our parents' ages."

"No, it's not," she says, rolling her eyes and shaking her head. "Here. Take a look at this." Bridget grabs Ollie's phone, plugging in his password and swiping through his pages.

"Hey." He reaches for it, but Bridget elbows him out of the way.

"I know you have one." Then a few seconds later. "Aha!" And she hands me the phone.

I take it begrudgingly, staring at the screen, which is filled with the photo of an incredibly busty blonde. I mean, could those things possibly be real? "What is this?"

"It's an app. I mean, this is Ollie's so I'm sure it's programmed to only show brainless girls, but we can download it to your phone and give it a try."

"I resent that," he says, reaching across the couch to snatch the phone from my hands. My heart jumps when his fingers brush against mine, but I shove that feeling down into the pit of my stomach.

No more.

That stage of my life is over. Ollie is my roommate and absolutely nothing more. Nothing. The crush is done. Long gone. Finito. And maybe if I tell that to myself enough times, it'll eventually be true.

"So," I say a little too loudly, trying to force my thoughts back on topic, "what do I have to do?"

A sly smile spreads across Bridget's face. "Surrender your phone."

I know that look. That look got me grounded one too many times. That look means trouble.

I give her my phone anyway.

What? I'm desperate.

A few torturous minutes later, Bridge hands my cell back. I close my eyes tight, torn. Do I even want to see what she's done?

I sigh.

Yes.

Yes, I do.

A moment later…

"Bridge!" I whine, half-wanting to close my eyes and forget this ever happened. Of course, she used the only photo ever posted of me in a bikini—spring break senior year, the one that came about a week after my split with John, the one where Bridget volunteered to take his place and help drown my sorrows, the one where in my weakened state she managed to take more blackmail-type photos of me than ever in the history of our friendship.

And now she's cashing in.

"What, you look great in that photo."

"I'm practically naked in that photo."

"What photo?" Ollie perks up, straining his neck to take a peek at the phone. My face goes beet red—or at least it feels that way from the heat crawling up my neck—and I hastily bury the screen against my chest, hiding it from him.

Bridget pushes her brother back down, turning to me. "Just keep reading."

"Reading what? I don't even know how this works."

Scoffing, Bridge takes the phone from me, switching positions so her feet are on Ollie and her upper body is snuggled against my side. "Here," she says, shifting her finger on the screen to bring up the text for my profile. "Skylar Quinn, 22. Columnist. Recent grad. Looking for romance in the city that never sleeps."

I shrug. "That's not bad."

"And I put up these photos too, the bikini one is just to grab the initial interest." Bridget flips her finger to the side, shifting through the photos to prove her point. There's one of me at graduation. One of me with my dog back home. One of me surrounded by a pile of books on our campus quad. One of me laughing at a party. A nice enough variation saying I'm intelligent but not stuffy, fun but not too fun.

"So, what now?" I ask, a little more intrigued by the idea. Maybe online dating isn't so bad. You sort of get to feel the person out first—a photo, a bio, maybe even a little conversation before the first date. That's not that horrible.

"Now, we search."

And the screen suddenly changes from my face to that of a relatively cute guy. Below his face is a green check or a red *x*. Before I even have a chance to read his profile, Bridget hits the *x*, shaking her head and muttering, "too jock."

Another image pops up of a different boy. And I suddenly realize what's happening. "Wait, so you just like, check yes or no? Pretty much entirely based on their photo? That's sort of horrible."

She ignores me. "Ooh, he's cute. Glasses, a little nerdy, but still sophisticated. I'm checking him."

"Wait!" I reach for my phone, but it's too late. The green check has been hit and his photo has disappeared into the void. "What did that just do? Did I ask him out? Isn't that, like, desperate or something?"

"Relax, he'll just get a notification that basically implies you're interested. And if he takes a look at your profile and likes what he sees, he'll send you a message to meet up."

"Hmm." I nod and lean back, letting Bridge continue to take the reins on this whole online experiment. She knows me better than I know myself, so really, she'll probably pick better guys for me than I would anyway. "This is way easier than I thought it would be."

"I told you."

But then my phone dings. And again. And a third time.

"What's happening?"

"Oh, nothing…" Bridget trails off, but I can't help but notice she is slowly pulling my phone farther and farther out of reach.

"Bridge, what's that noise?"

"Just guys responding."

Another ding. And another.

"Give me the phone!" I shout trying to yank it out of her grasp just as another ring chimes through. But her arms are longer than mine and she easily keeps it out of reach. "How many guys did you check?"

"Just two, the others are guys finding you."

I pause. Sit up. Guys are finding me? Guys are noticing me? They're singling me out based pretty much only on my photo? I mean, it's totally demeaning and a little gross, and I know it's really the pull of the bikini and not much else, but still. A sort of buoyant feeling trickles up my spine, puffing out my chest, bringing a slight smile to my lips.

Another ding.

My heart starts bubbling like champagne, fizzy and light. So what if it's the bikini photo? It's still me in the bikini, not some other person whose photo I stole. I feel pretty good right now. Confident, and dare I say, a little smug. "That's like seven guys."

"You know..." Bridget looks up from the search to meet my amazed gaze. "Guys hit on you all the time, it's not their fault that you tend to run away every time they say hello."

"I don't run away," I grumble under my breath. I walk...quickly...

But Bridge won't let me off that easy. "You do too. Ollie, back me up on this."

He remains silent.

"Ollie?" Bridget says again.

"Wh—what?" He snaps to attention, pulled from a daze. Was he looking at my phone? For a moment, it looked like he was staring at my phone.

"Tell Skye that guys hit on her all the time."

He turns his eyes to me. They're sparkling with controlled laughter. "Guys hit on you all the time."

"And that she's just too nervous to take notice."

"And you're too nervous to take notice," he repeats, eyebrows raised in mock admonishment.

"And that she should try saying hello once in a while."

Now he's nodding his head, fighting back a grin. "And you should try saying hello once in a while."

"And that she's beautiful."

Ollie pauses. Swallowing. Humor gone. "You're beautiful."

Was his voice breathy or was that just in my head?

"And that your sister is your favorite person in the world." Bridget turns to me with a wink.

But Ollie just ignores her and stands up, pushing her legs off of his lap. "I'm going to start dinner. I bought supplies for dumplings, can you guys help me wrap them? I'll do the rest."

"Oh, so we're your sous-chefs now?" Bridget teases.

I interrupt before this carries on for too much longer—between the two of them it could be hours before I eat. And my stomach is already growling. "Yes, Ollie. We'll help."

He holds my gaze for a moment before disappearing into the kitchen. I stare a little too long at the spot where his face used to be, pulled away only when Bridget starts giggling in my ear.

"What?"

"Um…" she starts. "You need to read these yourself."

"Oh god, what now?" I ask, grabbing my phone and looking at the screen.

At first I don't notice what she's laughing at, but then it hits me. I race to click on the little envelope at the top of the screen, dread tightening into a deep, dark pit at the bottom of my stomach.

Your place or mine?

That's all the first message reads. Your place or mine!

Are you kidding me? Is that serious?

I'll choose neither, thank you very much.

I delete his chat from my phone, erasing it completely before I click on the next message from a different guy.

Sex?

And that's it.

Delete!

I click on the next, heart racing, vision turning the slightest hint of red.

Your gorgeous... Okay, well that one's not so bad, except for the incorrect grammar. Not ideal, but at least he was trying. I scroll down and read the second half of the message. *I want to lick chocolate fudge off your body.*

What the?

I mean, does someone actually think that is a good pick-up line? Or not even a pick-up line, but just an acceptable thing to say to a human being you've never even met before? Scratch that. Even if we had met, heck, even if we were dating, I'm not sure I'd ever want to hear that from someone. Ever.

I turn off my phone.

"Bridget, is this for real?"

She licks her lips, a sorry expression creeping onto her face. "Well, it's not the ideal first online dating experience. But, what's that saying? My mom always used to say it. You have to kiss a lot of frogs before you find your prince?"

I gawk. "Kiss a lot of frogs…?" I trail off, shaking my head. "He asked me to lick chocolate fudge off of him. Not just chocolate, but chocolate *fudge*!"

"What?" Ollie shouts from the kitchen. A moment later, his head pokes around the corner. "Who? What's going on? I'll be back in a second, wait for me before you guys say anything else."

I ignore him. "This isn't a dating app. This is a sex app! You put me on a sex app!"

"I didn't know that…" Bridget cringes. "I don't have a profile. I just have friends who use it. Ollie uses it!"

Speak of the devil.

At that moment, Ollie walks in with a bowl of dumpling stuffing and empty wrappers, ears perked to listen in on the conversation.

The perfect unsuspecting prey.

"You let her put me on a sex app!" I shout and jump off the couch, slapping him repeatedly in the arm—crush completely negated by the fury scalding my blood.

"Hey, watch the food." He swerves around me, almost dropping the bowl.

Just what I need right now—pork bits splattering all over my apartment—not. I drop back, still fuming, but calmed somewhat after my outburst.

"What sex app? What's going on? All I heard was something about licking and chocolate fudge…" He trails off into a fit of confused laughter.

"This!" I shove the phone in his face. At first, he turns serious, focusing on the screen to read what it says. But then I watch him mouth the words *chocolate fudge* and a moment later he's convulsing again.

I snatch the phone back. "I'm deleting this app. That's it. Online dating is so not for me."

"Oh, come on," Bridget urges. "That was just bad luck. We could try a website instead of an app. It can't always be like that. I mean, right, Ollie?"

"I don't know, sis," Ollie teases. "I always start my conversations by offering to lick hot foods off of a girl. I mean, really, it's just good manners."

Can I hit him again? I really want to hit him again.

Bridget beats me to the punch—literally.

"Ow." He sets the food down and rubs his side. "That actually hurt."

"Good," Bridget and I mutter in unison. And then we lock arms and collapse back onto the couch. A sigh travels up my throat. I'm right back where I started.

Single. Prospectless. In need of a boyfriend, and ASAP. Well, except now I'm even more exhausted and even more hopeless. And I had thought the situation couldn't get any worse. Clearly, I'd been wrong. Oh, blissful ignorance, why did you abandon me?

"What am I going to do now?" I grumble, sitting up to reach for a dumpling wrap. Ollie scoops a handful of the pork stuffing onto my roll and I start folding, repeating the process over and over. It's sort of soothing in its monotony. Bridget joins us and the room goes silent while we work, folding and crimping, folding and crimping, over and over until a bowl of raw dumplings sits full on the coffee table.

"I have an idea." Bridget sits up straight, looking at me with a triumphant expression. There's a very high possibility that I won't like the sound of this, but I keep quiet. What do I really have to lose at this point?

Uh, do me a favor. Don't answer that.

"Ollie!"

What? Did I just hear that correctly?

Ollie and I make eye contact—panicked. I know I must look just as alarmed as him, if not more. Terror makes my hands tremble, sends a painful shiver down my spine. Bridget can't know… She doesn't know…

"Ollie can set you up with someone at his restaurant."

I yank my gaze to the floor, releasing a heavy breath, blinking and then swallowing before I lick my lips. "I'm not so sure that's a great idea."

"Yeah, me neither," Ollie says, and I don't hear any joke in his tone this time. Like me, he's dead serious.

"Oh, come on. I'd set you up with someone, but you know all my friends. They're all your friends. But Ollie can vet the guy, make sure he's not crazy."

"A blind date?" I ask, hesitant for oh so many reasons. That's just the easiest to voice to Bridget at the time.

"Come on, guys. For me?" Bridget pleads, pulling on both of our heartstrings. And like always, I doubt either of us will be able to say no. Especially because, according to Bridget, there's no reason for either of us to say no in the first place.

I look at Ollie.

He looks at me.

And at the same time, we give in. "Okay."

"Perfect." Bridget leans back, grinning, and grabs the remote from the coffee table, clicking on the television.

"I'll go cook these," Ollie says and lifts the bowl of dumplings from the table.

I bite my lip. Thinking. And then just go for it. "Can I help?"

He pauses, cocking his head, but then shrugs. "Sure."

I follow Ollie to the kitchen, unsure of what I'm really doing here. But it felt right, in the moment, to come with him. I watch from a few feet away while he turns on the stove, grabbing a frying pan and dropping in oil. It pops and sizzles, growing louder when a handful of dumplings are tossed in. His movements are fluid, utterly confident, lazy yet commanding. The muscles in his forearm flex as he rapidly shuffles the spatula around the dish, completely controlled.

Pulled by some unknown force, I step forward, closer, so I'm leaning over his shoulder, hardly an inch away from his body. My eyes are on the pan, but my attention is completely on him.

"So, um, thanks," I say, not turning my head.

"It's no big deal, I'm happy to help."

"Well, it means a lot, to me at least." I lick my lips, nervous.

Ollie steps back, turning to me. And even though I don't want them to, my eyes find his.

"You want to try?" he says after a moment, offering me the spatula.

"You're trusting me in the kitchen?" I mock.

He shrugs. "There's a first time for everything, Skye."

"Oh, this isn't the first time. Don't you remember when you tried to teach Bridget and me how to make crème brûlée?"

One corner of his mouth picks up, puckering a dimple into his cheek. "Giving the two of you a blow torch was the biggest mistake of my life."

"We almost lit your mom's Christmas towels on fire."

"Almost?" He lifts his eyebrows in amazement, aqua eyes shining bright. "I seem to remember burying a certain Santa-covered cloth in the backyard before she got home."

"Oh, yeah…" I trail off. "I might have forgotten about that."

"Well, I didn't." He snatches the spatula away. "Maybe I should rethink this offer."

"Come on." I jump forward, reaching for his hand. "Give me a second chance."

"A second chance?" he asks, stilling his body. The air feels charged.

I nod, not really sure what we're talking about anymore. But my answer would be the same either way, I think. "Yeah, a second chance."

Ollie hands over the spatula. I dip it into the pan, pausing to look at him before focusing on the dumplings. I get under one, flipping it onto the spatula and depositing it on our serving platter. So far so good. I get another. But when I try to go for the third, it's stuck to the bottom of the pan a little and I press too hard, sending it flying across the counter—airborne.

Ollie sighs. "Let me show you."

And he wraps his fingers around mine, gently gripping my hand. I close my eyes, reveling in his warm touch. He guides me, flipping and turning, as though we're dancing and not cooking. I'm lost in the movement, in the subtle rub of his skin on mine—soft yet coarse enough to be manly. I don't realize the pan is empty until he pulls away and the barest shiver travels up my arm.

I don't say anything as I turn around and leave. I just walk to the couch and snuggle under the blanket next to Bridget, suddenly ice cold.

Confession 6

I've never been on a real, one-on-one, first date! Pathetic, I know.
But all of high school was dominated by my obsession with Ollie.
And my nearly four-year relationship with John started as a month
of anxious flirtation culminating in a 2:00 a.m. make out session
in the basement of a frat house...the sheer definition of romance.

My palms are sweating. My boobs are sweating. I think even my butt cheeks may be sweating. Okay, sorry, that last bit might have been too much information. But, well, I'm freaking out.

I'm going on a date.

A blind date.

My hair was blow-dried. My makeup perfectly applied. My outfit carefully selected by Bridget with absolutely no say from me—and these tights aren't exactly helping the situation. Thank god I'm wearing black. She at least had the foresight to put me in something sweat-stain proof.

Okay.

Breathe.

It's just a guy. A date. No big deal.

If it works, awesome. If not, my boss might fire me and find a sex columnist who actually goes on dates and has a sex life. So, no pressure.

Way to calm yourself down, Skye.

I shake my head. Time to snap out of it. I'm about a block away from the restaurant, so it is time to put my game face on. Smile? Check. Alluring eyes empty of the terror coiling in my stomach? Check.

Then I pause, stumbling on the sidewalk before I regain my balance. What is his name again? I take out my phone, glancing at my recent text messages. Glenn! Glenn... What does the name Glenn say? Well, I guess it would say more about his parents than him, but still. Glenn. What about, like, Fabio? Or, I don't know, Ryder, or, ooh, Cole?

Then again, Skylar sort of sounds hippie, especially since almost everyone I know just shortens my name to Skye. Or, well, like a boy's name, which I've gotten before. So, yeah, I'm in no place to judge.

And on that note, I've arrived at the restaurant.

Taking a deep breath, I step through the front door, pleasantly surprised by how nice the place looks. I'm definitely not in college anymore... Crisp white linens cover the tabletops. A wine cellar stretches along the back wall. Soft, ambient light fills the space, made more romantic by sparkling crystal chandeliers and carved wooden moldings. And a hostess who is probably dressed better than I am greets me as soon as I walk inside, inquiring about a reservation.

"Oh, um, I think it's under...Glenn?" I ask, sounding like an idiot, because of course I don't know his last name.

"Glenn?" she asks, skeptical.

I lean in, whispering girl to girl. "Sorry, I can text him to see if he's here. I'm sort of on a blind date."

"Oh, Glenn!" she suddenly exclaims, with an excited tone that instantly has me on edge. "You're the girl who has a date with Glenn. Let me show you to your table."

I can't help but notice the emphasis she placed on *you're*, as though she had heard of me before, as though she somehow knew Glenn, as though he specifically mentioned the date to her. But when I sit down at the table, no one is there, so I flip absently through the menu while I wait. And about halfway through the entrees, the realization hits.

No…

No!

I'm sitting in a restaurant on Fifth Avenue.

A new restaurant that just opened up.

A high-end American steakhouse.

No…

But as I peek over my shoulder, watching the man who is undoubtedly Glenn walk through a door clearly meant only for staff, my heart sinks to the floor. This is Ollie's restaurant. Well, Glenn's restaurant, but he's not really the one I'm concerned with. And the closer he walks, smiling, waving in greeting, the more I want to crawl under the table, curl into a ball, and just disappear. Which is a shame really, because I don't get enough of these moments to waste them. You know, moments when a really good-looking guy is approaching and you know for certain that his charming smile actually is meant for you, and not some leggy blonde standing behind you?

Yeah, that doesn't usually happen to me, so I really would have liked to appreciate it.

But I can't. And I don't. My feet tap nervously on the floor and my heart leaps into my chest when he comes to a stop next to the table.

"Skylar?"

I hastily stand on unsteady feet, somewhat surprised I haven't fainted yet, and shake his hand. I was supposed to shake it, right? That wasn't like him going in for a hug or something? I sigh, too late, and stutter out a reply. "Uh, you can just call me Skye. And you're Glenn, right?"

"Yeah." He takes his seat.

I keep standing, frozen in place for a moment—caught between needing to stay for my job and wanting to run for my sanity. My job wins out. I sit. "So." I swallow. Be cool. Be casual. You're just making polite conversation. "Is this the restaurant you work in? I didn't realize that when you asked me to dinner."

"It is." He nods, not even bothering to pick up the menu. I can't help but notice he has a nice smile, warm and friendly. And really white teeth too. No dimples, though... Wait—where'd that thought come from? Ugh, not the time to think about Ollie. Especially when Glenn is still talking. I lean in, refocusing, trying to catch the tail end of his sentence. "...a little unorthodox, but I thought hey, why not? This way I could make our dessert beforehand and you could taste a little of my food."

I nod, furrowing my brows, pretending I understand, when really I'm grasping for what to say next. He mentioned dessert. His cooking. Oh, and what did Ollie tell me? Not that I want to think about Ollie, and then I remember.

"You're the pastry chef!" I blurt and then shift uncomfortably on my seat, hoping that didn't come out as loud and crazy as it sounded. Knowing my luck, it came out even louder and even crazier, especially since he's giving me a confused sort of look. And then I realize, he must have told me that already, during those few moments when I completely zoned out and stopped paying attention. Not the best way to start a date.

I swallow.

My butt is sweating again.

"So, what did you make? Or is that a surprise?"

"No, not a surprise." He shakes his head, but keeps his eyes locked on mine. They're a nice color, a milk chocolate brown that sort of works perfectly for a man who makes desserts for a living. "I made one of my specialties—a medallion of cheesecake resting on a cinnamon crumble, topped with raspberry compote and toasted coconut shavings. Oh, and a caramel, butterscotch drizzle."

Holy crap.

I gape.

That sounds amazing.

He just chuckles at my expression. "So, that sounds good?"

"Delicious." I grin back. Maybe I'm not so bad at this.

"So what do you do?" he asks.

Such a simple question, innocent really. It's not his fault that it sends me into a coughing fit as I choke on the water I just swallowed and try my best not to spit it out all over the table. So not attractive. "I'm a writer," I finally say. "I work for the style section of a newspaper. But enough about me, I want to hear more about these desserts. Are you a cupcake man?"

"I am," he says cheerfully. I silently applaud myself on the successful sidestep and try not to salivate as the discussion veers into his favorite flavors. And for a moment, I really think I might have found my dream man. I mean, hello, breakfast in bed eating red velvet cupcakes topped with homemade cream cheese frosting? Yes, please!

But my elation fades in the blink of an eye when a waiter stops by our table, setting down a little treat, roasted butternut squash puree "compliments of the chef." Oh, the soup, the soup looks great. It's what's on top of the soup that has me balling my fists under the table.

A pesto-drizzle winky face.

A freaking winky face—a smiley face that's winking. And there's only one person who could have put it there.

I spin in my chair, looking back toward the kitchen entrance, but Ollie isn't there. Coward! Hiding in the kitchen to escape my wrath—

"Everything okay?" Glenn asks.

"Oh, sure," I mutter and turn back around, quickly downing the little shot glass of soup to erase the evidence. "That was so nice of them, to do that."

"Yeah, the guys back there are great. Speaking of, how do you know Oliver?"

I swallow my anger, trying to bring the charming, first date personality back around. "His sister is my best friend, we all grew up together. I mean, he's practically my brother." Except…not at all. But Glenn doesn't need to know that. I quickly change the topic. "So, how do you like living in New York? I've only been here for about four months, but I love it."

And just like that, the date is back on course.

Turns out Glenn has been in New York for a long time, twelve years. He came here for culinary school when he was eighteen and decided to stay after he got a job at one of his favorite restaur—wait! Twelve years ago he was eighteen… He was eighteen twelve years ago… I quickly do the math—I may be a writer but that doesn't mean I can't add. Still though, I'm doubting my skills as the truth hits.

He's thirty?

He's thirty!

I try not to spew food across the table as internal sirens blare, instead nodding absently to give the appearance that I'm paying attention. But really the word *thirty* is jumping around my head, knocking everything else out of whack. And then my brain does that thing where the entire world seems to warp around my thoughts, and the longer I look at Glenn, the more distinct the numbers three and zero imprint on his forehead. And no matter how hard I try to listen, all I hear from his lips is, *I'm thirty. I'm thirty. I'm thirty.* And all the wrinkles I didn't see become more pronounced. Is that a gray hair?

Thirty. That's an eight-year difference. When he was eighteen, I was ten! Oh, great, I just cringed because of how disgusting that is, but come on, I was playing with Barbie dolls when he was in college doing college age things.

And now he's speaking but I don't hear anything. Wonderful.

Focus, Skye.

Focus.

"Are you okay?"

"Yeah," I blurt way too cheerfully. Calm down, just calm down. Thirty isn't that old anyway. He's more worldly. More sophisticated. I wonder how many women he's slept with…Oh god, if he ever hears that I'm a virgin, he'll think I'm an infant! A child! And suddenly it's not that thirty seems old, but that twenty-two seems way too young.

Oh thank god, the waiter is coming over. I sigh, saved for a few minutes.

"Are you ready to order?"

We decide to split a porterhouse steak and a few vegetable sides. I'm not even paying attention to the food—my thoughts are racing ahead for something mature to say. And then the waiter catches my eye before leaving, throwing a little side grin my way and I know, I just know, he's a little traitor passing information off to Ollie in the kitchen. I wonder what he's going to report? That I look pale and crazed? Probably accurate…

I take a sip of my water, tossing a nervous smile in Glenn's direction.

"Tell me about your family," he says.

Good, that's easy enough. Well, not really because my family is completely complicated, but it didn't used to be. We were a perfectly happy suburban family—that is until my father decided to cheat on my mother with the live-in babysitter next door when I was fifteen. And then my house became World War Three for a few months. He was kicked out. Then let back in. Then kicked out. Then let back in. I learned to ignore clothes dropping past the kitchen window when I was doing homework, to tune out the raging shouting matches before I went to bed. More often than not, I escaped to Bridget's house, relishing in the normalness of her completely happy parents. But how do you tell that to a relative stranger?

"It's just my mom and me," I say, settling on those less complicated words. "My parents got divorced when I was a teenager, and I don't really spend too much time with my dad." I shrug, ignoring the pitter-patter of my racing heart. "What about you?"

"I have a big family," he says, affection evident in his tone. And it's sweet.

For the next while, we compare holidays and childhoods before we move onto travel and hobbies—all things I assume are pretty standard first date topics. And Glenn is just as sophisticated as I thought he might be. In culinary school, he studied abroad in Italy for a year and I'm enthralled by his stories about Europe—the food, the people, the culture. I've only ever been to England, but I yearn to travel—to see all of the places he's telling me about, to taste every meal and know for myself if it's all as delicious as he says. Somehow, I already know it is. The next hour passes in the blink of an eye. I forget to be nervous because I'm actually having fun.

Until Glenn apologizes, retreating to the kitchen to put the finishing touches on the dessert. And left alone again, my eternal freak out begins anew. Is this actually going okay, or do

I just think it's going okay? Does he think I'm funny? Does he think I'm cute? I think he's cute. But, what if he doesn't think I am? Is this all in my head? And then, oh god, we ate creamed spinach. Why do I eat so much spinach? Do I have something in my teeth—again?

I dip down for my purse, pulling my phone out of the side pocket, and turn on the camera, discretely checking my teeth out in the image.

Phew. They're clean.

But then a text message vibrates my phone, popping up on the top of the screen.

Ollie: *Stop checking yourself out.*

I sit up straight, spinning, but I don't see him anywhere.

Ollie: *You'll never find me.*

Me: *Where are you!?*

Ollie: *Secrets of the kitchen. My lips are sealed.*

Me: *Jerk!*

Ollie: *Did you like the soup? It's a new recipe I'm working on.*

Me: *Soup? Yes. Garnish? No.*

Ollie: *Aw, come on. It was funny.*

I tell myself I won't respond to his goading and drop my cell in my lap. Radio silence.

Ollie: *Skye? You're not really mad, are you?*

Screw it. I'm all alone at the table, my water is empty, and I'm bored.

Me: *How does my dessert look?*

Ollie: *Horrible. You should just leave now and cut your losses.*

And suddenly, I'm grinning wider than I have all evening, buoyant. I look up, but Ollie is still nowhere to be seen. Where the heck is his lookout spot? I turn back to my phone, retorting.

Me: *You're just saying that because you want it.*

Ollie: *Maybe…*

Ollie: *But Glenn would stab me with the cake knife before he'd let me eat your dessert.*

Me: *You'd deserve it for stealing my cheesecake! I've been thinking of that caramel drizzle all night!*

Ollie: *I took a spoonful when the head chef wasn't looking. So good.*

Me: *Yum!*

Ollie: *So…*

Ollie: *Think you'll go out with Glenn again? How are things going?*

I bite my lip, thinking, sort of wondering why he's so curious. Then again, he works with Glenn, so it's not that strange to ask. But he's Ollie. And I'm Skye. And nothing is ever quite as uncomplicated as it seems between us. Or maybe it is, for him.

Me: *Yeah, sure. He's a great guy. Really sweet.*

Ollie: *You don't think he's a little old? Did he tell you he's thirty?*

And for the first time I wonder if Ollie maybe wanted the date to fail all along. I challenge back.

Me: *Well, you set us up, so obviously you didn't think the age difference was a big deal. Why should I?*

The little texting thought bubble pops up, showing me Ollie is typing something. But then it disappears. Pops up again. Disappears.

Don't look up. Don't look up.

I look up.

I turn.

And there he is, standing in the doorway—the same one Glenn first walked out of—casually leaning against the frame, arms crossed. His hair looks even darker against the crisp white of his chef's suit, his furrowed eyebrows look stark against his pearly skin, and his normally full peach lips are drawn in a thin line. But then again, mine are too.

The door opens behind him.

Glenn.

Available Glenn. Smiling Glenn. Excited Glenn.

Ollie moves out of his way and goes back into the kitchen, not bothering to look at me again. I just pull my lips wide, feigning enthusiasm as Glenn makes his way back to the table.

He's so nice. He's so kind. He's so fun.

But he's not Ollie.

I eat the cheesecake. I rave over how amazing it tastes. I thank him profusely for taking the time to make something so delicious just for me. And when the meal is over, I let him lead me outside even though the back of my neck tingles the entire time, alert to the fact that someone is watching me and I know exactly who.

When Glenn goes in for the kiss, I hesitate. The evening was wonderful and I haven't been kissed by a boy in months. But at the last second, I turn, offering my cheek. And he gets the message loud and clear, saying goodnight and hailing me a cab.

The whole way home, I tell myself over and over again that no, I'm not just sitting in silence waiting for my phone to vibrate. I refuse to take it out of my purse. Refuse to look at it.

Until, *buzz*, it moves on my lap.

I rip open my bag.

Bridget: *How'd the date go?!?*

I ignore the sinking feeling in my chest.

Me: *Great!!*

Confession 7

Beautiful, fashionable women scare the crap out of me. They're like a foreign breed I don't know what to do with. Well, aside from Bridget, but I think it must be because I've known her for so long. It's hard to be intimidated by someone you've had burping contests with...

"I love it!" Victoria exclaims, swiveling in her chair, grinning while she reads the last few sentences of my column for next week. For a moment, I sit up higher, ears perked. And then, as per usual, she places the papers on her desk, reaches for her red pen, and goes to town.

Each swish of her hand is a dagger to my heart. The swirls of crimson ink are my blood. And Victoria, in her crisp clementine dress and floral scarf, is my executioner. Not the most obvious outfit choice for a killer, I'll admit, but the woman is heartless as she tears my work to shreds.

I sink so low in my chair that I can barely see over the rim of her desk. Once, just once, I would love to have a column I don't need to write over and over—oh, I don't know, about a million times—before it's acceptable to print. But this week is not that week, and as she hands back her edits, I do my best not to crumple the sheets into a tiny ball with my furiously clenching fists.

I've gotten much better at doing that assistant smile the other girls do. You know, the one that says I love you and I want to kill you at the same time. You sort of grind your teeth and deaden your eyes, while also pinching your cheeks and lifting your eyebrows. Yeah, that one took me a while to master. I'm pretty sure for a week there Victoria thought I was deranged. But now all she does is return a pleasant smile of her own.

"Get me a new copy by tomorrow morning, all right?"

I take the papers. "Of course, Victoria. I'll start working on it right away."

And then she looks back down at her desk, shuffling through her folders to signal that I'm dismissed. As soon as I'm out of her office, the smile vanishes. I know it's not really her fault—she's just doing her job, and I'm a new reporter, and in the long run my writing will be better for it. But I can't help how my heart sinks when my eyes run across every red scribble decorating the page. Total overhaul.

"Oh, and Skye?"

Crap. I lift the corners of my lips—it's the best I can do at the moment—and turn. "Yes?"

"Are you going on a second date?"

"Ah, no," I murmur, not sure if I should tell her more.

"Good," she says and looks back down. But now I'm the one who's curious. Good? What the heck does that mean?

"Um…" I step back into her office. "Can I ask why?"

"Glenn, the pastry chef." Victoria shrugs and scrunches her face, not bothering to look up from her desk. "It's just not sexy enough, not daring enough to really hook readers. They want to live vicariously. You need to find someone more exciting, more alluring for the long-term."

Poor Glenn…sweet, kind, if slightly boring, Glenn. I wonder if his name has been what's holding him back all along. Something about it just doesn't scream *sexy*, you know? But then the meaning behind Victoria's words really sinks in and I understand what she's really saying, what she really wants—a train wreck. Not a good guy, not a stable relationship, but drama—full-fledged, on-again-off-again, I-love-you-I-hate-you, one second we're fighting and the next we're passionately kissing, soap opera style romance. Well, I must say, it's so nice to know my boss is looking out for my well-being.

I sigh as I sink into my seat, staring at my computer screen while my mind processes all the things I need to do before I leave today. Rewrite my column. E-mail a few freelancers for status updates on their articles. Answer dating advice questions for the website—which, really, I barely feel qualified for. Oh, and shuffle through the hundred unopened event invitations on my desk—the ones carefully stacked into a very precarious column that may or may not collapse at any second.

Leaning back, I close my eyes for a moment, wishing it were Friday. I had one of those truly terrible days where I went the entire morning thinking it was Friday, only to remember after lunch that it was Thursday, and there was one more insufferable day to get through before the weekend. Ever since, my mood has been terrible. Well, truth be told, my mood has been terrible ever since the end of my date with Glenn—Ollie hasn't texted me, hasn't spoken to me, and try as I might to stay up really late and catch him off guard, I inevitably fall asleep before he comes home from work. I don't even know what I want to say, so really, it's probably better this way. I mean, it's definitely better this way.

Maybe…

"What are you doing tonight?" I hear one of the other assistants ask behind my back, but I choose to ignore it. All four of us share a corner space, and they're always making plans and not inviting me. To go get drinks, to go to events together, to go shopping. It's nothing new. I don't really think they do it maliciously, but that doesn't mean it doesn't sting.

So I don't answer as I sit up and log into my account, ready to check the e-mails I must have received while in Victoria's office.

"Skylar?"

Huh? Is she talking to me? I glance at the twenty new messages and decide, screw it, they can wait.

"Yeah?" I ask, swiveling around in my chair, curious.

"What are you doing tonight?" It's Rebecca. She's definitely the kindest of the three, a little more down to earth. During my first week, she gave me some shopping pointers about what colors and clothes might look good on me. Looking to either side, I realize Blythe, the obvious ringleader, is nowhere to be found. And neither is Isabel. Something strange is happening.

I shrug.

"Nothing really. I'll probably stay late and get some work done. Why? Do you need me to finish something for you?"

Rebecca looks at me funny and then laughs. "No, I'm meeting the other girls downstairs in a few minutes. We're going to meet some friends at a happy hour downtown."

I nod, moving just slightly back and forth in my chair, completely unsure of what she expects me to do or say. There's a slightly elongated pause, as though we're both waiting for the other to speak. I give in. "Um, have fun?"

Rebecca purses her lips, staring at me, and then asks, "Do you have a problem picking up social cues?" Then, acting as if she didn't just ask me a totally degrading question, she reaches for her purse and pulls a scarf around her neck, tousling her hair in a way that looks styled rather than accidental. Now that's a skill I could use.

Then I remember her question—social cues. Me. Picking them up. Okay I admit, there may be a disconnect there...a small one, minute really, inconsequential...or you know, one the size of the Grand Canyon.

"Maybe?" I answer somewhat honestly.

"Well, when I just said the girls and I are going out for drinks, it was sort of an invitation. Do you want to come?" And she stands there in her high heels, looking down at me with perfectly ruffled brown tresses and an outfit that could be torn from the pages of a magazine, and I realize something. Have they been inviting me all along? Dropping hints that I just never picked up? Do they think I'm maybe the a-hole who keeps ignoring them rather than the other way around?

Crap!

My entire life has just been brought into question.

How many times have I misread people's intentions? How many parties was I invited to in high school without realizing, all the while using Bridget as my excuse to go? How many guys have potentially dropped hints and I've been too in my own head to take notice? How many times—

"Uh, Skylar?"

Double crap! I'm doing it right now…

"Sure!" I jump out of my chair, knocking it very ungracefully into my desk. A second later, the gentle ruffle of sliding paper trickles into my ear.

No.

I sigh, knowing what's about to happen right before it does.

And then envelopes rain down around my feet—the invitations. The ones I had so painstakingly stacked are tumbling like a waterfall over the edge of my desk, slipping across the floor—a flash flood drowning my newfound enthusiasm. I have so much work to finish. I have a column to rewrite by the morning. I have a mess to clean. I have a thousand things more important than drinking that I have to do right now.

Rebecca's still waiting for me, so I look up into her smiling eyes. She just shrugs, completely unconcerned. "You ready?"

I look back down at the mess of envelopes circling my feet, still shifting into place. As though the world is mocking me, one last one drops, sharp point landing squarely on the exposed flesh of my upper foot, stinging so bad it brings tears to my eyes—and I decide I've had enough. Of this day. Of this office. Of my lies. And of being the only assistant left out of the fun. I grab my purse. "Let's go."

When we make it outside to where the other assistants are waiting, Blythe raises one eyebrow in my direction, but remains silent.

Isabel on the other hand, waves enthusiastically. "You're going out with us? You never go out with us."

I choose not to point out that if they did in fact want me to come, they could have been a little more blunt about it in the first place. You know, especially after realizing that I'm socially inept. But instead, I let my mood stay light and cheery, answering with an enthusiastic, "Yup! Where are we going anyway?"

Blythe shifts her upturned nose in my direction, looking down at me from the precarious height of her four-inch heels. "To see my brother and his friends."

"You have a brother?" I blurt and then bite my lip, hoping it didn't sound as rude as it did in my head. But really, who expects the spawn of Satan to have a sibling?

Blythe rolls her eyes. "Yes. And he's waiting for us."

Before I have time to embarrass myself further by heading for the subway, Isabel raises her hand to hail a cab. As a former model and stunning beauty, it takes about, I don't know, less than a heartbeat for one to pull up. I take the loser seat in the front next to the driver, sort of feeling more like an explorer on an expedition into foreign lands than a girl going out with friends—well, acquaintances anyway.

For fifteen minutes, Blythe, Rebecca, and Isabel discuss weekend plans, their most recent dating adventures, their latest hook ups. I subtly take a few notes on my phone in the front seat—hey, this is good stuff for my column! But when the conversation becomes a venting session about work, and the editors, and our bosses, I join in wholeheartedly, putting my phone away. And it feels sort of nice to bond with the girls over some common ground—they may all be rich and beautiful and fashionable in ways I'm totally not, but at the newspaper we're all at the bottom of the pecking order.

As a solid pack of four, we casually step into happy hour, maneuvering through the crowd in search of Blythe's brother. I can't help but notice as I look around that we don't quite fit in here. Practically everyone else in the bar is a man, and practically all of those men are staring at us, studying us, checking us out. They're young. They're in suits. They all feel shrouded in a cloud of over-confidence, at least that's what their blatant stares seem to imply. Well, either that or just total arrogance, but I'll give them all the benefit of the doubt. And as I meet a few of the roving eyes, I realize I'm one of the girls they're checking out. Me! I must be hot by association! I should hang out with models more often.

A blush warms my cheeks and I look away, focusing on following Rebecca's back as we weave in and out of people. All the way in the corner by a booth, we stop.

"Blythe!" a boy shouts, waving us over. He's cute. Like really cute.

Angular jaw. Straight nose. Clean-shaven. Honey brown eyes with a hint of green. Soft brown hair. Sort of the all-

American boy look. And, oh man, that smile…open enough to be kind, thin enough to be mysterious, and—shoot! He caught me staring. Way to be subtle.

I quickly flick my eyes to the side, nonchalantly scanning the room. When I glance back, he's still looking, but this time that melt-your-heart smile is even wider and definitely pointed in my direction, with some blatant interest I might add.

The need to flee jets up my spine.

Run. Run.

Fast!

But I don't.

And I don't look away either.

What is going on? This is so not me… But for one night, maybe it can be. You know, for the research.

"Everyone, this is Skylar," Blythe announces somewhat begrudgingly, pointing a finger in my direction. At the mention of my name, I snap out of my somewhat stalkerish trance and look around at the rest of the group. There are two other guys, both dressed in nice suits with loosened ties. But my eyes are drawn back to the boy who is now standing, opening his arms to bring Blythe in for a hug.

Are they dating? Just what I need, to land a tweenage crush on Blythe's boyfriend. But as they pull away, I realize it's much worse. They have the same profile, the same nose, the same chin…

It's not her boyfriend.

It's her brother.

"I'm Patrick Keaton," he says, extending a hand in my direction. I numbly accept, shaking, all the while trying to figure out how someone so evil could be related to someone so…not. At least, I hope not. "These are my friends Dan and Josh."

Dan reminds me of a politician, you know, with one of those smiles that's just too perfect to be real and looks more like a fancy façade hiding a well of inner disdain? One of those, complete with sparkling white teeth. And Josh looks like a player, too good-looking to be a nice person sort of thing. He also has sunglasses on top of his head even though it's after sunset, and is currently guzzling his own pitcher of beer, so there are other signs.

"Nice to meet you guys," I murmur, letting the other girls squeeze into the booth first. But they all follow Blythe and I'm left taking the seat next to Patrick, which isn't really a bad place to be, except I'm suddenly hyperaware of really ridiculous things. Does my breath smell? Am I taking up too much room? Is my hair too flat? Am I too close to him? Should I fold my hands on my lap, or maybe put them on top of the table, or cross my arms? And then I do all three of those things…twice. Before I start to look like I'm having a seizure, I finally put one hand in my lap and one on the table as a compromise.

"So, Skylar," Patrick asks conversationally, "are you an assistant too?"

Before I can respond, Blythe chips in, "She's the sex columnist."

Josh perks up, lifting his head out of his pitcher and looking at me with newfound admiration. Well, thanks for that, Blythe.

"It's more of a dating column," I rush to say, biting back the rest of my nervous chatter before I accidentally confess how far from a sex columnist I really am. Hey, it wouldn't be the first time. I need to change the subject. "What do you guys do?"

"Investment banking," Dan responds.

"Ah," I sigh, looking around at the sea of pinstripes with understanding. Bankers. The unattainable group of Manhattan men single women seem to chase with total abandon—they're wealthy, good-looking, known to have a wandering eye, which in an odd way makes them all the more attractive. It seems like I've inadvertently found the jackpot—too bad those are all traits I've never really been interested in. Well, haven't been interested in until now, I correct myself, meeting Patrick's flirtatious gaze.

"Ah, what?" he asks, the hint of a friendly challenge in his voice.

"Oh, nothing." I shake my head. "I didn't mean anything by it. It's just, you know, now I get why you're all in suits."

He narrows his eyes, letting me know he sensed the sidestep, but then a waitress comes over to ask if we want anything to drink. Blythe gets a cosmopolitan. Rebecca orders a glass of white wine. Isabel decides on a dark and stormy, whatever that is. And then it's my turn and there's really no doubt what I need—a cold beer. It may not be the most fashionable drink, but as I take a long sip, relishing the citrus tinted taste swirling down my throat, all I can think is oh, yeah—this is what I've been waiting for all week. Instantly, I'm a little less on edge. It's really amazing what a little bit of cold beer can do.

While I'm still sipping, Patrick leans over and whispers, "You don't really seem like someone Blythe would normally hang out with."

"Why?" I ask after putting my cup down. "Because I'm not a size zero, and I think spending thousands of dollars on a handbag is insane?"

Whoa, where'd that attitude come from? I'm not really sure, but I sort of like it. Apparently Patrick does too because he laughs, not pulling away. The gentle caress of his breath tickles the spot of skin just below my ear, and I know if I turned to look at him, we'd be close enough to kiss. I mean, I won't. But just knowing that sends a little thrill down my spine and raises the hairs on the back of my neck. I take another sip, feeling flushed.

"No," he finally says. "You look like the kind of girl who could go sailing without worrying that the wind would ruin your hair."

Huh. A little random, but I'll go with it. "Do you sail?"

"Don't you?" he responds, as though the very idea of not sailing is utterly insane. But isn't it really the sort of thing only fifty-year-old men with too much time on their hands do? I try to picture it—the ocean, the sun, the idea of being all alone with no one and nothing in sight. Patrick's smiling face pushes its way into my imagination, but now he's wearing a bathing suit, six-pack abs, and nothing else. And I'm in a bikini—stomach maybe a little flatter than it is in real life, but hey, this is my fantasy! And we're floating, sipping on champagne. We're surrounded by sparkling sapphire blue, stuck in a gemstone.

I shrug. Suddenly sailing doesn't seem so bad. Actually, it sort of seems like the most romantic thing in the world.

"I could get into sailing," I say almost subconsciously, not realizing I spoke aloud until Patrick's grin deepens and I feel mine doing the same. I'm about to turn and look at him, finally meeting his gaze, when—

"Ow!" I howl, jumping about five-feet in the air as I reach for my shin. What the heck? I rub the sore spot. Someone kicked me. Someone wearing pointy-toed shoes. I look up.

Blythe is staring me down from across the table. She blinks and the look is gone, replaced by concern. "Oh my goodness, Skylar, I'm so sorry. I was just crossing my legs."

Little brat. Of course, I can't say that. So instead I do that secret loathing smile Blythe taught me—she is the master after all—and say, "Oh, don't worry about it. I'm totally fine."

But Blythe has already forgotten me, turning her attention on her brother. "So, did you hear that Dad wants us to spend Christmas with Grandma and Grandpa in Connecticut? I mean, how lame."

And just like that, I've lost him. Patrick turns to his sister, pulled into family drama, and I'm completely forgotten by his side.

Oh, she's good.

She's very, very good.

For the next forty-five minutes or so, I nod politely while Dan and Josh switch between arguing about some multi-million dollar deal they're working on and arguing about football. Then I try to edge my way into Isabel and Rebecca's conversation but fail miserably when I realize they're discussing designers I know nothing about. Blythe is still whining about spending Christmas outside of New York City, which really doesn't seem like more than a five-minute conversation to me or all that terrible, truth be told. And I realize my job here is done. I bonded with my fellow assistants a little bit, maybe have enough to pull some sort of column together for next week, and would rather go home to binge watch reality television with Bridget then remain here and feel obsolete.

"I'm going to go," I mutter and stand up. No one really seems to mind. They're all too deep in their own worlds and I wonder if this is one of those social cues Rebecca said I have a hard time picking up on.

Just as I'm halfway down the street, someone calls my name.

"Skylar!"

I turn, unable to stop the little flip my heart makes inside my chest. "Patrick?"

He runs over, completely confident as he lays a hand on my arm. "Why are you leaving?"

I shrug, sort of wondering the same thing as I start to get a little lost in the evergreen edges of his eyes. "I, um, I just have some work I need to do for tomorrow."

He nods, not hesitating for a second before replying, "What are you doing on Saturday?"

I gulp, unused to a guy with such unbreakable confidence. Is he even the slightest bit worried that I might turn him down? I mean, I won't—at least if my racing pulse is anything to go by. But I could. And against my normally neurotic nature, I decide to make him guess a little bit. "Why? What's happening on Saturday?"

He bites his lower lip, ensuring that my attention is brought to that exact part of his very kissable body. "Well, I sort of hope that answer will be going out with me."

Straight to the point, and I kind of like it.

Patrick is the sort of boy Victoria wants me to date. I can tell just by looking at him. Definitely sexy. Confident if not cocky. With deep enough pockets to take me on lavish dates that our readers will love to sit in on. And just far enough out of reach to make me insecure in where I stand—which, I'll admit, scares me. I mean, he's the opposite of my ex. John was steady. He was safe. But then I blink, heart-pinching—John broke my heart anyway.

"Sure," I find myself whispering, caution blown away in the wind. What have I got to lose?

Confession 8

I'm a total romantic. Flowers, chocolates, kissing in the rain—bring on the clichés! I pretty much spend all of December watching those made for TV movies about Christmas. The cheesier, the better.

"Wait, he's picking you up?" Bridget yells from her room. "What does that even mean?"

We've both spent the past hour speaking through the wall, comparing and contrasting outfits while we ready ourselves for our dates. I've settled on a curve-hugging midnight blue dress, obviously stolen from Bridget's closet, and even broke out my old push-up bra for the occasion. And the ladies look fantastic, if I do say so myself.

"I don't know," I shout while staring into the mirror. Do I like these pearl earrings? Or how about these gold ones? Though silver makes the grayish blue in my eyes stand out… "He just said to text him my address and he'd come pick me up at eight."

"Like, in a car?" Bridget is really stuck on this idea. "Or in a cab? Or are you walking? I just, I've never even heard of someone picking someone up for a first date in this city."

"I think it's sort of sweet," I say.

"Well, however he's picking you up, he'll be here any minute."

Crap!

I jerk away from the mirror, deciding on the silver earrings, and take a step back, pulling my dress down to smooth out the wrinkles, doing a little twirl, you know, surveying. According to Skylar standards, I went all out tonight. Wedges—the closest thing to heels that I can safely manage. Full makeup covering the spatter of freckles that span my cream cheeks. A little pouf in my hardly ever styled hair.

I look good.

"You look hot," Bridget says, echoing my thoughts as she peeks her head through the door. "How about me?"

"Gorgeous!" And I mean it. Soft curls lighten her thick red hair. The evergreen skinny jeans look fantastic against her natural coloring, especially paired with that black sparkly top. And next time, I need to borrow whatever eyeliner she's wearing because her eyes pop—in a good way!

The phone on my desk vibrates.

I freeze as nerves surge up my spine. He's here.

Suddenly I can't breathe. My eyes go wide.

"Uh, Skye?" Bridge says.

I shake my head. I can't speak. My voice has run away. It's in hiding.

He's here.

Oh my god, what was I thinking saying yes! He's so far out of my league it's laughable. So attractive. So good-looking. So going to break my heart.

"Skye!" Bridge runs over and grabs my shoulder. "Stop freaking out."

"I'm not freaking out," I squeak. My hands are shaking. I might be hyperventilating. Is the room starting to spin?

"Come on," Bridget nudges, grabbing my purse before taking my hands and tugging me from my room. I think she's going to let go when we make it into the living room, but she doesn't. She just keeps pulling me past our kitchen and right to the front door.

"Bridge, really, it's okay," I protest, but she just shakes her head, letting one hand go to open the apartment door.

"As if I'll believe you. The last time I saw you this nervous was junior year in high school when Chris asked you on a date. You told me you didn't need me to come over and help you get ready, then I find out from everyone later that night that you totally bailed on him. Well, if this guy is so chivalrous that he's picking you up outside of our apartment, no way am I letting you blow it by hiding in the emergency staircase or something ridiculous like that until he gives up and leaves."

"I wouldn't hide in the staircase…" Though I admit, now that she said it, the idea doesn't sound half bad.

Ignoring me, she continues to yank on my arm, practically pulling it out of its socket—which when you think about it really wouldn't be the ideal way to start my date. But a few minutes later, I'm in the elevator, purse in hand, watching in horror as the doors close, leaving me by myself.

"Bridge!" I shout, banging on the metal just as it seals shut.

How could she leave me like this?

I swallow. Heat rises under my skin. Suffocating. The walls start to close in. I watch as the numbers click lower and lower, butterflies zipping around my stomach. And not in that cute anticipating way, but in this painful, terror inducing way. And then suddenly, I visualize my escape—the perfect excuse for retreat.

My jacket!

I forgot my jacket! I have to go back. I have to!

Futilely, I press on the button for my floor over and over again, but the number won't light up. I've got a one-way ticket—down. And a few seconds later, the elevator stops. I'm just going to stay here and go back up. Just stay and go back up, and get my jacket, and then hide in my room until I can forget this night ever happened.

The door cracks open and I want to close my eyes.

But he's there. Patrick. Almost the same as when I last saw him, but this time, a perfect red rose rests in his hand. When our eyes meet, all of my nerves melt away, vanish in a split second. Instead, I feel warm and tingly all over, excitement tangible, an energy that crackles the air around me.

"Skylar," he says.

I shiver. My name has never sounded so good.

"Patrick," I sigh.

Then the elevator door starts to close, because I, like a star-struck idiot, forgot to get off. I reach out to catch it, but Patrick beats me, stopping the metal with his hand and pushing it back.

"For you," he says, and hands me the rose.

And even though I know this could easily be some move he does with every girl, a carefully crafted gesture to put me right where he wants me, I can't help it. I accept, bringing the flower to my nose and sniffing gently as a shy smile curves my lips.

He grabs my hand, easily taking charge in a way I'm not used to. John and I were dating for months before he finally felt comfortable enough to hold my hand, but Patrick does it effortlessly, a little too smoothly. But I don't care, because his hand is warm and where our fingers touch, a little fire ignites beneath my skin.

Oh yeah, this is bad. Two seconds into the date and I can already feel myself falling, hard. But if he's playing a game, then I'm pretty much guaranteed to lose, so I might as well enjoy it while I can.

"I have a car waiting outside," he says.

"A car?" I ask, sort of giggling.

"Well, if I work on weekends the company pays for a car service back to my apartment, so I figured I would take advantage tonight." He looks back at me and grins. I melt a little more.

Definitely bad…but in the best way possible.

True to his word, waiting outside is a black town car. I sort of feel like a celebrity when he jumps ahead and opens the door for me, letting me scoot in first. The seats are soft leather and there's a divider halfway up giving us privacy. I've never felt quite so fancy before. I mean, I grew up in Pennsylvania just a few miles east of farm country. We didn't exactly take limos around. I'm about to comment when I remember that

Patrick, born and raised on the Upper East Side, probably did.

I close my mouth, biting my lip. We're definitely from different worlds, but tonight I get to be Cinderella—and I don't want to ruin the magic before it really even begins.

"So, where are we going?" I ask as the car eases away from the curb. I've crossed my hands on my lap, unsure of where to put them. Patrick stretches his arm over the back of my seat, and I'm hyper aware of the inch between our skin.

"One of my favorite restaurants in the city, I go with my family all of the time. It's an Asian fusion restaurant in Columbus Circle, gorgeous views of the park."

It takes me a second to realize he's talking about Central Park, and my anxiety creeps back in—any restaurant with great views of that park is a restaurant that is far out of my price range. But—I sigh—Cinderella. That's going to be my mantra for the evening, because, well, if the prince fits... I peek to the side, taking in Patrick's strong profile, and oh, he fits all right.

Now, what to say, what to say... I want to be charming and cute, maybe with a splash of sexy and a hint of mystery. That's easy enough, right? But I think and think, and lick my lips, and nervously smile in his direction, and after a few seconds I'm still drawing a complete blank. My mind is utterly empty. My tongue starts to feel fat and useless. An awkward chill creeps across my skin. This is so the opposite of the effect I was going for.

"So." Patrick finally breaks the silence. "When did you start working for the newspaper with Blythe?"

"Well, I started with an internship for the editors of the book review—"

"Ah, a smart girl," he interrupts, which normally bugs the crap out of me, but I can't help but smile at the admiration in his tone.

"I guess," I admit a little shyly, not really used to bragging about that sort of thing. "But a few weeks ago right around the middle of August, a position opened up in the lifestyle section and they wanted me."

"To be the…" He pauses. "Dating columnist?"

My face goes a little pink. Thank god he didn't say sex columnist—we'd have a full-on tomato situation here. "Sort of. I do most of the normal assistant stuff too, but I also have a weekly column talking about the average sort of dating life for, you know, recent grads and girls in their twenties. That sort of thing."

"So," he leads and then turns to me, warm eyes narrowing, corners of his lips picking up just a little bit. "Will I be in this column?"

Okay—tomato situation might be happening after all. I look away, suddenly smoldering in the tiny space of the car. "Maybe…"

"Maybe?" he challenges.

I feed off the humor in his tone, using it to push my nerves away. "Yeah, that's right, maybe. I mean, we only just started the date, I need to wait and see if it's newsworthy."

He nods, pursing his lips, pretending to be very serious. I squeeze mine together to keep from laughing—I don't want to ruin the game! "So what would one need to do to be newsworthy? I've already got the fancy ride."

"And the rose," I add.

"Right, and the rose."

"No chocolates though," I gently accuse, frowning.

Patrick shakes his head, face full of remorse. "I'm clearly off my game tonight."

"Clearly," I concede. And though he's trying really hard to remain stone-faced, I hear a sharp exhale of air, the barest hint of humor escaping, and grin. "Don't worry, you could make up for it. Tell me something strange about yourself, something that would make my readers remember you."

"Hmm." He furrows his brows, thinking. "I slept with my baby blanket until I was twelve."

My heart melts picturing him as a little boy—for some reason I imagine a soft blue blanket with teddy bears on it. Ooh and maybe spaceships. Adorable! But this is too fun to let him know that. "Or how about something bad? Break any laws recently?"

"I did!" he says really animatedly.

I lean in, truthfully intrigued. "You did? What?"

He leans in too—this is top-secret information after all—whispering, "I jaywalk all the time. Really. I'm a serial jaywalker."

I press my lips together forcefully, presenting the best solemn face I can manage. "I should arrest you right now."

"Well, I imagine that would certainly make for a good column."

"So, I have your permission then?"

He holds his hands out in front of me, palms up. I search through my purse for a second before pouting. "Shoot, I must have left my handcuffs in my other bag."

"A common mistake, I'm sure."

"You have no idea," I say and roll my eyes.

He's about to answer when the car eases to a stop. "We're here," Patrick says and reaches for the door. And then, with his fingers still resting on the handle, he turns back to me, adding, "Oh, and Skylar?"

"Yeah?" I say, pulling my eyes away from the view of the fountain out my window. Let's be honest, his face is way more interesting anyway.

"You forgot to mention a kiss," he murmurs, vision dropping to my lips before returning to my eyes.

"What about it?" I whisper, a little entranced—caught in the force of his gaze, the heat of it.

"I think it'll make our date newsworthy." And then he's gone, opening the door and stepping out of the car.

My imagination takes over and instead of doing things like, I don't know, following, I'm picturing what it would be like to kiss him. To have those strong arms wrapped around me, pulling me close. To have those soft lips tease mine, pulling and pushing, slipping down to my throat, over to the soft spot below my ear, down a little more—

My face slams against the seat.

Ow.

I adjust, sitting up and rubbing my cheek, when *bam*! Realization hits.

I fell over.

I actually got so mesmerized just thinking about kissing him that I fell over…inside of a car. How is that even possible? My entire body still tingles from the imaginary kiss. And I have to admit—I'm a little nervous how I'll react if it happens in real life. Well, not if, when. Definitely when. Cue the heart palpitations!

"Uh, Skylar? You coming?" Patrick teases.

Shoot! Did he see me?

"Sorry!" I scramble to follow, mind not quite working right, and I bump my head on the door on my way out.

Ow. Again.

More lightheadedness is so not what I need right now.

Patrick offers his hand and I take it thankfully, leaning on him while my racing thoughts clear. We make our way to the elevator, up a whole lot of floors, and arrive at the restaurant. To my amazement, my conversational skills return and we chitchat about nonsense until we're led to our table.

The sight takes my breath away.

Oh, yeah. This date is definitely newsworthy.

Our table rests right next to a floor-to-ceiling window, and I don't think I've ever seen New York look more beautiful than it does right now. The sun just finished setting, illuminating a midnight sky with soft aquamarine light. Far above, the stars flicker to life, brightening with each passing second, and farther down, countless windows across the horizon resemble floating lanterns against the deepening dark. The park is a forest shrouded in bottomless evergreen, vivified every so often by the orange glow of a streetlight. From so high up, the city looks quieter, more peaceful.

"Patrick." I sigh, because I can't find any other words.

He pulls my seat out and for the first time I notice the candles in the center of the table. They're always there, I'm sure, but right now it just seems like another thing to add to the growing list of romance. And bubbling beside the flame, shimmering like liquid gold, are two glasses of champagne. Across the soft light, I meet his eyes, warm brown at the center then brightening to dazzling emerald, and I get the sense that though he's been to the restaurant a dozen times before, this time might be different, might be special for him too. We clink our glasses, neither bothering to look away. A few minutes later, we're interrupted by a waiter.

"Your first course," he says and begins describing some sort of tuna tartare dish. I look down at the spoonful of tiny maroon cubes garnished with vegetables I don't recognize because they're in miniscule shavings.

"Um," I murmur, looking up. "I don't think these are ours. We haven't even seen a menu yet."

He just looks at me like I'm insane.

"Thank you," Patrick interjects, dismissing him before turning an amused smile on me. "I forgot you've never been here. There's an a la carte menu, but the tasting menu is much better. Seven courses and I ordered the wine pairings too. Speaking of…"

I turn just as two quarter-filled glasses of wine are set on the table, I don't catch the full description—I'm too focused on trying to discern what food is about to go in my mouth— but I recognize the words *sauvignon blanc*. The wine, at least, I know I'll like.

Without hesitation, Patrick picks up his spoon and polishes off the food in one bite, taking a small sip of wine to wash it down.

I swallow, a slight sliver of dread tickling my throat, and glance back at my plate, wondering if Cinderella had to deal with raw fish for her prince charming. Somehow, I doubt it. I mean, don't get me wrong, I'm all for trying new foods, but I'm more of a burger and fries, spaghetti and meatballs, take-out Chinese sort of girl.

Laughter pulls my eyes away from the food. It's Patrick, watching me watch my plate. "Aren't you going to eat it?"

"Oh, sure," I reply, reaching for the spoon, trying to act braver than I feel. "I just like to get the full aesthetic experience before I eat."

He raises his eyebrows, grin deepening as I bring the spoon to my lips.

One.

Two.

Three.

I open and swallow the contents.

Not bad, but not really my favorite either. It's a little…slimy. I reach for my wine, downing it in one sip, before looking up at Patrick with a sort of apologetic expression. And the rest of dinner passes in a somewhat similar fashion.

There's a spot in the middle where I actually recognize what I'm eating—lobster tail and then some sort of beef—but for the most part, I grin and bear it, telling myself I'm becoming more cultured with each passing second. The wine though, the wine is absolutely fantastic. And after one glass of champagne and seven miniature glasses of wine, I'm more than a little tipsy by the time dessert—a strange tapioca ball concoction—is cleared off the table. What can I say? Lots of wine and teeny tiny little portions make for a drunk Skylar.

"So, what did you think?" Patrick asks as we exit the restaurant, making our way toward the elevator. I hold onto his arm, leaning into his body for support. Oh, I can walk perfectly fine, I'm not that tipsy. But the wine has sort of whisked my inhibitions far enough away that I give in to the desire to touch him, to hold him. Beneath my hands, his bicep flexes just enough to make me curious about what other muscles hide beneath his clothes. Note to self—tasting menus at very expensive restaurants are dangerous. Steer clear in the future! You'll find your hormones raging with reckless abandon in only a few short hours.

"Did you like the food?" Patrick asks again.

"It was different," I say diplomatically. "Not really like anything I've had before. But next time, I think I should get to choose the spot."

He doesn't answer.

And then I realize my mistake.

Next time! Why did I say next time? Stupid inebriated loose lips!

I close my eyes tight, letting him lead my steps, but then I give in to curiosity and take a peek up. He senses the movement and looks down.

"And what spot is that?"

I bite my lip, thinking for a moment, but really—it's a no brainer. "Shake Shack. Madison Park. We can wait in line for an hour and freeze our butts off, then chow down on burgers and fries, freezing a little bit more from the milkshakes. But in the end, it'll totally be worth it."

He tilts his head a little, eyes brightening as if that's the last response he ever expected, but then reaches out his hand. "Deal."

"Deal," I repeat and we shake on it as we make our way outside. The night air sends a chill down my spine, causing goose bumps to pucker my skin. Patrick shrugs out of his suit jacket, resting it around my shoulders, and I hug the edges tight, breathing in the subtle scent of cologne.

I look at him.

He looks down at me.

A nervous tingle tickles my neck, and I know this is that moment at the end of the night that I dread—that moment when I take a cab home by myself or toss my caution to the wind and go home with him. But even after the romance and the wine, my choice is clear. Still though, I'm not ready to say goodbye, not ready for the magic of this night to end.

"A carriage ride!" I blurt, completely ruining the moment.

Patrick recoils, surprised by my outburst. "What?"

I look to the right where horses and carriages line up at the edge of the park, just waiting for riders, and take his hand.

"Come on, I've always wanted to do one of these. I've seen it in the movies a thousand times."

Patrick sighs. "You know what's not in the movies? Something someone born and raised in Manhattan can tell you?"

I refuse to give in to his sarcasm, keeping my mood cheerful. "What?"

"Those things stink."

"Don't be a downer."

"No, Skylar, they smell. Horrible."

And as we walk across the street, I begin to see what he means. The overwhelming scent of manure seeps through my nostrils, ripe, harsh enough to cut through the buzz the wine has made in my brain. But it's too late. I'm already set on the idea. And Patrick relents.

We settle in the backseat and yes, it does stink. But as the driver eases off the curb and pulls into the softly lit park, Patrick wraps his arm around me and I snuggle against his side. My heartbeat quickens, pulse racing, as a familiar set of butterflies returns to my stomach. But these are nerves of anticipation, and a wave of excitement washes over me, standing my hairs on end, making my entire body alert.

I look up.

Patrick is already watching me.

Our breath teases, filling the minute space between our lips, tickling the surface of my skin. His eyes dance, twinkling like stars. They start to close and mine follow. Pulled together by the wine and the romance, his lips land velvet soft against mine, and we're kissing. A rush of pleasure curls my toes and I sigh as he pulls me closer, erasing the gap between our bodies.

Suddenly, the smell is the last thing on my mind.

Confession 9

I've never been one for public displays of affection. I mean, a little peck is fine, but when two people are eating each other's faces during my morning commute, we're going to have a problem. So you can believe me when I say I feel really, really guilty when, three make out filled carriage rides later, I meet the disgusted, judging eyes of our driver. But you'll probably also believe me when I say, oh man was it worth it.

I'm floating.

Really, I'm not sure my feet are touching the ground as I finally say goodbye to Patrick and slip into my apartment building, lips puckered and swollen from a night very well spent. I've never really understood that whole cloud nine saying, but right now I think I'm there.

"Skye!"

Scratch that…the cloud has just disintegrated and I'm making a rapid descent back to earth. Mayday! Help! Maybe if I just ignore him, he'll go away.

"Skye!" And then a warm hand lands on my shoulder, turning me around. Heart plummeting I give in and spin, meeting Ollie's curious gaze. "I thought that was you," he continues, and then looks over his shoulder and out the door, looking for something—or someone. "Who was that guy?"

I shrug out of his grasp, annoyance rising. For days, I've tried to talk to him—but no. He just has to show up at the end of the best night I've had in weeks—heck, and months—and totally ruin it!

"What's it to you?" I snap.

"That wasn't Glenn was it? I swear he was working in the kitchen tonight…"

"No, for your information, it wasn't." I walk to the elevator and Ollie follows, hot on my heels.

"Who was it?"

I press the button, giving Ollie the cold shoulder before responding, "His name is Patrick."

Ollie grunts.

I turn on him, sticking a finger in the center of his chest. "What?"

"Nothing, nothing," he says and steps back. Then under his breath mutters, "Tool."

"I heard that."

"Well, sorry," Ollie adds, in a voice so far from apologetic it's laughable.

I look back at the elevator door, wondering what could possibly be taking so long, and then give in to the question burning my tongue. "Why do you care, anyway?"

"I don't," Ollie growls.

"Well, good."

"Yeah, good." Then he takes a deep breath, and from

years of experience arguing with the McDonough siblings, I know there is more coming in three, two, one… "It's just, I didn't realize you had so many guys lined up. You were complaining about needing to find a boyfriend for your column, and here you are a week later coming home at three in the morning, letting some loser shove his tongue down your throat right outside our building for the whole world to see."

"Patrick is not a loser," I say just as the elevator opens before us. He was, however, shoving his tongue down my throat… But I'm too angry to give Ollie any sort of win. He steps ahead of me into the elevator while I continue ranting. "He's sweet, and chivalrous, and just treated me to one of the most romantic nights of my life. Which is more than I can say for you."

Okay, shut up, Skye!

I seal my lips, forcing them closed before I begin to move the conversation into topics better left unsaid. Ollie remains silent and I step onto the elevator next to him, crossing my arms.

But I can't help it, my blood is boiling and my throat burns to say more. Not about the thing, I don't want to talk about the thing—you know, that thing that happened four years ago that I don't want to ever think about again. So instead, I lean over and tersely whisper, "And there aren't *so* many guys. There were two guys, Glenn and Patrick, and that's it. So I don't need any attitude from you, okay?"

But at that exact moment, a hand stops the elevator from closing and I just know before I even look up who it's going to be. And I'm right. It's Neal—the spinach guy. Oh, for the love of god! I hit on a guy one time and it's like the world won't stop punishing me for it. Seriously! I can't escape him.

"Hey, Skye," Neal says kindly, completely unaware of what he just walked into.

I wince, holding back a massive sigh, and mumble, "Hey."

And then I wait for the inevitable.

And wait.

Ollie takes in a deep, sharp breath.

I sigh. Here we go.

"Oh," Ollie says in mock surprise, voice so smug I want to punch him. His eyes are two lasers pointed at my skull, painful. "Do you two know each other?"

"He lives in the building," I say. "Neal, Ollie. Ollie, Neal."

"Dude." Neal shrugs and holds out his hand. They shake.

"So, how'd you meet?" Ollie asks, tone far too light and far too leading.

I'm about to reply, but Neal, smelling like booze, jumps in first. I cringe. "On the elevator," he says. I breathe a sigh of relief. That wasn't so bad. But then he adds, "Her teeth were green. I thought she had a medical condition."

Oh god.

I want to disappear. Immediately.

Ollie snickers. "What condition?"

"I had spinach in my teeth," I snap.

Finally, the door opens to Neal's floor, and it takes all of my self-control not to shove him forcibly off the elevator.

When the doors close, I stare straight ahead, not daring to meet the challenge in Ollie's gaze.

"So, should we add Neal to the growing list of your admirers?" Ollie asks.

I remain utterly silent.

"Anyone else I should know about?" he continues.

Do not give in. Do not give him the satisfaction of a response. I just have to keep my cool.

"No? I just want to be aware if any lovesick guys are going to come knocking on our door at five in the morning, demanding to see you? I mean, if they do, I need to know how to handle the situation. Who to turn away…who to punch in the face."

I keep ignoring him until we reach our floor.

But as I begin to put the key in the lock, I stop, squeezing my eyes tight. Ollie is right behind me. Like always, I'm totally aware of his body and how close it is to mine, totally aware of the way I yearn for his touch even when I'm furious with him.

"What—"

"Ollie!" I interrupt, turning to face him. "If you have something you want to say to me, just say it. Because as soon as I go inside, I'm going to my room and going to bed, and you'll lose your chance."

His turquoise eyes brighten to clear crystal and he seals his lips, holding back whatever teasing remark he was just about to say. Our faces are only inches apart. I ball my fists at my side, holding them steady, keeping them perfectly still as a current tightens the air between us.

"I missed you," he finally says.

I suck in a breath. My chest burns. So do the corners of my eyes.

"You didn't talk to me for four years and I missed you."

I missed you too.

The words sit ready, waiting at the back of my throat, urging to be spoken. But I can't. Because I wasn't supposed to miss him. I was supposed to forget him. I want to forget him. And tonight, for a few hours, I did.

Instead, all I do is say, "Okay."

Ollie closes his eyes for a moment, holds them there, and then nods. But I can't help but wonder what is left unsaid, what words burn the back of his throat. I don't press though. Because honestly, I don't think I'm ready to hear them.

For now, this is enough.

So I turn, ready for the solitude of my bedroom and for sleep. But as I twist the key and push the door open, a surprised scream travels up my throat, popping out before I can stop it.

A bare butt.

My eyes zero in on the target and I can't look away. I mean, I want to. But I'm bizarrely mesmerized in some out-of-body experience—like, is this really happening? There is a naked boy walking across my living room.

And then it clicks.

Bridget's date. Bridget's naked date.

Oh god.

I slam the door shut, stumbling backward into Ollie, almost knocking both of us over. He catches me before I fall, wrapping his solid arms around my waist, holding me up. I turn in his arms, eyes wide.

"Skye? What?"

My head shakes. He didn't see. Thank god he didn't see. But then Ollie reaches into his back pocket, going for his keys.

"No!" I jump, regaining my balance and firmly holding his hand. There is no way I'm letting Ollie inside. No way.

He shakes my hold easily.

Time for a new approach.

I stand in the doorway, arms crossed. "Want to go find some pizza?"

"Pizza?" he asks, stretching his keys forward to open the door. "It's three in the morning."

"So? I'm hungry," I grumble, casually extending my arms and bracing them across the doorway, trying to create a human barrier. My stomach growls, nicely completing the act. Which isn't really an act—after seven puny fish courses, I could use a little pizza.

"Well, I just spent about fourteen hours in a kitchen, so I'm not." And he narrows his eyes, peering at the door, clearly on to me.

"You're not going to make me hunt for pizza at three a.m. on my own, are you?" I look up, batting my eyelashes, using all the feminine powers of persuasion I possess. He softens, body wilting just a fraction, and for a moment I think I've won. I let down my guard, releasing my hold on the door.

Ollie acts.

In one move, he grabs me around the waist and lifts me over his shoulder. Damn, he's still just a strong as I remember.

My hands land on his back, clutching for something steady to hold on to now that the floor looks precariously far away. But my fingers gain a mind of their own, traveling down his shirt, running over the contours of his muscles, farther down to the curve of his lower back.

Whoa, girl!

I gulp, shaking my head.

Freaking wayward hands! I curl my fingers in, realizing that the sound of jingling keys has filled the hallway.

"Ollie!" I kick out.

He just hugs my thighs tighter, holding them in place. I pound my fists on his back instead.

"Ollie, put me down."

"Not…" He grunts. "Until…" The shoulder below my abs dips for a second. "I open…" A resounding click makes its way to my ear. "The door!" There's no missing the triumph in his voice.

I wince. Waiting.

Ollie steps forward, still not letting me go, and hauls us both into the apartment. I peer around. Nothing in the kitchen. Nothing in the living room.

"Will you put me down now?" I ask, trying to maintain a little dignity. Which, you know, is really hard to do when you're upside down. And in a dress. And probably mooning the entire world…

"Okay." He shrugs beneath me. I wait for a second, expecting him to bend down and place my feet gently onto the floor. He dips. But a second later, his whole body shoots up and I know exactly what he's doing.

Soaring through the air, I yelp, "Ol—"

But before I finish, I land face first against the couch cushions. I stay there for a second, breathing heavily, rapidly pulling my skirt down. Unfortunately, this isn't the first time this has happened. I should have been more prepared.

"Ollie!" I gruff, flipping over, meeting his grinning face. Not surprising. "I'm not ten anymore, you can't just throw me around."

"I can't?" He looks pointedly to where he just threw me.

"Well, I mean technically, you can, obviously, but—"

I stop mid-sentence as the sound of the toilet flushing echoes across our tiny living room. I know who it is before the door even opens and I close my eyes in anticipation. I already saw his naked butt. I don't need to see anything else. Ollie on the other hand... I sigh.

Three.

Two.

One.

"What the hell!" Ollie bellows.

"Oh, hey man," the naked guy mumbles. "Sorry."

"Who the hell are you?" Ollie continues.

The guy shrugs, squirming around. "Bridget's date. Who are you?"

"Her brother," Ollie growls, utterly terrifying.

Silence falls. Naked guy subtly reaches behind him for something to cover himself with, eyes comically wide in any other situation. I just glance back and forth, keeping my gaze on their upper regions, unsure if I should laugh or get Bridget or maybe act as a human shield...

"Skye!" Ollie yells, exasperated.

I fasten my gaze on him. "Hey! How is this my fault?"

"Why didn't you warn me?"

"Oh, I don't know." I shrug. "Because I didn't want involuntary manslaughter to go on my permanent record."

"Out," he orders.

I scrunch my eyebrows. "Wait, are you still talking to me? Because I really don't think I'd feel good about abandoning the poor guy to your wrath all on his own."

"No, I'm not talking to you." Ollie sighs and turns, then points to naked guy, who has grabbed a towel from the bathroom to cover himself up.

My towel.

Ugh.

That might have to be burned.

"You!" he demands. "Out!"

I stand, wrapping my hands around Ollie's furiously pointing arm. "Ollie…"

He doesn't move an inch. "Get out of my apartment, now."

"Dude!" Naked guy shrugs.

"Ollie, he's naked."

"I'm aware," Ollie growls. I roll my eyes.

"No, I mean, he's naked. We can't just kick him out of the apartment."

Ollie lowers his arm. I breathe a sigh of relief, smiling apologetically toward the stranger still stuck in the bathroom doorway, afraid to move. And then Ollie charges across the living room, and I, still holding onto his arm, stumble behind.

"Bridget!" he yells, banging on her door. "Bridget, put some clothes on and get out here now."

I push him out of the way. "I'll go in, just cover your eyes for a second."

Using the opening, I squeeze past Ollie and slip inside Bridget's room, sealing the door shut behind me before closing my eyes and turning on the light.

"Bridge?"

"Yeah?" she says, mid-yawn.

"Do you have any clothes on?"

"What?" she mumbles, still half asleep.

I purse my lips, weighing the options, wondering how long it will take Ollie to kill Bridget's, uh, man-friend. Screw it. I open my eyes and pick her T-shirt up off the ground, handing it to her as I crouch onto the bed.

"Skye?" she asks, pulling on the T-shirt and sitting up, utterly confused. "Where's Tim?"

"Oh, is that his name?"

Realization dawns. Bridget's eyes grow wide, filling with horror. "Where's Tim?"

I shrug, wincing. "Well, I'm assuming you only have one guy here. So it's safe to say Tim is the one who is currently standing butt naked in our living room."

"Bridget!" Ollie calls through the door.

She drops her head into her hands, moaning. "Why is he naked?"

"Well, you probably know the answer to that better than I do." Our eyes meet, and we both bite our lips to keep from cracking.

"He's naked in front of Ollie?"

"Yeah."

"Is it so hard to put on a pair of boxers to go to the bathroom?"

I shrug. I mean, I would think it was obvious enough but… "Maybe make that more clear next time?"

She sighs, shaking her head. "Do I have to go out there?"

"Yes," I say and grab her hand, pulling her to her feet.

"Remind me again why I thought living with my brother would be a good idea."

I pause, staring at her. "I have no idea."

And on that subject, the two of us easily agree.

"Okay, okay, I've got this, I can do this," she repeats, giving herself a little mini-pep talk. In the meantime, I slip out the door. The tension in the living room is palpable. Ollie stands at the far side of the room, arms crossed, glaring. He and the naked guy, I mean Tim, don't say a word to each other.

"Bridget will be out in a moment," I whisper, speaking to both of them.

"Um?" Tim asks, hesitant. "Can I go get my clothes?"

"Yea—no." I change my mind mid-sentence after meeting the steel in Ollie's eyes, a crisp furious blue. "Why don't you just wait until Bridget gets out here and then you can go in."

Ollie nods, giving his consent.

And then the silence thickens. My eyes bounce around the room, not sure where to look. I tap my foot. The seconds crawl by.

Finally, Bridget emerges.

"Bri—"

"Ollie, shut up," she snaps. His mouth hangs open, halted mid-word. Heck, mine hangs open too. The fierceness in her voice is fantastic. She ignores her brother and walks over to Tim, handing him a bundle of clothes. "Here you go. It's probably best if you go now. I'm so sorry about this. Call me tomorrow and we can try to forget this ever happened."

He doesn't even bother to get dressed before leaving the apartment. He's gone, fast as lightning. I've had blinks that have lasted longer than his exit.

Bridget's expression sinks as she watches him go, and then it narrows, tightens, turning to Ollie. "You," she speaks through her teeth, hardly opening her mouth. It's frightening. "You asked to live with me, temporarily. You asked. And I, being the wonderful human being that I am, said yes. But if you can't deal, you can leave."

"Bridget, you're my little sister. I'm not just—"

"No," she cuts him off, shaking her head, and points a finger into the center of his chest. I stand in the corner, watching in amazement. "You might be my big brother, but we're both adults now and we can both make our own decisions. Tim and I have been going out for a few weeks and I really liked him and now he might never speak to me again. And it's all your fault. So you can shove it, because I'm going back to bed and I expect an apology in the morning."

And then she's gone, just like that.

"What just happened?" Ollie whispers, glancing in my direction.

I shake my head, lost for words. That was magical to behold.

"There was a naked guy walking around our apartment," he says with disbelief. "How did she turn that around on me? I mean, how? What? I'm not crazy, right?"

I bite my bottom lip, trying not to smile, and nudge Ollie with my shoulder as I walk past him toward my room. "Go to bed, Ollie."

But he grabs my hand, stopping me.

I turn.

My eyes flick to our intertwined fingers. Then they travel slowly up his arm, across his broad shoulders, over his pursed lips, and into his aqua eyes. They're cloudy, confused, full of the same unspoken words from before in the hallway.

My heart skips a beat.

He holds on. Not saying anything. But not letting go.

Then a shudder passes through him, erasing whatever I thought I saw.

"I'm sorry," he mumbles, dropping my fingers, releasing me. "For, uh, ruining your night."

I lick my lips, looking down at the floor, swallowing. Patrick, I remember. He's talking about what happened in the elevator, what he said about Patrick… Sweet, sexy, relatively uncomplicated Patrick.

I shake my head, bringing a smile to my face as I meet Ollie's gaze again. "You didn't."

"Good." He nods a few times, small movements while his eyes flick around the room, and then runs his fingers through his thick, almost black hair. "Because I want you to be happy. I hope you know that. And if this guy makes you happy, then, well, I'm happy for you."

"Thanks," I say. And there's this sinking feeling in my stomach, but I don't understand why, so I just say goodnight and leave Ollie alone in the living room. As I crawl into bed, I listen to him shuffle around for a little while, tinkering in the kitchen. Twenty minutes later, the light seeping through the space below my door finally flicks out and he goes to bed.

I wait for dreams of Patrick to come, to lull me to sleep. But they don't. Instead, I stay in the real world with my hand pressed flat against the wall, wondering what is happening on the other side of my lonely fingers. Wondering if maybe Ollie is pretending to sleep, pretending not to be thinking about me too.

Confession 10

I'm embarrassingly gullible. Really, tell me the sky is green and the grass is blue, and I just might believe you. But it sort of stinks, because I end up trusting in things I probably shouldn't. Like thinking for all of high school that I actually had a chance with Ollie. Or never once guessing that my ex John was cheating on me for years. And it sort of makes me wonder what other things I believe when I really, really shouldn't…

All Monday mornings are terrible. But as I walk into the office, bleary eyed and exhausted, I quickly realize this Monday is going to be far worse than I ever expected.

"Did you go on a date with my brother?" Blythe asks before I've even had a chance to remove my coat and turn on my computer. Before I've even had a moment to visit the fancy coffee machine and make myself a sweet hazelnut latte. Her timing couldn't be crueler. At least let a girl get some caffeine before you lock her into an interrogation!

But alas…

I sit down, shrugging out of my jacket, and turn in my swivel chair to face her. "Good morning, Blythe."

Her perfectly framed eyes are livid. The black eyeliner only enhances the force of fury. I sigh, leaning back in my chair, waiting for the onslaught.

Brothers? Why do I need to fall for people's brothers? Life would be so much easier if I could just fall for one of the, I don't know, three billion other guys on the planet.

"Where'd you guys go?" she asks, ignoring my hello.

I glance to either side, realizing I'm completely surrounded as Rebecca and Isabel casually twist their chairs and stop typing to listen in. Oh well, that was inevitable. "I don't remember the name of the place, but he said your family goes all the time. It was an Asian fusion restaurant in Columbus Circle."

Her eyes widen and she tightens her lips.

"Did you guys have a good time?" she asks, and I can't help but notice the somewhat hopeful tone in her voice—the wish that my answer will be no.

A small smile curves my lips involuntarily just thinking about the evening, and well, more importantly how it ended— the hours of making out part, not the Ollie-naked boy-Bridget part. Sigh. Patrick. Prince Charming. The words could really be synonymous. And my face must say it all, because before I get the chance to respond, Blythe rolls her eyes and scoffs.

"You're totally smitten," Rebecca chimes, now blatantly ignoring her computer to join in the conversation.

Isabel follows. "So, can we get details?"

"Well..." I trail off, not quite sure what to reveal. To these girls, an expensive restaurant and a private car are probably nothing unusual. "Well, he greeted me at my apartment with one long stemmed red rose and had champagne waiting at the table when we got to the restaurant. And after dinner, we took a few carriage rides around Central Park, and well, you know, one thing led to another, and..."

"Is he a good kisser?" Rebecca asks.

Blythe sneers.

I fold my lips inward to keep from giving too much away.

"Look at her face, of course he is," Isabel teases.

A blush creeps its way up my cheeks.

"Just try not to get too love struck," Blythe offhandedly comments before turning back to her computer. But she doesn't type anything, and I know it's just because she's waiting for me to ask for clarification.

I really don't want to give her the satisfaction.

But at the same time, what the heck did she mean?

"Um, Blythe?" I murmur, waiting.

"Yeah?"

I stare at the back of her head, imagining I'm burning a hole through those perfect blonde tresses. Through my gritted teeth, I respond, "Is there anything else you want to add?"

"Oh, I mean, I'm sure it's nothing," she says, spinning in her chair with a far too-innocent expression. Yeah, because I'd really believe she's looking out for my well-being. "He just loves the chase, you know? Romantic gestures, over-the-top dates. He loves reeling a girl in, and I'm sure you can guess what happens after he gets what he wants."

He cuts them loose with nothing but a broken heart? Yeah, I get the picture. And though it makes complete sense—

I mean, that would describe about half the boys I've ever met in my life—I just don't see him that way.

But maybe I should.

And this is exactly what Blythe hoped would happen—she planted a seed. I smother it, pushing the doubt far down into the pit of my stomach, and plant a fake smile on my face. "Well, thanks for the tip."

"I mean," she says, sitting up and putting a freshly manicured hand over her heart, "I'm not saying he'll do that to you, I just want you to be careful. I wouldn't want to see you get hurt."

Oh, I'm sure you wouldn't.

I ignore her and turn back to my desk, but I guess my sinking mood is sort of easy to see because Rebecca rolls her chair over in my direction.

"I really like your necklace by the way," she whispers, smiling.

I glance down, touching the beaded and bedazzled piece I bought just yesterday on a shopping spree with Bridge. I mean, it's still paired with my navy suit and crisp white button down, but it's something. And I appreciate that she noticed. "I was bound to pick up a few fashion tips at some point, right?"

Rebecca just grins and goes back to work.

I flee for the solace of the coffee machine on the opposite side of the floor, bringing my phone to text Bridget while my latte brews.

Me: *What would you do if you didn't like someone Ollie was dating?*

I wait for a few moments, idly tapping my foot and

hoping that Monday morning at the gallery where she works is as quiet as my section of the newspaper is right now.

The phone buzzes.

Bridge: *The real question is has Ollie ever dated a girl I've liked? And the answer is, hell no!*

I grin. I can't help it.

Me: *But if he did…would you try to sabotage? Or do anything?*

Bridge: *Eh, no. My brother can make a fine mess of things all on his own.*

Bridge: *Wait, what's this really about? You know he's an idiot as much as I do.*

Bridge: *Did the assistant from planet bitch say anything to you?!*

I bite my lip. Maybe this wasn't such a good idea. But I'm in too deep to stop now. Bridget, stubborn as she is, would text every hour on the hour until I finally gave in and responded. Or she'd just bombard me as soon as I got home.

Me: *Nothing really, Blythe just sort of suggested Patrick was playing me…*

Bridge: *Well, that's as good a sign as any that he's really into you! Or she wouldn't be so worried!*

Me: *You think?*

Bridge: *Definitely! You're probably just a little sensitive to the idea because of the whole John fiasco in college. But we're grads now. Much more mature dating standards.*

I sort of want to remind her that just two nights ago her date was caught walking around naked by her best friend and her brother, which really doesn't help us on the whole maturity level thing, but I let it slide.

Me: *Thanks, Bridge!*

And I slip my phone away before anyone in the office notices that I am clearly stationed at the coffee machine and not working by any standards. Taking one glorious sip, I shuffle back to my cubicle, careful not to let a single drop spill.

Bridget's right.

At least, I hope she is.

When I sit back down, I feel my butt vibrating and pull my phone out for a quick second, thinking it's Bridget. But to my surprise, it's not. It's him. Patrick. I immediately grin. Butterflies swarm in my chest. And I realize that even if he is a player, I don't really care. Hey, I've been a virgin for twenty-two years, I think I can wait a few more months to see if a guy is the real deal or not. But I remember our kisses, which did in fact wiggle their way into my dreams, and think, well, maybe not...

Patrick: *Shake Shack, tonight? I have a break in work from around 6 to 8, just enough time for dinner.*

I immediately start to text back that I'm in, but then pause.

Do I want to be so available? Do I want him to think I'm just at his beck and call whenever he wants? Or should I be busy? Should I make him work a little harder? Dating politics are the worst... And then another question pops in. Do I really want to eat macaroni and cheese alone tonight, wondering the entire time what it would be like to be out with Patrick instead?

Yeah, no...

Me: *Sure! I'll meet you there at six.*

Patrick: *Perfect.*

And it is, it really is.

Because now, for the rest of the day instead of obsessing over Blythe's snide remarks I'm daydreaming about milkshake kisses—which, really, does anything beat that? The answer you're looking for is no. Well, then again, maybe chocolate kisses. Really, I should run an experiment to figure this out. These are the sorts of things every girl deserves to know.

As it turns out, I don't have to wait too long for my answer.

"Skylar!"

I turn, glancing up from my spot in the line wrapping around Madison Square Park to see Patrick approaching with two paper cups in his hands. I got here first and decided to stake out a place in line—the sooner we get to the front, the better. The smell of burgers and fries has already got my stomach twisted in knots. It's only a matter of time before my body rebels against me and starts groaning embarrassingly loudly, demanding food.

"You know, this place always has a crazy line, but I thought in mid-October on a surprisingly cold night, we maybe wouldn't have to wait as long," he says, shivering for a second as he steps next to me. "Here."

I take the cup from his hand and my palm instantly warms from the heat. Bending down I smell the lid. "What's this?"

"Hot chocolate." He shrugs, but then grins deeply, honey eyes glowing. "You said last time I was missing chocolates, so I thought I would do the next best thing. I want to be newsworthy after all."

"Oh, you are…" I say and then trail off, holding his gaze, hoping I look at least a little flirtatiously mysterious, and not like, a serial killer with crazy eyes or something.

"I am?" he asks.

I shrug. "I may or may not have started working on my next column this afternoon and you may or may not be the subject."

"I'll have to remember to buy an issue to see how I scored."

I lean in, whispering, "I have some inside information I can give you."

He moves closer, meeting my eyes. "Oh yeah?"

"You scored pretty highly."

"Good," he murmurs and then winks.

And I can't help it. I close the gap and kiss him. His lips are warm and taste of cocoa, and as soon as we touch, I want more. But then my neurosis catches up with my body and I freeze. I just kissed him—kissed him. Was that too forward? It's only our second date, are we at this level? The making out in public before the sun has set level?

Shut up, brain!

I push the thoughts away, stretching on my toes as Patrick presses his hand into the small of my back, deepening the kiss. My free hand finds its way to his chest, tugging on the zipper of his coat to pull him just a tad bit closer. I'm lost in the chocolate and the heat and the buzz gathering beneath my skin.

"Is she peeing, Daddy?"

Well, that'll take the mood right out of a situation. But

then I pause, feeling a warm trickle slip down my thigh, hearing the soft pitter-patter of droplets.

Crap!

Am I peeing? I mean, I feel like that is something I would know I was doing.

Wait…

Is he peeing?

I pull away from Patrick, wide-eyed and beet red, and look down.

My hot chocolate.

I sigh. Relieved. But then I see that my cup was crushed between our bodies and both of us are mildly covered.

"Shoot!" I curse, wiping the liquid off my jacket, running my hand down the front of my pants, and swatting the spill away. Luckily, it's coming off pretty easily and after a moment I switch, rubbing Patrick's jacket, wiping the material clean, murmuring, "I'm so sorry. I'm so sorry."

But then I freeze. Because my hand is rubbing the bottom of his coat, which is on top of his slacks, which are over his, uh, privates… I snatch my fingers back.

Did I just feel Patrick up in public? Oh my god, did I just sexually assault him? And in front of a little boy too!

Petrified, I look up—right into his perfectly beautiful evergreen-tinted eyes. Now we're staring at each other in silence. He doesn't say anything. I don't say anything. An eternity seems to fill the air around us, creating a bottomless gulf between our bodies. An impassable divide. And everything in my body says to flee, to retreat, to get away as soon as humanly possible.

So I blurt, "Napkins!"

And then I run…like a five-year-old.

This is so not the second date I had in mind.

A few moments later, I'm cowering in the bushes on the side of the restaurant—stomach growling with the enhanced smell of delicious food—reminding myself to breathe, just breathe. It's not a big deal. I'm making way too much out of nothing. I mean, he probably didn't even notice. If he was fourteen, that might have just rocked his world. But he's twenty-four, and experienced, and now probably just thinks I'm crazy because of how I reacted…pull it together!

I take a deep breath, looking around, meeting the eyes of a few strangers tossing curious glances in my direction. I mean, I'm crouching behind a bush for crying out loud. Does it get any worse than this? Then I hear the ominous flap of wings and look up. I'm directly below about twenty pigeons, and each bulbous eye is pointed in my direction, shining with a devilish gleam. A whole new bout of terror clenches my gut.

Crap—literally!

I jump out of the way. Is that the splat of droppings landing on dry leaves or am I just imagining it? I don't turn around to find out. The world just sent me a message and I got it, loud and clear. Suddenly, facing Patrick doesn't seem so bad. Especially when the alternative is getting dumped on, like actually dumped on, by pigeons. I shiver, forcing the image from my mind, and grab a few napkins from the dispenser before returning to the line.

For a moment, I think he ditched me.

I mean really, who could blame him?

But then the crowd shifts a little, and I see that he's there, scanning the line and looking for me too. I smile when our eyes meet, a little more comfortable than before, and wave with my napkin-filled hand.

"Sorry," I murmur as I close the space. "You'd think for a place teeming with ketchup, napkins would be easier to find."

We both take a second to pat ourselves dry. And then the silence returns.

"So…" I trail off, unable to bear it.

"So—" he starts, but then a ringing cell phone interrupts and he digs his hand into his jacket pocket, pulling out a blackberry, scanning the screen. He cringes, looking at me with a sorry expression and steps out of line, whispering, "I have to take this."

I watch out of the corner of my eyes as he nods, says something, nods again. I've never wanted to be able to read lips more! But a second later he hangs up and I stare forward, pretending I wasn't completely eavesdropping on his call—not like it did me any good or anything.

"Work?" I ask.

"Unfortunately," he says, tone grim. I hold back my frown. "It was my boss. Something fell through on the deal we're working on and I have to get back right now. We need to completely overhaul our presentation for the morning, and it's going to take all night. I'm so sorry."

I shrug, pasting on a smile. "It's okay, I understand."

"Rain check?" he asks.

I smile and nod.

And then he turns around, walking away without so

much as goodbye.

My face falls.

I can't help but notice there was no time or place associated with that rain check. No specifics. And I have the unsettling feeling that I've just been dumped. Was that call even real? Did he just not want to ditch me outright and asked a friend to call to give him an excuse? I thought that was just something girls did... And I really thought things were going well this time. I mean, until the whole molestation incident five minutes ago, but that wasn't that big of a deal—was it? Am I crazy? I had the butterflies with him—butterflies! Those don't happen very often, at least not to me.

"Skylar!"

I look up, hope springing to life, a burning flame in my chest.

Patrick is jogging back toward me, shaking his head.

"You don't have to go?" I ask, internally cringing a second later. That didn't sound desperate, did it? Whatever. He came back! I don't really care how it sounded. Okay, well, *that* did sound a little desperate. Ugh. I focus on him instead of my incessant internal monologue.

"No, I have to go, I just completely forgot to ask you something."

"What?" I try to keep my voice light and casual. As though I'm not hanging on his next words. As though I'm not intertwining my fingers to keep from throttling him.

"Well..." he trails off, pursing his lips a little, thinking. "What are you doing for Halloween?"

I pause—I was not expecting that.

Halloween is in like two weeks. Does he want to plan something in advance? Guys never want to plan dates so far in advance—not this early on. Maybe he's not breaking up with me…

"Nothing!" I chirp, a little too excited. But who cares? He's asking me out again!

"My friend Dan is having a Halloween party on his yacht and he needs the final guest list by Friday, so he can give the full manifest to the crew. Do you want to come?"

"Your friend has a yacht?" I blurt. And then realize the correct response was yes—easy, simple, one word. Yes. But it's too late.

Patrick shrugs. "Oh, it's not his I guess, it's his parents."

Because that's totally normal…not.

I shake my head, refocusing, and say, "Yeah. I'd love to."

"Great." Patrick smiles widely, deepening the creases around his eyes as his whole face warms. And it's all for me. All because I agreed to another date. I flush.

He keeps talking, but my eyes are stuck on his lips, their perfect rosy color, and I'm distracted as I watch them move and pucker and widen. I'm not really listening, but am instead thinking about another kiss—a nice, sweet goodbye kiss. And I don't realize he's stopped talking until I notice his mouth has stopped moving.

I look up.

He's leaning forward, watching me—waiting.

"Oh, yeah, that would be great," I hastily reply, not sure what I've just agreed to.

An amused gleam shimmers to life in his eyes, and I wonder if he knows I have no idea what we're talking about. He raises his eyebrows, and says, speaking a little slower, definitely teasing me. "You said your friend was dating someone, right? They can both bring dates if they want, just text me everyone's full names by Friday so I can tell Dan. Okay?"

"Yes." I nod firmly—I heard him this time. I'm still not quite sure what happened or what I missed, but I did hear him. And then, just for extra emphasis, I add, "I'll text you."

"Sorry I have to leave," he says again, looking over his shoulder as though a giant clock is waiting there to show him that time is in fact ticking by.

"It's okay. Really."

And I mean it.

Unlike before, he doesn't just abruptly turn away and leave me. He leans in, closing the distance between us. But when he's just a few inches away, he pauses, peering at me mischievously.

"What?" I ask.

"No hot chocolate this time?"

I bite my lip, grinning. But I don't have time to reply, because he closes the gap and brushes his mouth against mine, kissing me. His lips don't taste like chocolate anymore, they taste just like him, and I might like that even better.

Too soon, he pulls away, saying goodbye. I watch him walk away. And yes, I'll admit that my eyes might dip to his butt just a little. Hey, who can blame me? If you saw it, you'd look too.

But as he disappears around the corner, a sudden realization dawns. Hits me like a ton—heck, ten tons—of bricks, knocking the wind from my lungs, leaving me gasping for a second.

He said *both*.

Before, when he said I should text him names, he said both people could bring dates. I rack my brain, thinking back to our first date and everything we talked about, shuffling through the various conversations, tracking any and all names I could have possibly said to him, and only two stand out.

Bridget and Ollie.

He had asked if I had roommates, and I said two—Bridget, my best friend, and Ollie, her brother. Two. Both.

Oh my god.

All my excitement vanishes—gone, poof, just like that. Replaced with gut-wrenching dread. Halloween. Me, Patrick, and Ollie. And Ollie's imaginary date. And Bridget. And, oh man, I bet Blythe will be there too.

All of us.

Trapped on a boat.

With no way out.

I mean, what could possibly go wrong?

I close my eyes, cringing, and then open, looking at the line before me. I could go home to the warmth, but I won't. I'll wait here for another half an hour on my own, because, really, I've never needed a burger, fries, and a milkshake more.

Make that a double milkshake.

And could they add a shot of vodka too?

Confession 11

Halloween is Bridget's favorite holiday, so almost by default it's one of mine too. I mean, I was more of a fan when it meant free candy and not sexy barely-there costumes, but still—playing pretend as a grownup is fun...usually, anyway.

"Oh my god, is that it?" Bridget leans over and whispers into my ear, pointing toward a massive, sleek white yacht at the end of the pier.

I swat her hand down. "Stop pointing, it's embarrassing."

"Your boyfriend is rich," she comments, gaping.

"It's not his boat... and he's not my boyfriend," I qualify begrudgingly, because really, I would love it if Patrick were in fact my boyfriend. But that's one of those things that's most often decided by a truly awkward conversation or a drunken slip up—either way, it hasn't happened yet. We've had three dates since the whole groping incident in the park, which makes this the second longest relationship I've ever had—but still, until he says it, I don't want to think it.

Bridge just rolls her eyes. "Well, none of my other

friends have access to multi-multi-multi-million dollar ships for parties. Although," she pauses, winking at me, "after tonight maybe they will."

Oh, right. I forgot to mention that Tim, the naked man, never called Bridget again, so she's flying solo for the evening—not that it dampens her style at all. Ollie, on the other hand, should be arriving any second with some girl named Aubrey. Not that I care or anything.

"Are you sure I don't look ridiculous?" I ask Bridget for maybe the twentieth time in the past hour.

She shakes her head. "I'm not responding to that question anymore."

"Bridge…" I whine.

Nothing.

God, so stubborn.

I flatten my hands against my stomach, running my fingers over the spandex that feels painted onto my body, and pull the fake leather jacket tighter around my stomach. Usually for Halloween, I take the easy road—*Mary Poppins*, *Breakfast at Tiffany's*, Dorothy. You know, the sweet, rated-PG look. Well, after Bridget's prodding and constant reminders that we may never find ourselves on a yacht ever again, I decided to step it up a notch. Or, well, she decided for me—lending me her clothes, curling my hair for about an hour, and letting me borrow her fiery red lipstick. Have you guessed yet? I'm Sandy, from *Grease*. And not the buttoned sweater, white sneakers, headband Sandy that I would usually play, but final scene Sandy—stripper heels and all.

And oh man, do I feel ridiculous.

I peek at Bridge, holding in a sigh. She's as confident as ever, marching forward, eyes gleaming as they stare straight ahead at the yacht. Then again, she looks amazing—as per usual.

Every year, Bridget uses some painting as inspiration for her costume. One year, she pulled off a Picasso look with some bizarre face paint that looked a little too realistic, like ear for a nose sort of stuff. Another year, she was one of those pop art comic book girls. But I can't help noticing that this year, rather than over-the-top face paint, she went a little sexier too. *Madame X* is her inspiration—I wasn't sure what painting it was so she had to show me. Apparently, back in the day it caused quite the scandal. All I know is that she's wearing a super tight, super low-cut black gown with sleeves that drape off her shoulders and a slit up her thigh that I sort of think wasn't in the original piece. Her bright red hair is pulled back and up into a bun, leaving a lot of cream skin exposed. Like I said, she looks fabulous.

"Name?" A man in an official-looking white button down asks as we approach the yacht.

"I'm Skylar Quinn and this is Bridget McDonough, we're friends of Patrick's," I murmur, fighting back a sudden bout of nerves that maybe we were accidently left off the list. Or not so accidentally left off...but that's just ridiculous. Right?

His eyes scan his clipboard and a few seconds later, he checks off two names from his list, looking up with a smile. I relax my shoulders, releasing the tension in my muscles, but then his gaze flicks to our feet. What now?

"No shoes on board. There's a basket where you can store them for the night," he says and points to the right.

I pause.

Did I hear that correctly? I'm not allowed to wear my heels? Hallelujah! Can I kiss him? I mean, I know I can't, but the urge to throw my arms around his shoulders and plant a big fat kiss right on his lips surges through my system. Quick as I can, I unstrap the four-inch death traps and free my aching toes, and then I sigh, a warm and joyous sound. Being barefoot is glorious.

The crewmember is ignorant of my sudden bliss and just keeps talking. "If you take a left at the top of the ramp, there's a staircase that will lead you to the second floor where the party is being held."

"Thanks," Bridget and I chime, and then look at each other, mouthing *second floor*, and arching our eyebrows with idiotic grins. Strains of music and the rumble of conversation guide us around the back of the boat to the gleaming white grand staircase partially hidden by orange and black streamers.

Bubbles of anticipation pop beneath my skin, putting me in the party mood, and an unusual bout of optimism shimmers to life in the back of my mind. I have an unclassified but really fun boy-thing, I have my best friend, and I have a once in a lifetime experience cruising the Hudson River on a yacht. Maybe I was dreading tonight for nothing...

"Skylar!"

Then again, maybe not.

I cringe, recognizing the voice, and turn. "Blythe, how are you?"

Immediately, her eyes scan up and down my costume, burning with judgment. And I think mine might do the same. For a second, I really have no idea what she is, except maybe a Victoria's Secret model. But above the booty shorts and bustier, I notice a little pair of ears. A cat. Why am I not surprised? She does have claws after all.

"How adorable, you're Sandy," she says in too sweet of a voice, stepping closer to run a finger over my jacket, instantly able to tell that it's fake leather. "I was Sandy for Halloween back when I was fifteen. Of course, not for the whole night. Just long enough to get past my mother, but then I changed into a real costume when I met up with my friends. Not that you need to change or anything. You look really cute."

How unusual. A backhanded compliment from Blythe. I open my mouth to respond, but Bridget beats me to it.

"I really love your costume too," she says, copying Blythe's tone almost exactly. "Considering how objectified female bodies are in the mainstream media, I think it's really brave to come dressed as a porn star. I really appreciate the political statement you're making."

I bite my lips, while my cheeks puff with contained mirth.

Hold it.

Hold it.

I breathe deeply, swallowing the sounds back down.

"And who are you?" Blythe asks, glaring at Bridge, crossing her arms.

"Bridget McDonough, Skye's best friend," she says sweetly, still not giving up the act, and offers her hand.

"Blythe Keaton."

They shake. And just like that, a new pair of archenemies is formed.

But I don't have time to separate the two of them before the catfight begins, because a pair of muscular arms wraps around my torso, pulling me back into a firm chest, and soft lips come to rest a teasing distance away from my neck.

"You look great," Patrick whispers, breath tickling my skin, brushing the sensitive spot below my ears. A tremor races down my spine and spirals back up again, deliciously hot.

I spin in his arms.

And then recoil, stepping back.

What the…?

I'm speechless

Patrick is wearing a headdress—a full-on Native American headdress with feathers that stretch all the way down his back. My eyes dip to his bare chest, a little farther to the nicely tanned and chiseled abs I've only ever felt through fabric, and then farther to fringe-lined chaps stretching down his legs.

"Please don't tell me those are assless…" I murmur.

"We're the Village People," he says, grinning.

"You and who?" I glance from side to side

"The guys, wherever they are, probably in the other room with the drinks. I lost a bet and had to wear this costume. I had my eye on the sailor outfit, but Dan got to wear it since he's captain of the yacht for the night. But, this isn't so bad, is it?"

I scrunch my brows tightly and then relax, stretching my fingers out to run them slowly over the contours of his six-pack. "No, not so bad."

"Hey, guys."

I jerk my hand back instinctively at the sound of Ollie's voice, and when my eyes land on him, my heart clenches, squeezed by an invisible fist.

Ollie is a T-bird.

Leather jacket. Black pants. White shirt. Hair slicked back. Brood—oh man, the brood. He looks good—really good. A little dangerous. But what else is new? And then it hits me, right as Patrick slips his fingers through mine, draping his arm across my shoulders, claiming ownership—it looks like we're here together. Like Ollie and I are the couple.

"What are you wearing?" I yelp and then slam my lips shut, wincing.

Ollie looks at me, confused. "What? This is what I wear every year." And then his eyes rake my entire frame, slowly, down to the tips of my toes, taking his time on the way up. And he grins. He actually grins. "Oh."

Patrick tugs me a little closer. And I let him.

"This might be my fault..." Bridget mumbles. I turn my glare from one McDonough sibling to the other. She's biting her lip. "I heard someone mention Grease and I just thought it was someone at work since I couldn't remember. And then I thought—Oh! Skye would make the perfect Sandy."

"Which she does," Patrick adds, squeezing me gently for emphasis. I smile up at him. Feeling a little better, until...

"Oh, everyone, this is Aubrey. Aubrey, this is everyone."

A girl steps out from behind Ollie and my jaw actually drops. I'm gaping. In awe. She's freaking beautiful. And her perfectly toned legs stretch as high as my neck. I'm not even kidding.

"Hey, I'm Bridget."

"Blythe."

"Nice to meet you, I'm Patrick."

And I hear them all speak, but my mind and body are completely disconnected. It might have something to do with the fact that my jaw is still nailed to the floor… But I can't move. Can't say anything.

Where did he find her?

Did he buy her? Is she even human?

"When she comes out of her coma, that's Skye," Ollie chimes. And I'm so transfixed I can't even glare at him. I mean, it's bad. So bad, that Bridge leans over and pinches me, hard. I twitch—growing painfully less attractive with each passing second it seems—and snap out of it.

"Oh, sorry, yeah, I'm Skye. I just love your costume," I add, trying to cover my tracks. And then I actually look at her costume, which is a black leotard showing a rather aggressive amount of butt cheek—really it might as well be a thong as far as I'm concerned—and then nothing but bare leg all the way down to the warmers scrunched around her ankles. Oh, I mean, she also has on a gray cut-off sweater that covers most of her torso and just falls off her shoulder a bit. But that's a lot of leg, like four feet of bare skin. And bum—bare bum too.

Okay, ugh, fine. She looks amazing.

Whatever.

"Oh, thanks." Aubrey shrugs. "It's *Flashdance*. I have so many old leotards laying around, I almost always use them for Halloween."

"Are you a dancer?" Blythe asks. The accusation in her tone makes the word dancer sound ugly and despicable. And you know what? I think I'm learning to appreciate Blythe in ways I never have before.

"Yeah," Aubrey says, smiling kindly, totally sincere in her sweetness. I could probably really like her, you know, if I didn't have a fiery level of hatred burning my insides like I do right now. "I'm a Rockette, actually."

Well, that explains the legs.

Blythe doesn't even respond, she just rolls her eyes and exits the conversation without so much as a goodbye. I need to steal that move. I mean, it's utterly rude, but completely effective.

Instead though, I swallow. "Who wants a drink?"

Because I need one, ASAP.

"Come on, I'll show you," Patrick says, slipping his hand under my coat to lay his palm fully against the small of my back. I focus on the warmth of his skin as he guides me through the crowd. "We have cocktails or Jell-O shots, pick your poison."

I look at the fully stocked bar with mixes and liquors of all kinds. And then my eyes drift down to the half-empty tray on the table. I grab two and hand one to Patrick.

"Happy Halloween," I toast.

And then we both slurp, downing the Jell-O in one easy move. And all I can think is, oh man these are dangerous.

Sugary and sweet, I barely notice the alcohol except for a bitter aftertaste. Patrick takes two more from the tray.

Oh, what the heck!

"Happy Halloween," he whispers after, leaning down to kiss me. And right when I think he's going to pull away, he deepens the kiss instead, arching my back. My hands grip his bare shoulders for balance, and I can't say I mind the feel of his smooth, warm skin or the firm muscles beneath it.

"Get a room!" someone calls and I pull away.

Bridget winks at us and I grin, knowing the catcall came from her. And that's pretty much where the party really begins. Bridget wants to do a Jell-O shot. And then Ollie and Aubrey join us, and they want one too. And then we all decide to test out the bar. The boat leaves the harbor and the gentle rock shifts people this way and that, so we all dance to counteract the motion. The music blares against the night and ever so often when I look out the clear plastic canvases zipped all around the deck, flashes of the Manhattan skyline poke through to remind me that this isn't a dream, it's the real world. So, yes, this is all really happening to me.

Patrick's hands barely leave my hips as we sway back and forth, bodies pressed tight. Even when we're just talking to people, when he's introducing me to friends, he's touching me. A hand on my back. Fingers interlaced through mine. An arm around my shoulder. And it's nice to be so wanted, to be joined with another person in that way. I don't miss my ex John, but I do miss this—the feeling of being connected to another person, of being a *we* instead of a *me*, and somehow Patrick and I have slipped into that role.

I even get used to Aubrey. I don't get used to the pangs of jealousy that pinch my gut when I happen to glance over and see Ollie's hands wrapped around her, when I see her smile after he whispered something softly into her ear. But I don't think I'll ever get used to that, from anyone. And she's nice enough, a good sport. As soon as the other guys find out she's a Rockette, they demand a performance and she's tossed into the middle of a dance circle to do high kicks and splits. Blythe scowls from the corner, surrounded by a group of girls I don't know. Bridge and I joke that we need to wipe the drool off the floor before someone slips and hurts themselves. But when I look at Ollie to gauge his reaction, I notice that he's not even watching. His eyes are drawn out the window, toward something I can't see.

And then everything changes.

Everything shifts.

Out of nowhere, a karaoke machine almost magically appears. Patrick is whisked away by his friends, ordered to don his headdress, and the Village People put on a show. I'll admit, when they start belting out "Macho Man" while simultaneously flexing their muscles, I get a little breathless. Who wouldn't? Even Bridge grows silent by my side.

But then Patrick's friend Dan, the leader for the night, starts pulling people up from the crowd. A couple dressed as Sunny and Cher. A girl who came as Britney during her "I'm a Slave for You" years. And I don't see it coming, I really don't, when suddenly a hand grabs my arm, yanking me toward the makeshift stage in the corner of the room.

"What? No!" I protest.

And in the confusion the buzz of alcohol has caused in my brain, it takes a second for me to process that the fingers wrapped around my wrist belong to Blythe. And even longer to realize that this could only be something bad. But by then it's too late. And I know what I'll see before my eyes fully focus.

Ollie.

Or not Ollie—Danny.

Danny Zuko. As in, Sandy and Danny, up on stage for a duet.

Stupid karaoke.

"Oh no," I say, turning around to flee.

But the crowd has become an impenetrable wall and no one will let me through. They sense my weakness and they pounce. Someone says it once, and then all of a sudden everyone on the yacht is chanting, "Grease! Grease! Grease!"

And I'm stuck. Trapped without an escape. Just like I knew at some point tonight I would be.

Ollie places his hand on my elbow, tugging gently, offering up a comforting smile before handing me the second microphone. The opening strains of the song begin. And suddenly I feel like a shy girl playing a character. I am Sandy— all dressed up with no clue what to do and an entire crowd of people watching.

I'm having an out-of-body experience. Ollie starts to sing, shrugging off his leather coat in a mini striptease and tossing it into the crowd. He screeches that I'm electrifying and then falls face first to the floor as my victim. And I know it's my turn next, but I have no idea what to do.

I turn. Searching for a solution, a clue.

Bridget's there, just like the girls in the movie, placing a fake cigarette in her mouth, dropping it to the floor, instructing me on my next move. And I do it. Then I put a foot on Ollie's chest, pushing him up, and his smoldering teal eyes land on mine. A shock travels through my system, a bolt of lightning igniting my every nerve on fire.

After that, the words come easily.

Because he is the one that I want. And right now, I have him.

I don't think we break eye contact for the entire song. We both know the lyrics by heart. At one point he grips my hipbone, twirling me around, moving my body in steps to match his, as though we're one person. I'm laughing for no reason, caught up in the moment and in the heat of his gaze.

Then it all ends.

As slow as a sunset, yet as sudden as a car crash.

The music dies out and we're face to face, inches apart, breathing heavily, unsure who is going to pull away first. I don't see the other people. I forget the rocking of the boat. All I see is Ollie. Time stretches, slows, so the second passes in what feels like an hour.

And then sudden. Snap. The moment races forward, faster than the speed of light. Ollie turns. Looks away first, bowing to the applause. The boat rocks and I stumble. But he's already walked away, stepped off the stage. And I'm falling, with no one there to catch me.

Confession 12

I've never been to the hospital. Well, I guess except when I was born. But that doesn't really count, right? I've never had any broken bones or emergencies or anything. Or, at least I hadn't. Because, well, crap—there goes my perfect record.

When I say falling, I mean literally, falling.

But my mind is so caught up with the Jell-O shots and that other more figurative falling, that the ground catches me before I catch myself. And by catches me, I mean rams into me like a freight train at full speed.

As soon as I can breathe again, I scream, and I mean scream, at the top of my lungs, in one long extended sound, a word I haven't said in years. Because it's vulgar, and I don't like it, and because too many yearly viewings of *A Christmas Story* have drilled the lesson home after so long. But I can't help it, it just pops out—a foghorn cutting through the party, reverberating around the walls of the yacht, echoing in my ears again and again.

"Fuck!"

And screw it, I mean it.

But then I stop. Pause.

My mind catches up to the pain, and I realize I just fell in front of the entire party. And not like a graceful tumble, but a full-on faceplant, a total wipeout. And I'm still lying on the ground in a heap of confused limbs. My butt is definitely straight up in the air.

Crap.

Nobody saw that, right?

I close my eyes, and all I hear is silence. No music. No conversation. Heck, no laughter even. There's only crickets and the slap of the wind against the side of the boat. Well, the crickets might be in my head, but they may as well be real. Slowly, I turn my head to the side, wincing as my forehead scratches against the wooden floor of the boat.

Eyes.

A hundred eyes all on me. At this point there aren't even bodies connected to them, they're just enormous bulbous pupils staring at me, judging me, illuminated with contained laughter and a shade of pity.

I scramble to sit up.

"Ow. Ow. Ow," I murmur over and over, clutching my wrist to my chest, smiling and cringing at the same time, trying to play it cool. My entire body screams at me to stay still, but the embarrassment burning my chest is stronger, and it's all I can do not to run from the room. The crowd divides, letting me pass easily, and somewhere in the middle, I finally find familiar faces.

"Are you okay?" Bridget whispers, stepping next to me, wrapping an arm around my waist.

"Mentally? No… Physically? Yeah, still no." I sigh.

Patrick appears out of nowhere, putting a hand on my arm. "Skylar, are you hurt? That was, uh, quite the fall."

We finally make it to one of the smaller living areas on the yacht, a place that is gloriously empty. I collapse on the couch, still cradling my limp wrist. "My hand is on fire."

Patrick looks down, wincing. "Do you think you broke it? It's starting to swell."

"Oh, good god," I murmur, letting my head fall against the back of the seat. Only I could break my wrist during karaoke. Let me just repeat that for emphasis…karaoke! I mean, karaoke night is my grandmother's favorite event at her nursing home—she even ditches her wheelchair to perform and has a dance routine. I've seen it! But I can't get through one measly song. What is wrong with me?

A high-pitched snicker makes its way to my ear. I drop my head to the side, meeting Bridget's eyes. Her mirthful eyes. Great. She's laughing at me. My best friend is laughing at my shame. Then again, if the roles were reversed, I'd probably already be rolling around the floor, so I can't really judge.

"I'm sorry, Skye," she says, and then stops because now that she opened her mouth, a stream of uncontrollable giggles has filtered through.

I glance at Patrick, and Bridge has set him off too.

And now they're both cracking.

I turn my gaze back up to the ceiling, rolling my eyes. "Really, guys? I'm in serious pain here."

Patrick stands, shaking his head and sighing. "I'll go find you some ice and see how far away from port we are."

As soon as he's gone, I turn back to Bridge. "How bad was it?"

She bites her bottom lip, raising her eyebrows.

Crap. That bad?

"I'm a hazard to myself," I murmur.

"No," she says and then drops her head on my shoulder. "You had some drinks, you're on a boat, and you slipped. Grace has never been one of your strong points."

"Gee, thanks," I say wryly.

Bridget just raises her eyebrows even higher.

"Okay, okay, you're right. How's that little thing called empathy working for you?" But I'm grinning too.

"Great," she chimes.

Patrick strolls back in bearing gifts—a bag of ice and some chocolates. Have I told you he's prince charming yet? I've mentioned it, right? Because I don't think he's ever looked so good, Halloween costume and all.

I greedily steal the candy, and then remember I only have the use of one hand. Bridge unwraps a piece of chocolate and hands it to me.

"See, empathy," she whispers.

I snatch the candy.

"Good news," Patrick says and gently lays the bag of ice over my wrist. For a moment, it stings, but then the freeze feels good, numbing some of the pain, cooling the fire beneath my skin. "Apparently, the party was about to end anyway. We're five minutes away from docking. So as soon as we get off, we can take you to the hospital to get your hand checked out."

"You don't need to do that," I say, turning to him. "Bridget can take me, I don't want to ruin your whole night."

But he doesn't respond, he just leans forward and kisses me instead. I'll take that reply anytime! Suddenly, the pain doesn't seem too bad anymore. His lips are the perfect distraction.

"I'm going to go find Ollie," Bridget murmurs, easing off the couch.

Normally, I'd feel bad forcing her from the room, but I'm too wrapped up as Patrick slips into her spot, hardly breaking the kiss as his arm lands across my shoulder, gently tugging me closer without jostling my wrist.

But then he pulls back, eyes focused on mine.

"So, you and that guy?"

"Huh?" I whisper, in a daze, completely confused by the shift. "What guy?" And then I remember the song, the duet, Ollie and I on stage but in a world all our own. I bite my lip, widening my eyes and trying to look shocked. "You mean Ollie?"

"Is something going on?" he asks with a hint of vulnerability in his tone, one I'm not at all used to from him.

I place my uninjured palm against his cheek, locking our gazes so he knows I'm telling the truth. "No. There's nothing going on. Ollie is practically my brother. I've known him for my entire life."

And I think for the first time, I actually really want to mean those words. They're not an afterthought or an excuse, they're more like a prayer, a hope that one day they'll honestly be true.

"Good." Patrick lifts one corner of his lips, cockiness back full force. But I prefer it that way—on him, it looks good. And then he kisses me again. But it ends far too soon when a cough in the corner of the room pulls both of our attentions away just a moment later.

And of course, it's Ollie.

How long has he been there?

"Hey, *sis*," he says.

Wonderful. I guess that answers my question.

"Bro!" Bridge slaps him on the arm as she walks past, pushing him out of the doorway, before taking a seat. "We're pulling in. Ready to make our grand exit?"

"I'm not so sure I'm ready for a grand anything," I mumble.

"I heard your stage exit was pretty grand," Ollie drawls, grinning. "I'm heartbroken I missed it."

"Where did you run off to so quickly?" I ask.

But before he can answer, the boat shudders, coming to a somewhat jerky stop. And a second later, partygoers stream in, searching for coats and purses, taking one last drink, and then trickling out, asking each other where to go next.

Anyone up for the emergency room?

No? No takers?

I ease off the couch, using Patrick's hand as an anchor as he helps pull me up.

"I have your purse," Bridge says, coming to my other side. Ollie and Aubrey follow silently behind. And then all five of us join the masses and walk slowly down the steps, across a ramp, and back onto solid ground.

Poof. Just like that, the magic of the night is over.

"Shoes?" Patrick asks, looking at the footwear lined up along the edge of the dock. Most of it is picked over, and he finds his boat shoes easily. Bridget eases into her heels. Ollie finds his boots. Aubrey slips into a pair of sneakers. And me? I stare at the red pumps Bridget forced me to don for the evening, wondering if I can put enough hatred into one glance to set them on fire. Or maybe telekinesis. I would happily send them tumbling over the edge and into the river if I could.

Bridge follows my line of sight. "Oh…right."

"Yup." I sigh. Bring on the pain. But a moment later, I'm airborne. "Wha…?"

I look up into Patrick's smiling face, nice and cozy in his strong arms. Which really—the boy's got muscles. He doesn't look strained at all. Let me just say, John tried lifting me multiple times while we were dating and I'm lucky to still be alive. But Patrick…well, he can whisk me off my feet any time he wants.

"You already broke one wrist this evening, I think we should cut our losses," he says. I just shrug, happily kicking my bare feet, and wrap my one available arm around his neck. And though I feel Ollie's eyes boring a hole into my side, I don't give into temptation to turn around and look.

He has Aubrey.

I have Patrick.

Everything is exactly how it should be…until we hail a cab.

"I'm coming," Ollie growls as Bridget pushes him away from the door.

"Just take Aubrey home, or go out and have a good time. Either way, we're fine. Skye has me and she has Patrick, really you don't have to come."

I sigh from my spot in the cab, watching the meter begin to tick, and am half tempted to close the door and leave all four of them behind.

Ollie scoffs in Patrick's direction. "She's known him for, what? Three weeks? I don't trust this guy. I'm coming."

"Back off, man," Patrick growls.

Bridget just rolls her eyes. "Stop being so overprotective. We're fine."

Ollie ignores her, stepping closer to Patrick—a little too close, challengingly close. "Look, I've known Skye since she was five, and I've never let anything happen to her." Well, that's not exactly true, I silently charge—he knows exactly what he's let happen to me. We both do. But Ollie doesn't even pause, he just barrels on. "If anyone is going to help take her to the hospital to make sure she's okay, it's going to be me."

"Well, Patrick is her boyfriend, so I think he can handle it," Bridget says, tugging on Ollie's arm.

And then everyone pauses.

I start silently choking in the backseat.

What did I say before, about the boyfriend conversation only happening in awkward sober conversations or totally drunken slips? Yeah...crap.

"Bridge!" I hiss. She looks at me with a broken expression, clearly aware the situation is getting away from her.

"Since when are you her boyfriend?" Ollie spits.

"Since now," Patrick replies.

Wait, what?

I grin.

"Oh, give me a break." Ollie crosses his arms. I can't help but notice Aubrey is shrinking in the corner, looking at me with some concern.

Okay, time for me to step in.

"People!" I shout, a little louder than I intended, but the ice has almost completely melted and the pain in my hand has turned to a throbbing pulse. "Remember me, the one who needs to go to the hospital?"

They all jolt, shocked, turning to look at me. And I realize—yes, they did completely forget about me. Wonderful. What better saviors could a girl ask for?

"Okay, Patrick, get in the car," Bridget says, giving him a shove and then blocking the doorway. "Don't leave, just give me two minutes to talk to Ollie." And then she slams the door on his face. Well, almost.

"I do not like that guy," Patrick mutters. And I mean, I can't say I blame him.

"He just…" I trail off with a sigh. How do I finish this? He just what? Truthfully, I have no clue what could possibly have gotten into him. Ollie was the most popular guy in high school. The captain of the football team. That guy every girl was in love with and every guy wanted to hang out with. He didn't get in fights. Ever. Well, except with some of Bridget's boyfriends, but that was like a macho big brother thing…

Wait?

Is that what's happening? Does Ollie really think of me like a little sister? I mean really? After everything…

I shake my head.

Doesn't matter. For now, it's as good an excuse as anything.

"He's just really protective of Bridget and me. Like he said, he's known me since I was five. And I mean, Bridget and I were best friends from the start, playdates every day, doing all the same clubs, and Ollie was with us most of that time. He's always been super overprotective about any guys Bridget or I see, and," I pause, biting my lip, unsure of how much to say. But the words just tumble out anyway. "And Ollie was there when my parents got divorced, there to cheer me up when I snuck through Bridget's bedroom window at two in the morning because my mom and dad were fighting again. He saw me cry, a lot, and I think he just doesn't want to see me get hurt like that again."

And I know what I'm saying is true. But when I think of the top three worst times of my life, there's no question what they are—my parents' divorce, when my grandfather passed away, and how I felt after everything went down with Ollie over four years ago. Which is funny really, because I dated John for more than three years before I found out he cheated, and what Ollie did was still worse—far, far worse to my heart.

And now he's here. Pretending like a few weeks of living together has erased all of the history, has given him back the right to be overprotective of me, when it hasn't. Not by a long shot.

"Okay," Bridget says as she opens the door, shocking me from the dark direction of my thoughts, pulling me back to the real world. "So, Ollie and Aubrey just left. And to top it all off, I think I thought of a great way to solve this whole mix up."

Patrick and I look at each other, both slightly confused.

"What mix up?" I ask.

"Well, I mean," she says with a shrug, "isn't it obvious? The whole Patrick, Ollie mix up. Clearly the two of you haven't gotten off to a great start, which trust me, my brother can be an ass sometimes so I totally understand. But if you and Skye are going to keep dating, then you and Ollie need to be friends. Well, not even friends, just civil with each other."

"Bridge…" I growl. "What did you do?"

"Nothing, I just set you all up on a double date for next weekend. That way all four of you can get some quality time. Though, between you and me, I don't really think Aubrey is going to last." She rolls her eyes, frowning as though to say *typical*.

But I'm still caught on her last words. "You set us up on a what?"

"A double date, the four of you. Ollie has an early shift at the restaurant on Saturday, so I thought dinner or something that night would be perfect. I mean, if you can make it, Patrick."

I glance at Patrick, whose jaw has also fallen slack. His eyes find mine, widening with some alarm.

"You set me, Patrick, Ollie, and Aubrey up on a date?" I repeat.

"Did you hit your head during the fall?" Bridget asks, eyebrows rising higher by the second. "A double date. Yes. You, Patrick, Ollie, and Aubrey."

"And Ollie agreed to this?" I question.

"Actually, he came up with the idea."

I lean back against my seat, deflated. Why am I not surprised? More importantly, what the heck is he planning?

"Saturday night you said?" Patrick asks, turning to Bridget. She nods. "I can do Saturday night."

And there's just a little bit too much joy in those words. My questioning changes—just what in the heck is Patrick planning?

"Skylar, does Saturday work for you?" he asks. I narrow my eyes, trying to read his expression. But I can't. He might apparently be my boyfriend, but I still haven't known him long enough to decipher what meaning hides behind the green flames in his eyes, sparkling with some sort of mischief.

Every fiber of my being urges me to say no. No! Just say it, come on. Nip it in the bud. But of course, this pops out instead, "Um, sure."

I really am a glutton for punishment.

Ugh.

A few minutes later we arrive at the emergency room, which really looks more like rejected circus performers anonymous with all of the bright colors and costumes. Patrick, Bridget, and I settle in between Dracula and Medusa, waiting our turn to see a doctor. And all I think as I ease into my chair, is holy crap, it's going to be a long night. And I'm not sure if I'm talking about this one, or the double date I just barricaded myself into.

I repeat. Ugh.

Confession 13

There is one benefit to knowing someone for your entire life. Sure, Ollie has dirt on me. And well, a lot of it, because as you know, I have issues. But I also have dirt on him. Oh you know, just little things like he used to let Bridge and I braid his hair—butterfly clips, fake pink hair strands, glittery ties, the whole shebang. And, yes, before you ask, I have the photos to prove it. Dirt!

"Do we need to lay some ground rules for the evening?" I ask Ollie as we step onto the elevator. My nerves are totally shot. I've been worrying about tonight for the past two days, ever since I last saw Patrick on Thursday. Which makes it even more infuriating that Ollie seems completely at ease by my side—lazy smile, lazy gait, suspiciously good-natured attitude.

I want to throttle him.

"What sorts of rules?" He leans forward to press the button, just barely grazing my shoulder with his arm. I step away, out of reach.

"Hmm, I don't know, maybe that you aren't allowed to shout at Patrick or go psycho big brother on him?" I accuse, glaring at him.

"Okay." He shrugs, turquoise eyes slipping over to mine, hidden under the layer of dark hair that's fallen over his forehead. "Then rule number two is you're not allowed to gawk at Aubrey."

I step back, arching my eyebrows. "I did not gawk!"

He drops his jaw, staring at me with a vacant expression, letting his entire body go slack, drooping his head forward. And okay, I admit, it's a rather good impression of what I probably looked like on the yacht, but still.

"Stop," I murmur.

Ollie just widens his eyes, continuing to gape at me.

"Ollie…" I shift on my feet, uncomfortable with the attention.

Of course, he doesn't break character at all.

I shove him. "Ollie, stop!"

The door opens and he finally straightens, grinning, slipping past me with an air of victory. I jog to catch up, following him through the front door of our building.

"Okay, fine, whatever. Here's an actual rule, no telling embarrassing stories about me."

Ollie just shakes his head. "That's never going to happen."

"Why?" I ask, glancing up at him with pursed lips.

He meets my gaze, eyes twinkling, dimples out full force. "Because, Skye, embarrassing you is one of my favorite things to do."

I sigh, fighting the urge to shove him again. "Come on, Ollie. Patrick and I have only just started dating, and even with my broken hand, he somehow finds me attractive. Right now I think I'm in that cute place where my clumsiness is charming. I don't want the bubble to burst."

"That's insane," he mumbles.

"What is?"

"That mentality," he says, with a note of bitterness in his tone. "If you really like this guy, don't you think you should know he appreciates everything about you? Not just the parts you want him to see? You shouldn't be afraid to be yourself."

"I'm not..." Am I? I mean, I'm trying to be a little more confident and a little more suave to fit in next to Patrick, but with the accidental groping and the broken arm, I'm pretty sure the real Skye is leaking through.

I nibble my lip as we step down the entrance to the subway and swipe our cards, shuffling through the turnstile. Five minutes for the next downtown train.

"It's not that I'm afraid to be myself," I finally say, still bothered by the idea. "I just, I think it takes time for two people to get to that place where they're close enough to be their true selves with each other. And Patrick and I are moving in that direction, but we haven't quite gotten there yet."

"Okay." Ollie shrugs, not looking at me and instead leaning over to peek down the tracks, searching for the next train.

But I'm not finished yet. For once, I want to be the one who wins the argument. "Come on, Ollie. Don't tell me it's not the same for you with girls."

"It's not," he responds, still not looking at me. "If I found someone I really liked, I'd be myself. I'm pretty charming, you know."

But I don't take the bait. I want to stay here in this more serious place. I want a real answer from him. "Have you ever really been yourself with a girl?"

And I think we're both aware that I'm included in the question.

Ollie finally turns, just as the rumble of a train shakes the ground beneath our feet, a thunderstorm barreling forward. "Once," he says, brutally honest. And I really don't know if that one time was with me. Then he mumbles something, slipping his head to the opposite direction so I can't decipher the movement of his lips.

"What?" I ask, shouting over the screech of the brakes.

Ollie doesn't respond. He just keeps his eyes focused on the doors coming to a slow halt right before us. Silently we both board the train, shuffling forward, grabbing onto the pole in the center of the floor for balance. I don't know what to say, so I remain quiet, thinking. A few seconds later, Ollie's finger brushes mine, slipping ever so slightly down the metal, just enough that his pinky lands on my thumb.

Ignore it.

Don't look up.

Don't show him you noticed.

I hold my hand still, but every ounce of awareness in my brain is focused on the small centimeter of skin touching mine. And I can't take it. Can't take what it makes me think about. So I move, drop my hand down an inch, and suck in a deep breath, glancing out the windows and away from Ollie.

A few seconds later, I feel him again.

Pinky to thumb.

The smallest connection, but enough to make my nerves go haywire. To make even the hairs on the back of my neck stand alert, to make my mouth go dry. My stomach fills with flutters, alive, sending thrills up and down my chest. I slip my hand down, farther this time, a few inches, only able to breathe when our contact is broken.

Then I wait, wondering if it will happen again. One time is chance. Two times, an accident maybe. But three and it starts to feel like a choice, a decision he's making, a signal he's maybe trying to send.

The train stops, more people get on, and I'm pressed into Ollie's side, feeling the warmth of his body through my coat. The air fills with an awkward tension I can't ignore, and I know one of us needs to speak, to fill the silence. But I don't know what to say.

And then his finger lands on mine again.

I lick my dry lips.

Even with the crowd and the murmur of conversation and the thrum of the train, the moment feels intimate. As though we're alone. Skin to skin. Bodies pressed tight.

I give into temptation.

I look up only to find that Ollie is already watching me. His jaw is tense, tightened, as though he's clenching his teeth to keep from speaking. His normally grinning lips are drawn thin, tight. And his eyes are shaded, heavy behind slightly closed lids, below furrowed brows. But the longer our gazes hold, the more the tension eases from his expression, melting away.

The doors behind us ding, opening. It's our stop.

We hold for another moment, neither breaking. And then one side of Ollie's lips rises, smirking. And I can't read why. The grin turns mysterious, alluring, as his bright eyes shimmer with a secret he doesn't want to let me in on—not yet.

This time I look away. I break the moment. I walk off the train, leaving him behind. Because whatever that secret is, I don't want to know it. I'm tired of being confused, of being left out. I'm tired of the games.

I want easy.

I want Patrick.

And right now, I know exactly where to find him.

Ollie eventually catches up to me when we're above ground, crossing the street, but I don't bother to say anything. One block and one quick elevator ride later, and we've arrived. Patrick and Aubrey are already here, making polite conversation, and it's all I can do not to run over and throw my arms around him. I do however plant a big one on those smiling lips when I get close enough to close the distance.

Easy. Sweet. And exactly what I need.

"I reserved a lane for an hour," Patrick tells us. Before you ask, yes we're going bowling. And yes, my arm is broken and currently wrapped in a cast. And no, it wasn't my idea. Do you think I have a death wish?

The cashier gives me an incredibly dubious look as Patrick helps me shrug off my coat, and I walk up to the counter asking for a size eight shoe.

"I'm right handed," I mumble with a shrug, holding up my broken left hand. She doesn't say anything. She just hands me the shoes with a smirk. I snatch them and walk away, following Patrick to our lane and leaving Aubrey and Ollie to follow behind.

"One hour, huh?" I ask Patrick as we sit down.

He smirks. "I figured we might sneak away after and grab some dinner on our own."

"Sounds perfect to me." And really, I couldn't appreciate him more in that moment. One hour. I can make it through one measly hour. No big deal.

"So, who wants to go first?" Ollie asks when he and Aubrey arrive.

Patrick is already working the monitor, setting up our names. "I thought you might," he says, overly generous. And I look up to see the order is Ollie, Patrick, Aubrey, and then me—last, just like I asked. I mean, really it's just prolonging the inevitable. But still…

Oh, did I not tell you I can't bowl?

Well, we'll get to that.

Ollie walks up, grabs the heaviest ball on the rack, and steps forward smoothly, releasing. Strike. Aubrey lifts her hand for a high five and the two of them smile at each other.

My stomach recoils.

"Nice shot," Patrick murmurs, standing.

Ollie raises his eyebrows, gesturing to the lane. "All you."

I'll admit, a tingle of nerves pricks my heart as Patrick steps up and a strange sense of competitiveness tightens my chest. I want to win. I want to beat Ollie. I want Patrick to be better.

He grabs the same ball as Ollie and lines up. Step. Step. Step. Release. His leg swooshes back in perfect form and...

Strike!

I jump up, cheering, and give him a kiss as soon as he turns around, throwing my arms around his neck. Okay, maybe a slight overreaction, but every nerve in my body snaps all at once, and there's nothing else I can think to do to release all of this pent up energy. And besides, he just looks so adorably kissable when he turns around with a look of complete triumph.

But as soon as we break away, I can't help it. A blush creeps all the way up my cheeks and embarrassment warms my skin. My eyes slip to the side, running into Ollie's furious glare. A thrill shoots up my spine, bringing a grin to my lips. But I break contact, tearing my gaze away and turn around.

Whoa—what the heck did that mean?

Did I make him jealous? Was I trying to make him jealous? Or was that just overprotective Ollie once more— older brother Ollie?

I sit back down, folding my hands in my lap, biting my lip as I stare at the floor. Patrick follows, wrapping an arm around my shoulders and easing back as Aubrey takes the floor. She bowls a spare. I wince. Does the girl need to be stunning and talented and a good bowler? Aren't the first two enough?

"You're up, Skye," Ollie prods, teasing. His turquoise eyes dance in the dark, fiery with anticipation.

Patrick gives my shoulder a squeeze, whispering, "You got this."

I walk up, every step a resounding thump in my chest as the rest of the room goes so silent that I can hear myself breathe.

Seven-pound ball? No. Hot pink and way too girly.

Eight-pounder…okay, never mind. Whose fingers are that small?

I grab the nine-pound ball, not really at all sure what I'm doing as I slip my thumb and two other fingers into the slots.

Be the ball.

Breathe.

Be the ball.

Okay, let's get back to what I said earlier. I have no idea how to bowl. I mean, sure I've gone before—with Ollie I might add, hence the smirk burning my back right now—but the whole one-handed throw thing has alluded me for my entire life. I'm more of the squat and use two hands sort of bowler, but the cast wrapping around my left hand has kind of made that option obsolete.

How hard can this be, really?

Just breathe.

I line up, copying everyone else's movements and hold the ball up at my chest. Okay, step. Step. Step. Swing. I throw my arm back.

Whoa!

That ball is way heavier than I anticipated and I stumble, squeezing my fingers for dear life, just barely able to keep the bowling ball from flying backward out of my palm.

Someone snickers.

I don't need to turn around to see who.

A moment later, after a few shaky steps, I try again, a little more prepared. Step. Step. Step. Swing. Release!

And I do it, the ball actually leaves my hand and lands in the center of the lane with a resounding thud. And it rolls. And it rolls.

Oh no.

It's sliding. It's slipping. It's—

Gutter.

I deflate.

"You can do this," Patrick says from behind. I close my eyes, grabbing a different ball, and wait for the light to go back on at the end of the lane. I line up again, throw…

Gutter.

This is going to be a long night.

"Good try," Patrick says, smiling as I take my seat.

"When did you start bowling one handed?" Ollie asks.

I turn to him, glaring under hooded brows. "You missed a lot while you were living in California."

"Maybe." He shrugs, easing up from his seat. "But some things never change, Skye." And then he turns his back on me, stepping onto the lane to bowl. Strike.

Why am I not surprised?

"So, we're supposed to be getting to know each other, right?" Ollie says as he sits back down, a little smug with his scorecard. "Well here's a juicy tidbit. I was Skylar's first kiss."

I immediately jolt out of my seat. "You were not!" Is he seriously bringing this up right now? Here? "Charlie Saunders was my first kiss. Ninth grade, truth or dare, and it was horrible."

I sit back down, breathing heavily, and realize a thick silence has settled in the wake of my outburst. I glance at Ollie and his eyes are wide, shocked, a little troubled. I flick my gaze to Patrick whose eyes have narrowed to pin pricks. Aubrey is chewing her lower lip, eying me like new competition. And then I understand. Idiot!

Denial.

Denial was the correct approach. Because now, hanging unsaid in the air between us, is the question of what number Ollie was. I never said that it didn't happen. I just said that it didn't happen first. And that's a huge difference.

Crap.

"I mean, what are you even talking about?" I continue, mumbling, hoping my voice doesn't sound as shaky as my fingers. "We've never kissed ever." The words sound lame even to me.

But Ollie takes it in stride, leaning back with a wide smile. "Of course we have, I'm heartbroken you don't remember. Fifth grade, Valentine's Day…"

I release the tension in my body, breathing normally again—of course he's talking about that and not the other thing. Of course. Ollie likes to tease, but he's not mean spirited about it.

I smile as the memory trickles to the forefront of my thoughts. "I was in second grade and you were in fifth grade, and in the middle of recess, Bridge and I snuck onto the big kid playground to give you our valentines."

"And," he says, taking over the story, "Bridge gave me a big kiss on the cheek when she gave me her valentine, so when you gave me yours you leaned in for the same, copying her, but you missed and hit my lips instead."

"I think you're forgetting the ending to that story..." I trail off, waiting.

But Ollie looks at me with a blank expression. He doesn't remember! I bite down my grin at having one over on him. "And as soon as I leaned back, giggling, you shoved me and yelled, 'Ew! Girls have cooties!' And then ran away."

"I did not," he says, sitting up.

"You did too," I challenge, "and I fell on the pavement and scraped my knee and had to go to the nurse's office for a Band-Aid."

His jaw drops. "I don't remember that at all."

Aubrey chimes in, "You know, they say when little boys do that it's because they secretly have a crush on a girl."

Seeing Ollie's mounting embarrassment, Patrick leans in. "Speaking as someone who may have pushed a few girls and called them mean names when I was a kid, that saying is completely accurate."

And I can't help it. Witnessing his desperation is like a drug—I'm always on the receiving end of this. And for once, it's fun to give him a taste of his own medicine. I ask, in a jokingly sing-song voice, "Are you guys saying Ollie loved me?"

"Okay." He falls back, exasperated. "Now you guys are just being ridiculous. Have you ever seen Skye as a little girl? She was a freckle-faced pipsqueak!"

"Hey!" I lean forward, pointing at him. "You're one to talk, four-eyes."

"You wear glasses?" Aubrey asks, turning with surprise.

"I used to," he grumbles. By my side, Patrick is grinning wider than I can ever recall seeing.

"Oh, now he hides behind contacts. But for all of elementary school and all of middle school, Ollie didn't just wear glasses. He wore black, wide-rimmed glasses that were larger than his face. And they always started slipping, so he had to push them up his nose all the time."

Ollie crosses his arms, glaring at me. I raise my eyebrows as if to say, *what?* I mean, hey, I tried to take embarrassing stories off the table. He's the one who wanted to use them against me. Well, not this time buddy. Not this time.

"Okay, so I wore glasses," he says, "but then I became the quarterback and the captain of the football team, and I started wearing contacts. Did I mention I played in college for a year? Before dropping out to go to culinary school?"

Oh, I see what he's doing. Trying to change the subject to something cool—football, culinary school. Nice try. Not going to happen.

"You know, Aubrey," I say, dismissing Ollie's previous words, "I have an interesting tidbit for you, in the efforts of getting to know one another of course. Ollie used to be a dancer."

His teal eyes practically turn red with the heat of his glare.

Aubrey grins, slapping his arm. "You didn't tell me that."

"It's nothing really," he murmurs, and then says louder, "Who's up? Patrick?"

But Patrick shrugs. "I can wait, I want to hear this. Skylar?"

I pause, letting the suspense build, looking around, taking in the moment—more especially, taking in the subtle shake of Ollie's head, the silent plea to stop. Yeah. Right. "Well, I don't know if you know this, but Ollie and his family are 100 percent Irish and very proud of it, so when they were little, Ollie and his sister learned Riverdance. They used to perform in all of our school talent shows, up until what, Ollie? Eighth grade? Oh, I mean when I was in eighth grade, so that was actually eleventh grade for you, right?"

He peers at me suspiciously, because of course, that's not really the embarrassing part. We used to love it. He and Bridge are actually really talented dancers. No...I haven't gotten to the embarrassing part yet.

"Wow, that's amazing," Aubrey says, and I can see the admiration mounting in her eyes. I wonder if all of these stories are just making her like him more. Eh, doesn't matter. The expression on his face is worth it.

"Actually, Skye," he says, still unsure of where I'm headed, "it's not called Riverdance, that was just a famous show. It's just called Irish Step Dance."

"Right, sorry," I apologize, and then press forward. "But my favorite part is that Bridge said Ollie wasn't flexible enough and used to get really mad at him for not being able to do the high kicks—"

"Skye..." he interrupts, tone drenched with warning.

But I'm not afraid of him. What's that saying? Payback's a... Well, you get the idea. "So Bridge and his mom forced him to go to ballet class with us when we were little. You should have seen him in his black spandex tights!"

Silence.

Wait for it.

Wait for it.

There we go—the image of Ollie in glasses and tights has fully sunk in. The chicken legs. The thick rims. The awkwardly long limbs. Let's take this a little further and picture him working the ballet bar, glaring at his younger sister as he dips into a graceless plié, maybe bringing his free arm over his head, channeling the beautiful swan he was supposed to become. You know, the good old days, when Ollie was just Ollie. Just Bridge's brother. Just my friend. Back before he turned into the disarmingly handsome high school guy I couldn't get my mind off of. Or, well, the annoyingly handsome man I—on second thought, let's not go there.

I spare a glance at him now, noting the dark gleam to his normally bright turquoise eyes, and can't help but smile a bit smugly. Finally, after so many of my attempts, I think he might understand what it means to be on the short end of the stick—at least, if his sour expression is anything to go by.

Shaking his head with a happy sigh, Patrick stands to take his turn bowling. A spare. Not equal to Ollie's strike, but that doesn't matter anymore. For some reason, the competitive knot has left my gut, replaced only by mischievous anticipation.

Aubrey bowls a nine.

And then I'm up again. But this time, my nerves are gone. I'm barely thinking about the game as I step up to the lane, position myself, and throw the ball—actually knocking a few pins down!

My mind is somewhere else, sifting through my memories for what story to tell next. There's the time Ollie got stranded naked in a field during football hazing. Bridge and I snuck into the back of her dad's car when he went to pick him up, trying our best to keep the giggle fits quiet. Ooh, or how Ollie used to play pretend with us—his Luke Skywalker action figure always ended up married to my Little Mermaid Barbie. Oh yeah, tonight is going to be fun. Much more fun than I ever thought possible.

Confession 14

Have you ever found yourself playing a game you're not sure you want to win? I mean, I'm relatively competitive I guess. I like winning. But sometimes, it's like, everything's over and you're just left in this limbo—did I win? Did I lose? What was I even fighting for in the first place? I mean. Ugh, never mind. I don't know what I'm talking about...

I'm sipping on a glass of champagne, casting furtive glances around the room trying to find a familiar face in the crowd. Where'd Bridge go? And when is Patrick going to get here? And isn't Ollie coming?

Oh crap. Eye contact with a total stranger.

Whoops!

I smile meekly and flick my head in the opposite direction, sending what I hope is a clear message—don't come talk to me!

Really, I'm not sure what I would even say to these people. I'm hunched in the middle of the art gallery where Bridge works, trying to enjoy the opening night celebration she's helped coordinate for the past month. The artist on display is a modernist painter—pretty much blobs on a canvas as far as I can tell, but that just proves how little I know about this stuff.

I mean, I can just picture it now. Someone steps over making polite conversation, saying, isn't this piece wonderful? I look at the splatters and the plops, a mush of colors spaced between blank spaces of white, and nod confusedly, biting my tongue as I wonder if I could have done better. Or, you know, if a fifth grader could have...

"Hey," a low whisper filters into my ear.

I spit my champagne back into the glass, choking on it just a little as I turn. The picture of grace, as always. Cringing inwardly, I smile at Ollie. "Hey. You surprised me."

And then I wait for the snappy retort. He isn't one to ever let me get away with anything. Spitting up in public? Perfect fodder. But to my surprise, the joke never comes.

"So what do you think?" he asks instead. And I can't help but notice that his body is turned mostly away from me, hands in his pockets, as though he's uncomfortable. But aren't I supposed to be the one who's uncomfortable around him?

I furrow my brows. Something is definitely wrong here. "Um," I say and shrug, following his lead as I turn toward the painting on the opposite wall. It's an almost but not quite symmetrical circle of blue on a white backdrop. Mind-blowing... "It's nice."

He cracks a little, lifting the corner of his lip. And I wait for it, for the teasing. But his mouth evens back out and he nods seriously, still keeping his eyes locked on the painting. "Yeah."

And then silence descends. But not like a nice silence between friends. It's the sort of silence that expands with each passing second, that ginormous elephant in the room kind. I lick my lips, heartbeat surging a little faster as my anxiety starts to seep in. What's going on? Where is this coming from? I haven't seen Ollie since our double date, since the quick goodbye outside the bowling alley as Patrick and I went our way, and he and Aubrey went theirs. Overall, I thought the whole night went pretty well. I never learned to bowl any better, but you know, I wasn't expecting a miracle.

Maybe something happened at work? It's been about a week.

Or did he an Aubrey get into a fight? It's possible, I guess.

I lean over, needing to at least say something, hoping to cheer him up. "You know, Bridge told me some of these are worth more than I make in a year. Some might be worth more than I'll make in the next ten years."

His eyes widen disbelievingly, and then he shakes his head, releasing a tight breath. "Clearly, I went into the wrong career."

And well, I sort of agree. So I just nod, prolonging it as much as I can, but then, oh shoot, the silence is back. Only this time, I think I've been brought down to Ollie's level. I mean, really, when you think about it, that is a little absurd. I knew going into it that writing wasn't exactly a lucrative profession, but come on.

I peek sideways, taking in Ollie's profile, the clench of his jaw.

My curiosity gets the best of me.

"Ollie, are you ok—" I start, but an excited voice drowns mine out before I can finish.

"You made it!" Bridge chimes, appearing almost out of nowhere. "Are you having fun? What do you think of the party? Isn't the artist just amazing? A real genius? We were so lucky to nab him from the other galleries."

I process each question one at a time, a little lost in the whirlwind of her enthusiasm, which is about as far away from where I was thirty seconds ago as you could possibly get. But I know from the impatient bounce of her toes exactly what she wants to hear.

"Oh my gosh, he's fantastic," I gush, bringing a wide smile to my lips. "I mean, I don't even know how he comes up with these ideas, they're magnificent."

"I know," she says, speaking insanely fast. "I mean, the composition is incredible. There's a perfect balance in the imbalance. The way he plays with light and darks, with emptiness, with colors. It's so simple, but so complex. I could stare at these for hours."

I nod along, sipping my champagne because I don't really know how to respond. I mean, I took a lap around the room when I first got here and was pretty much done after that.

"You know, I think I've seen these somewhere before," Ollie chimes and for the first time tonight, there's humor coloring his words. I can't help the grin that pulls at my cheeks as I wait to hear how he's planning to end that sentence. Bridge glances at him with her eyebrows cocked. He just points toward the blue circle behind us. "Didn't you paint something like that back in kindergarten? I'm pretty sure it was on our refrigerator for months."

Bridge just rolls her eyes, exasperated. I meet Ollie's gaze, silently agreeing with him, overjoyed when I spot the twinkle in his cerulean irises, the one that was missing before. He's not complete without it. And all I want to do in this moment is make sure it stays there.

"Ollie," I start in a sort of chastising manner. "Don't be ridiculous. Bridge wasn't in kindergarten when she painted it…she was a preschool prodigy."

Bridge glares at me and I know exactly what that look says—traitor. And even though I probably should, I don't really care.

"She was a master of the potato stamp," Ollie adds, tone dramatically serious.

I lean in, adopting the same persona. "If you ask me, finger-painting was her true art."

"It's a lost art, really," he comments sadly.

I nod. "Definitely underrated."

"Say what you want," Bridge interjects before Ollie has a chance to speak. "I'm going to find two people who aren't such smartasses to talk to."

And then she leans across the space, grabs my glass of champagne from my hand, takes a long sip, and saunters off. I mean, you have to hand it to her. The girl knows how to make an exit.

I'm left shell-shocked, holding the empty air, peering at my fingers a little sadly. That was great champagne—and more importantly, it was a great excuse to not speak. Something I'm in dire need of as the air between Ollie and me stretches to a taut tense once more. I smile at him, but the spark has already disappeared from his eyes. And I can't help but wonder if it has something to do with me.

"So," I start, trailing off. When exactly did things get so strange between us? Did I miss something? When did Ollie decide it was no longer fun to ridicule me? To tease me? Because I tried for about a decade to make him stop, and now that it's gone, I sort of miss it.

"Evening, everyone," I hear over my shoulder, just as an arm wraps around my waist. Just like that, I'm saved from the overwhelming awkwardness and confusion of the situation.

"Patrick!" And then I stretch up, kissing his cheek.

He glances around, scrunching his forehead. "Where's Aubrey? And Bridget?"

"Bridge is schmoozing the crowd," I say and then turn expectantly to Ollie.

He coughs, clearing his throat, before running a hand through his lusciously dark hair. I hate how that move always makes it look better than it did before. With my luck, if I even tried to sexily flip my hair, I'd end up getting my fingers stuck in a web of knots. But Ollie just makes it look easy, like being drool-worthy is second nature to him. Which it probably is...

Wait.

How did this train of thought start again? It's veering off into wildly dangerous territory.

Oh, right. Aubrey.

And Patrick!

My boyfriend, Patrick, whose hair is the only hair I should be thinking about. I lean into his side, enjoying the warmth of his body.

"Aubrey couldn't make it," is all Ollie says.

"That's a shame," Patrick says politely, clearly making small talk.

But it seems like that's the only kind of talk this conversation has any hope of having, so I just try to keep it going. Any talk is preferable to cringe-worthy silence. "Yeah, that stinks. It's your first Friday off in weeks."

Ollie just shrugs.

I want to throttle him. Work with me here!

But then his gaze sharpens and he looks at Patrick with interest. A small knot of dread churns my stomach. What's coming?

But all he does is ask, "So, what do you think of the artist?"

Patrick glances around, eyes zipping from canvas to canvas, taking the paintings in. "I'm not really into all of this stuff, but it seems pretty good to me. I think my parents might have some of his work at our beach house."

"Well, I think it's a little overhyped, to be honest," Ollie murmurs, and then his eyes flicker over to me. I try to keep my heart from leaping out of my chest. Just from nerves. Obviously. "What do you think, Skye?"

Cue penetrating bright blue stare.

I fidget under Ollie's scrutiny, looking up at Patrick instead, moving just a smidge closer to him. And even though I'm not looking at him anymore, the intensity of Ollie's gaze burns my skin. "Well, you heard Bridge, he's a genius. I don't really know much about it either."

I peek to the side, just quick enough to see a hint of disappointment line Ollie's eyes before he turns them away, out toward the window. A sinking feeling lurches in my chest, but I'm not sure why or what it means.

"Champagne?" a man asks, leaning a tray into the middle of our group.

God, yes. It's sad how little hesitation there is in my movements. But hey, I'm desperate for a distraction. Almost immediately, the glass is at my lips and I'm taking down a long sip, rummaging through my thoughts for something to say once the bubbles dissipate.

Luckily, Patrick beats me to it. He leans in, speaking more to me than Ollie. "How long are we going to stay here?"

I purse my lips, thinking for a moment. "Well, we don't need to stay for the entire thing. Bridge will be here for hours, I think she needs to stay to help clean everything up after. Maybe another hour or so? Just so we can talk to her some more?"

He nods. "Okay. Some friends of mine are at a bar around the corner from here. Want to meet up with them after?"

I smile. Um, duh. But I have to play it cool. "Sure."

"You can come too, man, if you don't have plans," Patrick follows up, looking past me. And for the second time that night, I almost spit out my champagne as I jerk my head to the side. Freaking Ollie. I totally forgot he was here for a second. It was an easier time.

"Nah, I'm good," he murmurs with a shrug.

Thank god.

Before anyone has time to say anything else, I notice a red head barreling toward us with a wide grin.

"Patrick, you're here," Bridge calls, closing the distance. "How's my favorite investment banker?"

He throws her an amused grin. "Good. How's my favorite slightly inebriated art salesman?"

"Wonderful," she chirps. And then leans in conspiringly. "Keep the inebriated thing on the down low. I have to maintain a professional aura."

"I'll take this then," Ollie says and plucks the half-full champagne glass from her hand, downing it in one gulp.

"Hey!" she argues. But it's too late anyway.

He just smiles. "You'll thank me tomorrow, sis."

She raises one eyebrow, holding Ollie's gaze for a long moment before turning back to Patrick. "So, see anything here you like? If anyone asks, just make sure you tell them Bridget McDonough sold you on a piece."

He winks. "Will do."

"We were just talking about what we're going to do later tonight," I say, changing the tide of the conversation from Bridge trying to pawn off a multi-thousand dollar painting on my boyfriend. "When do you think you'll be able to break free of the gallery?"

She shrugs. "Not anytime soon. But let me know where you go and I'll try to meet you out later. Oh—" And then she stops, looking over my shoulder, gazing really intently at whatever is behind me. A second later, a little twinkle lights her eyes. "Excuse me. I've got to go talk to people who might actually buy something, like the lady in a fur coat who just walked in. I'll see you guys later. Enjoy the free champagne!"

I toast her as she walks away, taking my next sip in her honor.

"I think I'm going to head out too," Ollie says.

Immediately my heart jerks. "No!" And really, I have no idea why I say it—especially not so wholeheartedly. "I mean, you should stay. You never know when you'll get to see Bridge in action again."

He holds my gaze for a moment, blue eyes intense, before flicking his attention to Patrick. "No, really. I'm beat from the work week. All I want right now is my bed."

"It was good to see you again," Patrick says, reaching out for a handshake, which Ollie returns.

"See you later, Skye," he mumbles.

But I have no response.

I'm just so utterly confused.

Who is that guy? Because it's not Ollie. Not the Ollie I've known for almost twenty years. He would never leave an event his sister was throwing early. Would never be so quiet, so absent. Would never be—I don't know how to describe it except to say defeated. Dejected. Everything in his person just looks so down.

"Should we take a walk around the room?" Patrick asks, placing his arm around my shoulders.

I rip my gaze away from the lone figure of Ollie walking away, trying to diffuse the cloud hanging over my mood. "Sure."

"I'll keep an eye out in case there's anything my father would want. I'm actually surprised they're not here," Patrick says, leading me around the room. "Have I ever told you about our summer house?"

I shake my head.

And as he launches into a description, my mind rebels against my better judgment and completely tunes him out. Then my body follows. Against my will, my eyes creep over to the door just in time to see it shut behind Ollie's back. I spy on him, watching as he stops, shoulders rising in what I think is a long, deep breath. And I keep looking as he steps farther into the night, across the street, disappearing around the bend. And even then, I just stare at the empty spot his body used to fill.

Something happened.

I don't know what or when or how. But I do know Ollie looked lost, not himself. And even though I don't want to admit it, the pinch of my gut tells me I'm the reason for the change. If I dug a little deeper, I'm sure I'd understand. But I don't know if I'm ready for the answer.

Confession 15

Memories are really easy to bury—at least that's what I always thought. My dad. The divorce. Ollie. All those sad moments are trapped under layers and layers of happy ones. Like the old saying, out of sight out of mind. But ever so often, you see something, or smell something, or hear something, and the dam breaks. Just like that, the moment you tried so hard to forget comes flooding forward, washing over you and pulling you under.

Home.

I feel like home is one of those things that is so underrated until you don't have one anymore. Before the divorce, I took my family for granted. Two loving parents. One child. Happy. I never dreamed it wouldn't stay that way forever. But until the papers were finalized, my house became a warzone. It wasn't until I left for college and realized how strange a place the rest of the world could be that I relearned to love my house, my home, minus its one former occupant.

But Bridget's house is sometimes what I really think of when I think of home. It's where I came for solace. Where I went to escape. At least it was, before everything happened with Ollie. But no one knows about that except for him and me. So for the past six years, ever since my parents' divorce, it's where my mom and I have come for most of our holidays, including Thanksgiving. And this year is no different.

But I can't shake this uneasy feeling as Bridget's dad pulls into the driveway after picking us both up from the train—and yeah, you read that correctly. Both of us—two of us. Believe it or not, Thanksgiving is a really busy day for restaurants, which is why Ollie hasn't been home for Thanksgiving four years in a row. And truth be told, I'm a little thankful he's not here this year.

For the past few weeks, everything has felt off between us. That uneasy tension I noticed the night of the gallery party hasn't gone away. I mean, I'm getting used to Ollie's presence, to having him back in my life—at least, I think I am. But something shifted during our double date. Ever since, the air between us has been awkward in a way it never has before. He's talking to me less, paying attention to me less, which is fine, I guess. It's just strange. Just something I need to get used to.

On the other hand, everything with Patrick has felt just right. I mean, the broken hand has put a little damper on everything, but in all honesty, I don't mind. I'm a little thankful for that too. Everything has been brought down to my pace, which I'm sure is much slower than he's used to. But so far, he hasn't complained. So far, he's been the best boyfriend any girl could hope for.

For the most part, my life is exactly where I want it. Which is why I don't understand the clump of nerves tightening my stomach as I step out of Mr. McDonough's car and make my way up the front steps of Bridget's house. And the more I try to ignore the mounting fear, the more intense it becomes. Making my hands tremble. My palms sweat. My tongue dry. But the front door flies open before Bridge's dad can even pull out his key, and I don't have time to uncover the source of my anxiety, because two motherly embraces quickly steal my attention.

"Mom!" I exclaim, falling into her arms and wrapping mine tightly around her. She visited Bridge and me back in early August and we talk at least once a week, but still, it feels like I haven't seen her in forever.

"I missed you," she whispers into my ear.

"I missed you too," I say back, squeezing a little tighter for emphasis.

Behind me, Bridge yells, "Mrs. C!"

I break away, letting her take a turn hugging my mom. The *C* stands for Cooper. She switched back to her maiden name after the divorce. Joanna Cooper—I've always preferred the change. It sounds more like her anyway.

"Hi, Mrs. McDonough," I murmur as Bridge's mom, Claire, pulls me in for a tight embrace.

"We've missed seeing you around here," she says. And I guess it's true. Ever since Bridge and I went to college, I haven't been coming around as much. Just a few times a year instead of an almost weekly basis. But, you know, the whole avoiding Ollie like he was the plague for four years sort of does that.

"The house smells amazing," I say as we all step inside.

The scent of turkey, gravy, and stuffing immediately fills my nose, warming my heart. That. That is what I think of when I think of home.

"Seems like you outdid yourself this year, Mom," Bridge comments, moving swiftly to the kitchen.

"Hey, I helped, young lady!" her father, Sean, calls after her. But he's a little busy bringing our bags in through the front door. Which, well, whoops! I guess old habits die hard. As soon as I come home, even though I'm a fully functioning—well, mostly functioning—adult, I resume the role of dependent child when I cross state lines into Pennsylvania.

All five of us wander into the kitchen, taking our usual places around the snacks set up on the table, munching but trying not to get too full. Bridge's mom stands at attention over the burners and the oven, circling the kitchen like a hawk, keeping an eye on all the dishes still being prepared. And I can't help but be reminded of Ollie, who looks so much like his mother. Same dark brown hair. Same bright turquoise eyes. Same love of the kitchen. And then there's Bridge and her dad, the two redheads reaching for the same snacks at the same time. Well, and then you have my mom and me. We used to be completely different—she was loud where I was quiet, confident where I was shy, popular where I was nerdy. But after the divorce, something shifted, and now she's more like me, sitting in her chair, happy to listen while everyone else speaks.

"So, how's living with your brother going? I'm amazed you haven't killed each other yet," Mr. McDonough asks between crackers.

Bridge just rolls her eyes, following his hand to the cheese plate and letting him cut her a slice. "God, he's so overprotective. I feel like I haven't had a date in months."

"Good," her father murmurs. "That's exactly how he should be."

"Dad," Bridge whines, lifting her brows at him while she bites into her cracker. And then mutters, "Yeah, well, say that to Skye's boyfriend cause Ollie almost got in a fight with him."

Bridge!

I widen my eyes, glaring at her. But it's too late. The damage is done.

"You have a boyfriend?" my mom says, shocked.

"Ollie almost hit him?" Mrs. McDonough calls from the other side of kitchen.

"Sorry," Bridge mouths in my direction, cringing. It's not really her fault. I forgot to tell her my mom doesn't know that much about Patrick. Stupid, stupid mistake.

"Um," I say, and then swallow, hoping everyone else didn't hear that resounding gulp. "Well, Mom, I've mentioned Patrick to you before, I told you we went on a few dates."

"You didn't tell me he was your boyfriend." And yes, there is an undercurrent of accusation in her tone. Not that I blame her—I always tell her everything. Well, almost always...

"Haven't you been reading Skye's—" I kick Bridge under the table, cutting her off. And she coughs, face burning red, glaring at me this time.

Oh, right, I probably should've mentioned that I never told my mother about the style section or the, uh, sex column. She may think that I got hired full-time for the book review section, but, well, can you really blame me? Who wants their mother to read all about their dating life every week? Especially mine, which is half-fabricated with frisky details that are utterly false. I mean, do you really think my mom would believe me if I told her those more suggestive elements of my column are complete fiction? That Bridge helps me write them? Uh, yeah, she'd just think I was trying to pull a fast one. Heck, I'm pretty sure I've convinced most of New York that I have a raging sex life, why wouldn't my mom think the same?

Yeah… don't want to go there…

"Skye's what?" my mom asks, eyes narrowing.

"My blog," I interject before Bridge has to say anything else. She looks relieved. "I was, um, writing a blog about life in New York, but then work got a little too hectic and I decided to delete it. No big deal."

"Well, I wish you'd told me. I love to read your writing…" She trails off, a little dejected.

Crap.

Now I feel guilty.

"I'm sorry, Mom, really. I would have told you, but it didn't really seem like something worth telling. Anyway, yes, Patrick is officially my boyfriend, so now you know that. And it only happened yesterday, so it's not like I was keeping a secret from you." A little white lie never hurt anybody, right?

"When did Oliver try to hit him?" Mrs. McDonough asks, and something about the way she says Oliver makes me a little nervous. It's that whole full name thing. Parents only say full names when you're about to get in trouble. It's like an unwritten rule.

"Bridge is just exaggerating," I say, keeping my voice light. "You know how she loves to dramatize a boring story."

"Hey," she calls, defending her honor.

But the protest is sort of undermined when her mom chimes in with, "Oh, yes, well that's our Bridget. But I'll give Oliver a good talking to if you need me to."

"No, really, nothing happened."

She goes back to mashing the potatoes. Thank god.

Phew. That was close. Subject change needed immediately. "Hey, Bridge, why don't you tell everyone about the gallery opening."

"Ooh!" She sits up, spitting some cracker crumble out. "It was so cool."

"Swallow, kid," her dad teases, receiving another exasperated eye roll from his daughter.

I sit back, off the hot seat for a moment, breathing a sigh of relief. But the longer I tune out the conversation, the more I notice the tingle of anxiety still funneling through my veins, the slight discomfort, as though something just isn't right.

My mom must notice, because she leans over and nudges me with her shoulder. "Come on, I have something for you in the car."

We excuse ourselves and I follow her outside, hugging my arms around my midsection to fight the cool air. "What's going on, Mom?"

"Nothing, sweetie," she says, and I can't help but notice that like her daughter often does, my mother didn't really think this plan through. We're standing in the cold, teeth chattering just a little. Not exactly the ideal place to have a heart to heart. She nudges her head in the direction of her SUV. "Come on, get in for a minute."

"Everything okay?" I ask.

"Yeah."

"So, where's this mysterious thing you have for me in the car." I raise one eyebrow in her direction.

"You know, you're a terrible liar for a reason. Me." But then she grows quiet, and I know exactly why. I must get my terrible lying ability from her, because we both know my father was a pro. Then again, the whole virgin sex columnist thing is pretty under-wraps. So, maybe I'm more like my dad than I care to realize…

Ugh.

Don't want to follow that line of thinking.

My mom interrupts, reaching out for my hand. "You just seem a little down, I thought we could come outside in case there is anything you want to talk to me about."

Hmm…let's see. Things I would love to say to my mom. Yeah, I've racked up quite a few of those. But for some reason, nothing comes to my lips. I've had so long to talk to her about Ollie, about my job, heck even about the good stuff like Patrick. I'm just not really sure where to even begin. And I don't know why now, after a few weeks of pure bliss, my mood has tanked. "No, Mom. Really, I'm just a little tired."

"Nothing with Patrick…"

"No, he's practically prince charming. So sweet to me."

"But?"

I bite my lip.

Is there a *but* at the end of the sentence? He's perfect. That's the truth. I smile, glancing up from the dashboard to meet her warm gray-blue eyes—something I definitely got from her. "No buts. We're happy together."

"Good." She nods, accepting my response. But I can tell something is still bothering her, something she comes really close to saying. But then she shakes her head a little, and shrugs. "Come on, let's get back inside. Dinner is almost ready."

I nod, but I suddenly find I can't speak.

I'm staring at the tree in the McDonough's front yard, and a memory pushes its way to the front of my thoughts. Bridge, Ollie, and I are playing in the shade of the leaf-filled maple. Ollie keeps stealing our dolls and tossing them away, so to get rid of him, Bridge and I bet that he can't climb all the way to the top of the tree. He tries, obviously, like any obstinate little boy, and then proceeds to fall about twelve feet to the ground, breaking his leg. I still remember the fear that enveloped my entire being as Mrs. McDonough ran outside, hearing her son cry.

But in real time, my mom has already gotten out of the car and she's staring at me from the front of the walk with furrowed brows, wondering what's keeping me. I shake my head, clearing the memory away and hop out, stepping quickly to her side.

"Sorry," I murmur.

But then my eyes drift to the driveway and I'm pulled back into the past again. Bridge and I are sitting next to a bucket of chalk, carefully covering the pavement in pastel flowers and hearts. We don't even see him coming. All of a sudden, water drenches us from above, soaking our T-shirts, and washing all of our hard work away. Bridge immediately goes on the assault, smacking her brother, but he's prepared with a water gun and chases us around for the next twenty minutes. Until we find the hose and absolutely destroy him.

"Skylar?" my mom asks.

I blink and our child selves disappear, the driveway is empty except for two cars. Then I realize I'm grinning and laugh a little, releasing the energy.

"You sure you're okay?" my mom asks.

I nod.

We walk up the path and slip through the front door. But as we pass by, my fingers reach out, running over the pane of a glass window, remembering a day that happened fifteen years ago, and my gaze returns to the yard. Ollie is teaching Bridge and me how to play baseball, but he's showing off and throwing really hard fastballs that we have no hope of hitting. His dad tries telling him to cool it, calling Ollie *slugger*. But he won't. And then it's my turn at bat and I swing, actually closing my eyes because I'm so afraid of the ball. The smack reverberates up my entire arm, shaking my whole body, and I hear the crash of glass before I even open my eyes. I think that was the first time I distinctly remember hearing an adult curse. The whole window shattered, sending glass everywhere. Of course, the three of us ended up running to the backyard, giggling, while their father continued shouting curses in the front yard.

And suddenly I realize what's happening.

Why I feel off.

It's this house. It's these memories. It's Ollie. Spending so much time with him. Seeing him again. Being so confused by him again. Right now, standing outside the McDonough house, I'm closer than I've ever been to reliving that night— the one that happened four years ago, the one I've been trying to forget ever since.

I walk inside the house.

"Where are you going?" my mom calls to me.

I'm marching up the steps. I didn't even realize I'd stopped following her, but I'm already halfway to the second floor.

"Just using the bathroom," I murmur and keep moving.

Part of me wants to stop. But I have no control. My body is moving on its own, it's taken control. My heart isn't ready, but every other part of me is screaming that it's time. Time to go back. Panic mounts underneath my skin as a sea of memories part, exposing the barren landscape of all the hardships I've buried deep below. Once tightly packed sand is now soft enough to slip through my fingers, revealing what rests beneath.

And then I'm there.

The door still has a sign that reads, *Oliver's Room! Keep Out!*

And I have. I've walked past this sign a dozen times. I've heeded the rules for four years. I've denied everything. I've tried to forget. But I can't.

My fingers stretch for the knob. They turn.

No.

I shake my head.

No.

But as soon as the door swings open, the world stops. The water rushes forward. And I can't move as the memory crashes over me, taking my breath away.

Confession 16

I bet by now you're wondering what happened with Ollie four years ago. Well, I guess I can't ignore it any longer. It was the night before Bridge and I were leaving for college, the night of our last high school party, the night before Ollie was leaving for another year at culinary school. And, well, here. You'll see...

"I can't believe you guys got so drunk tonight," Ollie murmurs from the driver's seat, running a hand through his hair. I'm mesmerized by the way the moon bounces off each strand, flickering from shadow to spark so quickly. But Ollie keeps his eyes on the road, just shaking his head in our direction.

"We're not that bad," Bridge mumbles, and even in my slight haze, I hear the slur to her words. Well, and then she convulses into a fit of giggles, undermining her argument just a little. Ollie looks to the side, rolling his eyes at his sister.

I don't realize I'm staring at him in the rearview mirror until his gaze flicks toward mine, grinning, but then he looks back to the road. A thrill spikes down my chest, burning from how much I want him. From how much I've always wanted him. But the fire is made painful from his oblivion.

Tonight. Tonight.

I've been telling myself for the past three hours, with every sip of beer, with every ounce of liquid courage—tonight. I have to tell Ollie how I feel. I have to. Because tomorrow I leave for college and who knows when I'll see him again. Desire coils in my stomach, a stiff bundle of nerves—one that's been there for way too long. And it consumes me. I can't think when he's home. I can't think when he's away at school. Every time I even talk to another boy, a sour taste taints my tongue, a little voice whispers, *sure he's nice, but he's not Ollie.*

I have to tell someone. And I can't tell Bridge. So it has to be him.

My head falls back, heavy from the alcohol, and I let my gaze slip out the window, tearing my eyes away from the reflection I've practically memorized—the face that stars in my dreams. My heart is pounding. But I have to. Tonight.

"You guys are going to be so miserable tomorrow," he teases, "arriving for your first day at school with a hangover. God, the car ride is going to suck."

"Ollie…" Bridge whines. "Turn on the music, I want to be loud for a little while longer."

He sighs. The sound makes me shiver. But then the music takes my attention away. Bridge leans forward, fumbling with the buttons, twisting the knob to an almost deafening level. She jumps in her seat, bopping with the beat, singing. But I keep staring at the darkness, watching shadowy shapes creep by. Pop music wraps around us, cocooning the car in notes and tones and crescendos vastly different from the silence beyond these doors.

And then it's gone. Disappeared.

I blink my blurry eyes, realizing we've reached Bridget's house.

Ollie deftly hops out, circling to his sister's door. Ignoring him, Bridge slides out, wobbly on her high heels, teetering before Ollie grabs her around the waist, holding her upright.

"You coming, Skye?" he teases, glancing over his shoulder to where I'm still waiting in the car. He holds out his free arm, offering it to me. "Come on."

My breath hitches as I slip against his chest and the warmth of Ollie's body curls into my side. I'm hyperaware of the position his palm secures against my stomach, of the pressure he uses to help me walk, of the attention he gives. I trip over my own feet. He clutches me tighter, making my heart flutter even faster, a hummingbird alive in my chest. I can't focus on anything except for the fact that he's touching me, can't think beyond the sensation of his fingers grazing the bare skin just above my jeans.

"You know, I thought better of you, Skye."

I look up, struck dumb by the twinkle in his moonlit eyes. "Wh—what?"

"I knew Bridge would get bombed as soon as I saw you guys sneak out for the party. But you? I thought you were supposed to be her good influence."

I smile, biting my lip. It's the only response I can muster because my eyes sink down to his lips, stuck.

"I'm not that drunk!" Bridge cries, tearing out of Ollie's hands to race up the walk.

"Shh!" he hisses. "Do you want to wake up Mom and Dad?"

Bridge responds by throwing out her arms, twirling around, faster and faster.

"Stay," Ollie orders, pointing at me before turning. I obey, standing still, swaying just a little with the wind, or maybe, well, with the booze. A few steps later and he's there, catching his sister as she loses her balance, crashing to the ground. Bridge yelps and Ollie rushes to cover her mouth, holding the shout in, sighing heavily.

"How do you get away with this when I'm not around to shut you up?" he murmurs, shaking his head.

Me.

I want to tell him, but I can't find my voice. I'm always the sober one, the designated driver, the responsible one. But not tonight. Because tonight, I'm on a mission.

"Come on, Skye," he whispers, gesturing for me to walk over.

I take each step slower than the last, one foot in front of the other, holding my arms out for balance. When I close the gap, Ollie puts his arm around me again, carrying both Bridge and me to the door, easing us inside and plopping us down on the steps in the front hallway.

"Wait here." And then he disappears, only to return a few minutes later with two full glasses of water and two pieces of bread. "Drink and eat this now."

Bridge and I listen. Something about the quietness of the house calms her rebellious mood. I gulp down the water, throat dry from all the words I want to say. When we're done, he leans down, holding us by our waists again, taking each step one at a time as we climb achingly slow to the second floor of the house. A few minutes later, and Ollie releases us at the edge of Bridget's bedroom.

"If you think you're going to be sick, knock on my door, okay?"

I nod, biting my lip.

He walks away, disappearing into the dark hall.

"Ollie!" I whisper.

He stops, turns. "Yeah?"

Say it!

Say it!

But Bridge is by my side, hanging on my arm, dropping her head against my shoulder, already sleepy.

Say it!

I open my mouth, chest clamped by an invisible hand. I'm trembling.

"I—"

All the courage leaves my body in a whoosh, leaving my limbs heavy with failure. I'm not strong enough. Not brave enough. I'm…nothing. The invisible girl with invisible dreams and not enough nerve to reach out and grab them.

"Thanks," I mumble.

Ollie grins. "Any time. Now please help put my sister to sleep before she passes out on the carpet."

I nod.

He's gone.

Bridge is practically snoring into my ear, so I hold her, stumbling for the bed, tripping so we both collapse onto the mattress in a heap. Only half awake, Bridge crawls to her side of the bed, rolling under the covers. But I stay where I am, staring at the stars twinkling on the ceiling, stickers I've wished upon more times than I can count. The neon green mocks me, an illusion of everything I could have if I only tried.

"Skye," Bridge whispers beside me. "We're going to college tomorrow."

"I know," I tell her, finally turning away from the ceiling, joining her under the covers.

"College," she sighs, blissful.

College. But my heart sinks with the idea. College. Where I'll still be pining after Ollie. College. Where I'll be haunted by the what ifs of tonight. College. Where every boy will continue to fail to measure up to the crush I've glorified in my head.

I've run through what will happen if I tell him a thousand times. Shock and desperation, the gentle let down, the way he'll never look at me the same. But at least then I'll know there's no chance. I'll know he'll never see me that way. I'll know it's hopeless. I'll get over it. I'll be done. I want so much to be done. I want so much for the constant ache to disappear. For the pining to go away.

My eyes shoot open.

I have to do this.

I have to.

Bridge snores beside me, and I almost hear the word *go* in the rumble—an urging for me to leave, to go, to find answers.

I listen.

Quietly, I drop my feet to the floor, ease off the bed, and walk to the door. The knob clicks when I turn it, making my pulse jump, but I press forward, tiptoeing across the carpet. And then I stop, my hand an inch away from his door, hovering.

I bite my lower lip.

Close my eyes.

Breathe. Inhale—one, two, three. Hold. Exhale—one, two, three.

My chest burns with nerves, with fear. My hands tremble. But if there's one thing worse than fear, it's regret. And I know if I don't find the courage to walk through this door, I'll never stop thinking about what could have happened if I did. My fingers twitch. Everything in my body pauses, stuck in this moment, in this decision.

And then in a rush it happens.

I open the door, step inside, and close it behind me.

"Hello?" a sleepy voice asks, followed by the movement of rustling sheets. The light clicks on, bright against the dark. And I feel caught. Trapped. "Skye? Are you okay? Is Bridget?"

"Yeah," I murmur, suddenly unsure, antsy as my hands wring in and out, pulling my skin tight.

He gives me a confused look, made all the more adorable by the disarray of his hair. And then the corner of his mouth lifts. "Did you walk in here by accident coming back from the bathroom or something? Are you that drunk?"

I just shake my head.

My throat is caught with indecision, clogged by trepidation.

Ollie sighs and rolls off his bed, somehow graceful as he lands on his feet in one swift move. Then he's walking toward me. Each step echoes against my heart, one heavy thud after another. "Come on, I'll take you back over to Bridget's room."

He places his hand on my arm, guiding me gently to the door.

"Oh, Skye, I can't wait to see your face tomorrow morning when the hazy memory of tonight returns. Mortification is such a good look on you."

He reaches for the knob.

"Ollie."

He doesn't react. He's twisting now.

I grab his fingers, holding them against the door, stopping him. And then I look up at the face that's only a few inches away from mine, drawing strength from the warmth of his hand, from the touch I so desperately crave.

"Ollie," I whisper.

He turns, meeting my gaze, looking down, enchanting me with those deep turquoise pools. But his expression is empty, unaware, not pining like mine. Not craving. My focus shifts to his lips, tantalizingly close, a distance that would be so easy to close if I weren't so afraid.

"Skye?" he murmurs.

I can't do this while we're touching, I can't think straight when his skin is pressed against mine. I can't think straight at all. My mind is running a hundred steps ahead of my body. What will he say? What will he do? Will he ever talk to me again? Will things ever be the same? Will Bridge find out? Will I lose them both?

The pressure beneath my skin mounts, boiling over. I'm a bubble about to burst. A volcano about to erupt. A bomb about to explode. My entire body tenses with anticipation. And I know Ollie must feel it, because his eyes narrow, growing more intense, more concerned. My ears buzz, drowning out the world, growing louder and louder.

And then everything stops.

I'm calm.

Clear.

Every ounce of fear evaporates for one split second, and in that second, I let go. "I'm in love with you," I whisper.

My heart surges forward, racing, thumping. But at the same time, I feel free.

I said it.

After so many years, I finally said it.

"You're what?" he murmurs.

"I'm in love with you," I repeat, and this time all of the hesitation is gone. The secret is out. "I've been in love with you for my entire life, and I had to say something before I leave tomorrow. I don't expect anything from you, I just needed to say it, to have you hear it, so I can move on with my life."

And then I wait, running over every possible outcome in my mind. Ollie will reject me, of course. Maybe he'll say I'm too much like a little sister, that we've known each other for too long, that he's never thought of me that way, that we've always just been friends. He'll be kind, he'll be gentle, caring like he's always been to me. But no matter how he says it or what he does, it will all mean the same thing—no. No, I don't love you too. No, I don't like you like that. Just no. And even though my heart sinks just thinking about it, it's okay. It's what I expect. It's what I need to hear to get over this—it's the whole reason I came to his room tonight, to hear the *no* I've imagined a million times in my dreams.

But he doesn't say no.

He doesn't say anything.

He blinks. And then he moves. Closer.

I can't breathe.

Ollie shifts his hand, lifting it from the doorknob, turning it so he brushes against my fingers. Those clear cerulean eyes hold mine enraptured. Butterflies flutter to life. Every rub of his thumb against my wrist sends fire up my arm. And then he leans down, led by his lips, closing the already small gap between our bodies.

My eyes shoot wide. I can't move. Can't react. I've envisioned Ollie's response for years and never once did I let myself believe he might actually say yes. Might actually feel the same. Might actually—

Ollie kisses me.

And I can't think anymore.

In a rush, our bodies melt together. My hands run through his hair, slipping past each strand, holding the back of his head. His fingers draw a burning trail up my arm, setting fire to my skin as they come to a rest just below my jaw, drawing circles on the soft skin of my neck, driving me wild. His other arm molds to my back, holding me close, skin slipping beneath my shirt, sending a shiver up my spine.

And I want to ask what's happening. What this means. What he means.

But I can't.

His lips trail across my jaw, down to my neck, eliciting a little gasp of pure pleasure from my lips, and I admit to myself that if I'm dreaming, I don't want to wake up. If this is a trick, I don't ever want to know the truth. I want to stay here, in this moment, finally living everything I never dared hope could be real.

I let my fears go.

And everything moves fast forward.

Somehow, my shirt ends up on the floor, followed by my bra, and in a few moments I've gone farther with Ollie than I have ever gone with anyone before. We still don't speak. Everything is quiet, as though being pulled along by fate. No questions. No awkwardness. It's just happening, smoother than anything I've experienced before. His skin feels made to touch mine, to hold mine, to caress mine. Ollie's shirt tumbles to the ground. My fingers trace the groove of muscles cutting into his chest, to his back, tracing the lines along his skin, exploring places I've only ever explored in my mind. All the while we're kissing, tasting.

Then he steps.

I step.

He falls.

I fall.

We land in a tumble on his bed, a mess of limbs, but nothing pauses. Ollie rolls, tucking my body beneath him, and then sinks down with utter control, pinning me against the mattress. His hand travels down my side while his lips still dizzy my brain, sending my nerves haywire.

But as his fingers dip just barely below my waistband, tickling my untouched skin, I break away, sobered.

"Ollie?" I murmur, breathing heavily.

He stops.

Everything.

"Ollie?" I whisper again.

In one motion, he jumps from the bed, walking to the other side of the room, turning his gaze away from me, staring at the wall instead. And I understand. The spell is broken. I broke it.

"You should leave," he says, voice dark, tone dead. I've never heard him like this before.

"Ollie? What just happened? Why?"

"You should go."

I stand, pulling the sheet with me, suddenly shy. I reach out to touch his back, golden in the soft midnight light, but he turns before I do. I snatch my fingers to my chest, hugging the sheet, and meet his empty expression. There's no hurt. No confusion. No anger. Nothing.

He's blank. Emotionless.

"Go."

But I can't. I won't. He felt it too. Feels it too. Or he wouldn't have kissed me. I shake my head. I love him. "Ollie, why are you doing this?"

"Doing what?" he asks, tugging his shirt back over his head, sitting on the bed, casual.

"Why did you kiss me? Why did you—why?" And my voice sounds weak, trembling, on the brink of tears—which must be the burning sensation around my eyes.

"Because I wanted to see if I felt something, and I don't. So it's better for both of us to forget this ever happened and move on. Friends, like we've always been."

I lift my foot to step closer, but I can't move. My head swivels back and forth, frantic with denial. "I don't believe you. There's no way you felt nothing just now. You can't kiss someone like you just kissed me and feel nothing."

He sighs, teal eyes colder than I've ever seen them. "You're just a kid, Skye. You have no idea what guys can or can't do."

"I know you," I whisper, desperate to cling to something.

"Do you?"

"Yes." I step forward, still wrapped in his sheets, clutching them to me like a life raft. "And I know that if you felt nothing, you would have said that in the first place. You wouldn't hurt me like this. You wouldn't be so cruel."

He pauses.

Doesn't respond.

And then he rolls over and turns his back to me, settling in against his pillow and reaching for the light. "Go to bed, Skye. You're drunk. You'll barely remember this in the morning."

Darkness floods the room, surrounds me. I blink through the black, trying to see past the mortification burning my eyes—to see past the fact that I'm half naked, standing in the middle of Ollie's room, utterly heartbroken. Even in the dark, I hold the sheet over my chest as I feel for my shirt on the floor. My throat clogs, stopped by a painful lump beginning to form. Tears drop soundlessly to the ground. I try not to sniffle, not to give him a clue, but I know some sighs leak out, loud in the silence.

Ollie doesn't say a word.

He's a statue in his bed. Made of stone.

My fingers brush the soft cotton of my shirt and I pull it over my head, forgetting about my bra as I rush for the door. I don't look back as I leave.

Confession 17

The next morning, I waited in Bridget's bed until I heard the front door open. I crept to the window, watching Ollie leave for the airport with his mother, waiting for him to look back and find my face in the window, to show me he was sorry. He never did. And I told myself I was done. That I never wanted to see him again. That I never wanted to hear his apology. Then I walked downstairs with a grin on my face, hiding the heartbreak inside, and moved on. At least, I thought I did.

I have that panicky feeling again. Why does this keep happening to me? My hands tremble in my lap, matching the bounce of the taxi as it races over the city streets. No matter how fast the cab moves, my heart surges faster, a constant pounding in my chest.

"Skye?" Bridge asks beside me. "Are you okay? You've been really silent all day. You barely spoke on the train."

I swallow, finding my voice. "I'm fine. I think I'm still working off my stuffing hangover, too many carbs. It makes me sleepy." Which would have been a great excuse if it were Friday, but it's not. It's Sunday afternoon and the leftovers ran out yesterday morning.

Bridge raises her eyebrows. "You're not sleepy. You're fidgety."

And as she says it, I notice my thigh is bumping up and down on the seat, nervously ticking. I stop.

"If you don't want to tell me what's bothering you, it's okay," she says, though I can hear the soft disappointment in her tone. "But I'm here if you need me."

I scan my brain for something to say, something to lift her downcast eyes, to prove to my best friend there is nothing in the world I wouldn't tell her—except, you know, the truth. That I'm terrified to see her brother. That a wound I thought I had sealed shut four years ago ripped back open and it burns, a fresh sort of sting.

"My dad," I finally say, remembering something else that threw me for a loop this weekend. "My dad wants me to go to his house for Christmas, to celebrate with his wife and her son."

"Really?" Bridge lets out a slow breath, nodding. "What did you say?"

I roll my eyes. "No, obviously. I would never abandon my mom to survive Christmas alone. So then he asked if we could maybe all take a trip together this summer."

"Wow, he's laying it on thick."

"Yeah," I growl, shaking my head. "For years, all he did was send cards for my birthday and over the holidays, maybe a visit once a year. And now he wants me to go on a family vacation with them? I should have known this was coming."

The cab rolls to a stop outside our apartment building and a spike pierces my chest. We're here. Distraction over. My palms clam up on the handle of my suitcase as I roll it over the sidewalk, through the doors and to the elevator. Bridge doesn't comment on my silence. She leaves it alone.

And then we're at the apartment door.

And then it's opening.

And then he's there. Grinning. Shouting hello. Reaching in for a hug.

I'm numb, stuck in the doorway.

Ollie leans in, hesitating just a moment, barely enough to notice, but I do. I see the hitch in his movement, normally smooth. But a second later, his arms wrap around me, pulling me close.

I forget to breathe.

In a flash, my mind imagines another time when we were this close. Skin to skin. No clothing between us. No tension.

But now I'm stiff as a board.

"Hey, Skye, welcome back," he whispers into my ear. And then he pulls back, eyes the color of a stormy sea as they squint at me, confused.

My grip on my bag tightens. A lifeline.

"Hey, Ollie," I murmur.

Breathe.

Walk past him and breathe.

I do, beelining to my room, gulping in air as soon as the door closes behind me.

Get a grip, Skye.

I shake my head, pulling my hair tight as I run my fingers through it. Just ignore him. Ignore that feeling. I've done it before and I can do it again. I have to. Still whispering a pep talk, I change into sweatpants and then straighten my shoulders, feigning confidence as I march back into the living room.

"Everything okay?" Ollie asks, eyes finding me before I've even stepped fully through the doorway, as though he was watching and waiting for me.

"Yeah," I sigh, energizing my tone. "I was just telling Bridge about some news with my dad, no big deal."

His eyes brighten. Relief flashes over his irises, lightning to break up the clouds. At least, I think it was relief because his entire body slackens, tension unraveling, and he tosses a heart-wrenching grin in my direction, lifting just one corner of his lips.

My gaze stays on his mouth, feeling the ghostly touch of those lips pressed against mine, trailing a line across my skin, making me shiver. But then I remember something else, the words that fell out, the few sentences that managed to break my heart more thoroughly than any other words I can remember.

I drop my eyes to the floor.

"Skye?" Ollie asks, stepping closer, voice full of concern.

I snap up, smiling. "What?"

"Nothing." He shakes his head. "Nothing."

"We need a Christmas tree," Bridge announces as she steps into the room, decked out in red snowflake pajamas and reindeer slippers. I step back from Ollie, needing space.

"That's a great look on you, sis," he mutters, shifting his expression to a more humorous one.

"Skye has the matching set," Bridge says, shrugging.

I nod, regretfully. "I do. We bought them for a party in college."

"Put them on," Bridge urges. "I have a surprise."

"A surprise that requires me to wear reindeer slippers?" I mutter. Bridge glares at me. I sigh, rolling my eyes, and return to my room, happy for the moment away from Ollie to breathe, to bring my body speed back to normal. When I emerge in my matching set—can I just say I forgot how ridiculously comfortable these slippers are—Ollie is standing in the middle of the room wearing a Santa hat and a pained expression.

"Do you know what she's doing?" he asks.

I shrug. "Nope."

But the distraction of Bridge and of the holidays is welcome, necessary to keep my mind busy, to prevent it from wandering. A moment later, a scratching noise catches my attention. The scrape of plastic on wood. Then an exerted grunt. And then, Bridge calls from her bedroom, "Um, a little help here, guys."

"This seems like a job for an older brother," I say to Ollie with a teasing grin.

He rolls up his sleeves, flexing his muscles. I try not to stare, but I can't help it. He's gone before he's even got the chance to notice my attention, and for a moment, it feels like high school all over again. Me pining. Ollie ignorant of the attention. And I'm not sure what that means. But I don't have time to harp on it, because two seconds later, the McDonough siblings emerge with a huge plastic box.

"What the heck is that?"

"My surprise," Bridge exclaims, excitement bubbling, contagious.

I grin, suddenly recognizing where I've seen that box before. "You brought that thing all the way to New York?"

She nods gleefully.

"What?" Ollie asks.

But it's too late, Bridge and I are both reaching for the lid, ripping it off, revealing the bright white artificial pine underneath. An uncontrollable smile widens my lips and I realize I'm giggling as I dig through the contents, pulling out tinsel and garlands and strands upon strands of lights.

"What in god's name is that?" Ollie asks from over my shoulder, disgust heavy.

"Our Christmas tree!" Bridge chirps.

Ollie just shakes his head. "Christmas trees should be green. And real. No pine smell, no Christmas tree."

"Lighten up," Bridge says, rolling her eyes. "Skye and I got this two years ago. The theater kids were going to throw everything away since the university decided to cut any shows that weren't secular, so we grabbed all the Christmas gear they had."

"Yeah, Bridge was working as a set designer, so they let her take everything. And then we threw an amazing holiday party—the white tree was a hit. Everyone said we were so vintage."

"More like cheap," Ollie mutters.

Bridge and I both shake our heads, smiling to each other. And for a second, life seems to go back to normal.

Three amigos just like Bridge is always saying.

"Okay, Ollie put the tree together. Skye, start unraveling the lights. I'll supply the tunes."

"Why do I have to put this atrocity together?" Ollie asks, crossing his arms. But even he can't hide the little smile pulling at his lips.

Bridge hands him the base of the tree. "Because you're a pain in my ass. Just do it."

He crouches down, separating the many individual branches by size, unfurling the wires, and shaking his head. "How old is this thing? Don't they have fold out ones now? You know, pull a crank and voila—Christmas tree."

I nudge his shoulder with my hip. "What's the fun in that?"

He meets my gaze and winks. I try to ignore the sparkler bursting to life in my chest, sending a wave of thrills down my arms.

Concentrating on the lights proves to be a welcome distraction, and I lose myself in weaving through knots, pulling wires through loops, undoing the web. Christmas music fills the apartment and soon enough the smell of sugar cookies drifts to my nose. Bridge has a weakness for cookie decorating. I shake my head as the sweet scent grows stronger—how in the world did she sneak all of this stuff in here without my realizing?

"Almost ready with the lights?" Ollie asks, catching me off guard.

I flinch, eyes lifting from my lap to find the tree perfectly constructed and ready to be decorated. It takes up about a third of our living room, but I don't care. Holiday cheer has wiggled its way into my heart, and it sort of makes everything seem okay. "Sure."

I walk over, handing Ollie the strand of lights I just neatly looped around my arm—which really, this is the first time my cast has come in handy. But that thought vanishes as our fingers graze. My heart flips, stilling my breath, as he takes the strand from my hold.

"Do you want to help?" he murmurs.

I nod.

We stand on opposite sides of the tree, and for the next few minutes, only the soft strain of caroling fills the room. Ollie and I pass the lights back and forth, fingers touching, igniting sparks along my skin each time. We finish one strand, add another. And then we move to the rest of the room, using clear tape to line the walls, finding one of those icicle strands for the space above the television.

"So, how was your Thanksgiving?" he finally asks, breaking the silence.

I shrug. "Good." But my mouth has suddenly run dry. "We ate at your house. It was really nice to see your parents. They missed you." Did I miss him too?

I push the question away.

Ollie lifts the corner of his lip somewhat sadly. "Yeah, the one downside to being a chef. Holidays are sort of the busiest time of the year for work."

"Do you think you'll be able to go home for Christmas?"

He nods. "Yeah, I hope so."

223

"What'd you do here? All by yourself?" And then I wince, because I didn't mean to make that sound so pitiful, but it sort of does.

"Honestly? Sleep." He releases a soft laugh. "And think. I did a lot of thinking."

"No Aubrey?" I ask, not really sure why.

"Uh, no," he murmurs. "No, I ended things with her. There just wasn't that spark, you know?"

I don't reply. Because of course, I know. And that's the whole problem.

I place tape over the last inch of the lights, trying to ignore the questions springing to life in the back of my thoughts. Ollie presses his fingers over mine, helping to push the tape down. The warmth from his skin radiates. Familiar. On fire.

A spark.

And I can't help it. I glance up. Maybe it's the Christmas colors blinking all around us, but his eyes have never seemed so green before, so rich.

He licks his lips.

Neither of us moves.

And I can't help but notice that the song playing in the background has shifted to Mariah Carey's Christmas classic, "All I Want For Christmas Is You". And if I wasn't entranced by the white lights flickering in Ollie's eyes, I might just roll my own with an exasperated sigh. I mean, the world is totally against me.

"You almost done in there? Cookies are about to go in the oven," Bridge calls from the kitchen.

I step back, snatching my fingers from beneath his. "Yeah!"

Bridge pokes her head through the doorway, grinning as she scans the room. "A winter wonderland!"

I try to copy her attitude, but my heart is pounding and I don't know where to look, where to go, what to do. In the end, I kneel over the box of decorations, pulling ornaments to hang on the tree, silent once more. Ollie helps. But the tension that surrounded us before Thanksgiving has returned, and I'm even more acutely aware of his every move than I was before. We're dancing around each other, afraid to get too close—two magnets working on opposite charges, with a certain amount of space constantly between us. While I'm standing by the tree, Ollie waits with the box of ornaments. When I'm done, we switch, maneuvering around the small space with self-conscious chuckles, little sighs that do nothing but hang in the air around us, making it thicker.

And then Ollie breaks the pattern.

"What's this?" he asks, walking to the tree, standing beside me. I look at his hand. My heart skips a beat.

"Mistletoe," I whisper. Because of course, he would find the mistletoe—the one single strand in a huge box of other Christmas decorations. Just my freaking luck. Then to fill the lingering silence, I add, "Bridge and I hung it over the doorway when we had that party."

He nods, runs a hand through his hair, fussing it up perfectly. And then he walks over to our door, hanging the strand above the frame. "Well?"

"Wh-what?" I stumble over the words.

He looks over his shoulder, eyes a clear turquoise once more. Piercing. "Tape?"

"Oh, right." I flinch, remembering the tape dispenser in my pocket. I rip off a piece and walk over, handing it to him.

But Ollie doesn't take it.

He waits. Watches.

I reach up, careful to avoid touching him as I secure the mistletoe to the door, just barely able to reach the height. And then even though I know I shouldn't, I shift my eyes, gliding ever so slightly from the uncomplicated view of the door to the very complicated view of Ollie's burning expression.

He acts swiftly. I don't even have a chance to move.

We're kissing.

Before I even realize his lips are touching mine, they're gone. And I'm left with only the aftershock, the fire blazing on my skin, sizzling and tingling even though the contact lasted for less than a second and is already gone. I swallow, pulling my trembling fingers from the door, moving in slow motion. The warmth still lingers, mocking me, mocking the feelings I thought I'd gotten rid of a very long time ago.

"Skye," Ollie whispers, voice softer than I've ever heard before. "I'm—"

"I have to go," I interrupt, stepping away, backing up, fleeing to my room. Because I know what he was about to say. *I'm sorry.* All he ever has for me are apologies that come too little too late. And I don't want to hear them.

"Skye!" he shouts, but I'm already behind the closed door, heaving in air.

"What's going on?" Bridge asks, muffled from the door.

My heart sinks. What was he thinking? What was I thinking? Did I know that would happen? With Bridge only ten feet away!

"Nothing," I say back, trying to keep my voice steady. "I just forgot I told Patrick I would come see him tonight. I have to go."

"What did you do?" Bridge asks quietly, but I still hear, and I know exactly who that question is directed to. I stop midway through pulling a pair of jeans on. Ollie takes a moment to answer and I wish I could see his expression, but it's far away, on the other side of the door I felt was necessary to put between us.

"Nothing." He sighs. Denial. Good. But then he adds, "Nothing I regret, anyway."

Well, great. What the heck does that mean?

"What are you talking about?" Bridge asks, voice as sassy as ever. And really, I want to hug her with gratitude. Go get him!

But I'm too furious to speak.

How dare he kiss me! How dare he, like nothing happened, like it's no big deal, with his sister—my best friend!—in the next room. I mean, the nerve! The sheer arrogance!

I shove my pants on, wincing a little as the zipper pinches my skin, but I'm in lightning speed mode. I need to get out of here. Away from him. Before I punch him in the face, and then Bridge will really know something is going on.

I take a deep breath, letting my hand hover over the knob, and then open the door. Bridge is glaring at Ollie. And

Ollie, well he looks confused. His brows are pinched tight with concern, but a smug smile widens his lips. And that just makes the anger raging beneath my skin burn brighter. But I shove it down and smile because there is one thing more important than my fury and that's making sure Bridge remains ignorant of the situation. Because she can never, never know.

"Bridge, honestly, Ollie didn't do anything. I just realized I'm late to see Patrick. I totally forgot." My voice is surprisingly chipper, deceptively easygoing—something I've never been able to attribute to my words before.

Ollie's eyes darken.

For the first time today, I successfully ignore him, throwing my arms around Bridge's neck and squeezing her for a tight hug. "Thanks for being the best roommate ever. Save me a cookie for when I get home tonight."

She clasps her hands behind my back, returning the embrace. "Will do. Have fun with your hunk of a man. If I had one, I'd be doing the same thing."

I roll my eyes but can't stop the little grin that sprouts, puffing my cheeks. And then I leave, walking out the door without a single look back. As soon as I make my way to the elevator and out the lobby, I can breathe again. I suck in deeply, letting the crisp winter air fill my lungs, liberating me from the stale air of the apartment a few stories above my head. My heartbeat slows to normal, and I feel free for the first time in days.

I don't really know what I want to do or where I want to go. My goal was just to escape, and I have. But I find myself wandering to the pharmacy, grabbing a few little Christmas decorations from the dollar shelf, and then boarding the subway heading uptown.

I've only been to Patrick's apartment once before—he cooked me dinner. But I think I know the way. And a little while later, his charmingly surprised face opens the door, mouth dropping before widening to a swoon-worthy grin. And I might swoon, just a little.

Before he can say anything, I plop a Santa hat on his head and hold up the gingerbread house kit I bought at the store. "Surprise?" I say and shrug.

"Best surprise I've had in a while," he murmurs, grabbing my hand, pulling me inside and against his chest. The heat from his skin is warm, comforting. Not a raging inferno, something more manageable. Something I can handle. And when his lips land on mine, I sink into the kiss instead of running away, because his touch sends a little spark down my spine. Not enough to drive me wild, not enough to make my brain stop functioning, but maybe it's better this way. He's not a storm pulling me under against my will. He's a choice I'm making for myself.

And as we fall onto the couch, lips still locked, my thoughts have a second to wander to another choice I could make. To the clothes packed in my handbag just in case I decide to spend the night. Just in case I decide I'm ready.

Confession 18

So…I wasn't ready. Big shocker! What is wrong with me? I'm twenty-two. It should not be this hard. I ended up staying the night, cuddling against his chest under his surprisingly cozy blankets, waking up to a kiss and a hot cup of coffee. I mean, the boy is perfect. So I say again—what is wrong with me?

"Skylar, any updates?" Victoria asks from across the conference room. We're having our weekly meeting with the Style team, only it got pushed back from the normal time on Tuesday mornings to Thursday afternoon.

I spit the sip of latte I just started to take back into my cup, coughing. And then look down sadly. Ew—backwash. I read somewhere once that the last tenth of any drink you consume is all backwash. I mean, how nasty is that? You end up just drinking your own spit. Disgusting. And yet…I don't think I have the heart to say goodbye to my nutmeg laced coffee just yet.

"Skylar?"

Oh, right. My boss!

"Yes," I say quickly, covering up for the space out. "I

just finished a new column, all about date night ideas to spice up the holiday season. On Sunday, I surprised Patrick by showing up with a few lights, candles, and a gingerbread house kit. With romantic lighting and soft Christmas music, any setting can become magical. I ended the piece with a few more ideas, ice-skating or a movie night, things like that. And added a part about how to seal the deal before the night is through, or just bring new heat to a long-term relationship. I think the readers will definitely swoon." I mean, I know I did.

"And it's on my desk?" Victoria asks, scratching down some notes.

"Yup."

"Good. And how about holiday gift guides? What are your ideas?"

I bite my lip, closing my eyes for a moment. When I open, Blythe catches my gaze, smirking. Did I mention I'm meeting Patrick's parents for the first time tonight? Who also happen to be Blythe's parents? And did I also mention that she's been dropping hints all day, you know, about the utter sabotage she is about to lay down?

Well, she is. And guess what? I'm terrified.

I mean, meeting the parents for the first time is always a little nerve-racking. But when you're a sex columnist who's sort of totally embarrassed about being a sex columnist, that little feeling of nerves gets blown up to full-on panic attack pretty quickly. And right now, Blythe is subtly rubbing her wrist—a gentle reminder that the day ends in fifteen minutes and then the two of us will be alone for however long it takes to get to a brownstone on the Upper East Side.

I look away, back to Victoria. "Well, for the gift guides, I got assigned to gifts for style-savvy techies, so I put together a list of about twenty-five different ideas and put that on your desk to review. iPhone cases, monogram decals, adjustable camera lenses for your phone, various gadgets."

And then I wait. Because I have a feeling I know what's coming next.

"Great." Victoria nods, and for a moment I really think what I was afraid of might not happen. That I might be in the clear. But then she opens her mouth, still holding eye contact with me, and my heart sinks. "For your next column, I want you to put together a sexy gift guide. Costumes. Toys. Accessories. Things like that. Okay?"

I swallow, trying to cover the gulp. "Of course."

Ugh.

I knew it. I knew this would happen.

I have to talk about toys. Toys? The only toys I know about are Barbie dolls and video games. And that's fine with me.

"Okay, that should be it, everyone. I'll see you all tomorrow. Skylar, can you come to my office with me?"

I subtly spit my coffee out again, holding back a sigh.

Goodbye, nutmeg.

"Sure," I mumble and then toss the paper cup in the trash, following Victoria out the door. My heart starts beating fast—Victoria wants me to come to her office. Why? Am I underperforming? My columns have gotten great traction so far. I even have a little following on a Facebook fan page I created for my penname. I mean, I wasn't going to write these under a real name! But still, the anonymous fame is pretty fun. Even if I find myself answering sex questions nonstop. Sometimes, I feel a little guilty handing out totally false advice. But I always ask Bridge for her opinion, so at least my responses themselves come from a place of experience—even if I have none.

"Skylar, I want you to look through these for your gift guide. A couple of different retailers sent them to our office as samples," Victoria says when we step into her office, and she hands me a loosely sealed cardboard box. "When you're done, just get rid of everything. I don't really find these sorts of things appropriate to keep in a newsroom."

My smile wavers.

Good god—what's in the box?

For a moment, my fingers flinch, ready to drop the thing like it's a bomb about to explode, but I hold on.

Stay professional.

You can do this.

"Thank you, Victoria. Have a wonderful evening," I say, doing that smile I've mentioned before—the sweet killer look.

"You too," she says, but her attention is already on the e-mails waiting in her inbox and I know I've been dismissed.

As soon as I get back to my cubicle, I drop the box loudly on my desk with a heavy sigh, and take a step back—staring at it as though it might bite.

"What's in that?" Rebecca chimes. Isabel is out today, so it's just me, Rebecca, and Blythe in the assistant corner.

"I don't really want to know," I mumble. "Just some things for my gift guide."

Rebecca immediately perks up, rolling her chair closer. "Ooh, let's take a look. This could be good."

I step back, giving her room, and she keeps wheeling slowly closer.

Okay. I'll admit it. I'm curious. Not curious enough to get any closer, mind you, but intrigued enough not to stop a girl on a mission.

Rebecca stands, slowly opening the cardboard flaps, and lets out a laugh. "Oh my god."

Blythe jumps into action, crossing the small space and taking a look. Even the permanently composed ice queen cracks a smile, glancing at me with humor dancing in her irises. Then they both look at me expectantly, waiting for me to join them. And dang it...I sort of want to. But I remain seated, holding my ground.

Rebecca breaks, reaching into the box to pull out a see-through red lace bra with a matching thong. "Patrick will love this," she says and winks.

Blythe just makes a noise of pure disgust, muttering, "Tacky."

"And these," Rebecca keeps going, pulling out a set of fuzzy handcuffs next.

My face starts to redden.

Next out is a bottle of some sort of lotion, and I don't want to know more than that.

"Oh my god, look at these," she exclaims, holding out a box of Santa hat pasties.

My cheeks are on fire. Literally. I think I might self-combust in the middle of the newsroom. Just poof, vanish into a cloud of ash, dying from embarrassment.

"What about this?" Blythe remarks. And her tone is way too nice, way too cheerful to be sincere. So I jump out of my seat, snatching the cardboard flaps and slamming them closed. Blythe barely has time to jerk her hand out of the way lest it be chopped off in my speed. And hey, I'm moving pretty well for a girl with a broken wrist. But I know one thing for sure—I do not want to see whatever Blythe was about to pull out of my little box of horrors.

"Okay, time to go," I say, shutting down my computer and tucking the box safely under my desk, as far away as I can hide it.

"Are you so eager to meet my parents?" Blythe comments while buttoning her red peacoat.

"Is there any reason I shouldn't be?"

"No, of course not…" she trails off. I bite my tongue, waiting, because obviously, there's something else she wants to say. Wait for it. Wait for it. Blythe throws her purse over her shoulder and then looks back at me, smiling. Here we go… "It's just, they loved Patrick's last girlfriend. Her parents were diplomats. She graduated from Harvard last year, neuroscience major, pre-med. They were heartbroken when he ended things."

Wonderful.

I sigh.

Future doctor, phony sex columnist—those are practically on equal playing grounds, right?

Right…

Not.

I follow Blythe to the elevator, squeezing in with the crowd, thankful for the silence. Speaking on the elevator always just seems a little strange to me, awkward, you know? I mean, come on. All anyone does on an elevator when two people are having a conversation is listen in—you're stuck in a box, there's nothing else to do beside eavesdrop!

"Uh, Skylar?" Blythe calls to me when we step outside the office. I've already turned toward the subway station. But I pause, spinning. She's standing next to a black town car, shaking hands with a driver in a suit, conversing like they are best friends. "My mom sent her car to pick us up."

I mean, duh. Obviously.

Why didn't I think of that?

"Thank you," I murmur to the driver as I slip through the door, which he shuts behind me. The seats are a fine tan leather. The handles are mahogany. There are even new bottles of water waiting in the cup holders for us.

I fold my hands in my lap, unsure. Blythe and I don't really do one-on-one girl time. I'm too afraid of her for that— and for good reason.

"So," Blythe chirps, bouncing on her seat to shift directions, facing me. "Before we pretend to be best friends for my parents, I just want you to know one thing. I'm on to you, Skylar."

I gulp at her ominous tone. Did I suddenly get thrown into a James Bond film? She's on to me? On to what? "Uh, I'm not really sure what you mean, Blythe."

"I've never known a sex columnist who loves to play innocent so much," she drawls.

And I can't help it. I throw on a snarky attitude and smile. Maybe Bridge is finally rubbing off on me. "How many sex columnists do you know, exactly?"

Her eyes narrow. "You blush like a fifteen-year-old girl every time we have to discuss your columns in our weeklies. You can't even say the word sex without smiling self-consciously. And the only R-rated stories you tell are in writing. Not once have I heard you say any of this out loud, because you can't. You're just lucky my brother isn't one to kiss and tell, or one to rat out a friend."

My heart is pounding, but I try to keep my voice as steady as possible. "What exactly are you accusing me of?"

"Oh, you know," she whispers, and I find I'm leaning in to hear every one of her words. "We work for a newspaper. We're supposed to work in journalism, not fiction."

"Everything I write in my columns comes from my heart," I say, and it's not a lie. Really. All the sentiments I put on paper are real, it's just the details that are a little, well, embellished. "It's just easier for me to write about these things, rather than talk about them out loud. That makes me shy, not a liar."

Blythe just nods, smiling sweetly. "Okay…"

Except she says it in a way that means everything but. Maybe if I get her angry, she'll crack. I lick my lips, nibbling on the lower one a little, thinking.

Just go for it.

"You're jealous," I remark flippantly. "You were working there before me, and instead of giving you a column of your own, Victoria hired me."

"Jealous of you?" Blythe asks, only it's not a question, not at all. "Please. I just don't like the entire city reading about my brother's private life every week."

"I don't even write out his name, only initials. There is no way anyone knows who he is unless he wants them to."

"I know who he is," she says just as the car pulls to a stop outside of a gorgeous brownstone on Fifth Avenue, right across the street from Central Park. "And as soon as I can, I'm telling Victoria who you really are. I just have to wait for my brother to break up with you first. And trust me, Skylar, it's only a matter of time."

And then the driver opens the door so Blythe can make a perfectly grand exit, while I scoot ungracefully across the seat, catching my coat button on a buckle and practically falling out of the car. By the time I get to the front door, Patrick is already there holding it open for his sister.

"Hey, Skylar." He leans down, giving me a quick kiss on the cheek.

"Hey," I murmur, trying to hide the fact that anything is the matter. "I was worried you'd be late."

He shrugs. "I actually have a conference call in about half an hour, so I thought I would come for the introductions and then while you guys have cocktails, I can take the call from my father's study."

My heart sinks. Feed me to the wolves, why don't you? But on the outside, I just smile warmly, pretending it doesn't bother me.

"Where are Mom and Dad?" Blythe asks, handing her coat to a maid who just appeared out of nowhere. I do the same, unused to being helped with such menial tasks. I mean, I can hang a coat on a rack myself.

"Upstairs," he says, taking my hand and leading me to the grand staircase a few feet away.

Now that I have a second to look around, I have to admit, I'm pretty much speechless. This house is amazing. Like, could have its own television special amazing. The Queen of England would find this place impressive. The walls are covered in warm, rich wood. The ceiling is painted—painted! Artwork is displayed in intricately carved golden frames. The upholstered furniture is crafted of shimmering silk, pin tucked and with feet carved like little claws. I can just tell that everything in here is from an auction house, infused with history. The grandfather clock. The grand piano. The marble fireplace. And when I look up, the stairs keep winding for at least two more floors. I mean, it's a mansion—a mansion in the middle of one of the most expensive cities in the world. A dozen of my apartments, heck maybe more, would easily fit in here. I knew Blythe was a socialite, I knew Patrick had some money to burn, but I had no idea they came from this.

"Blythe," a voice calls softly.

I look toward the sound to a woman dressed in a beautiful green woven dress with a matching jacket, and I've learned enough at the style section to know it's vintage Chanel and crazy expensive. By her side is a man in a dark gray suit, complete with a tie.

I swallow, smoothing my hands down the front of my black work dress—from the sale rack, obviously. At least I wore a bright scarf with it today to add a little color, Bridge's suggestion of course. And I'm in designer flats—I mean, they're a few years old, and a gift from my mom, but still recognizable with a bright gold buckle over my toes. For me, this is about as dressed up as it gets. But I feel a little bit like a toddler in a room of adults.

"And you must be Skylar," the woman says, giving me the once over. I can't decipher her expression enough to know if she approves or not—I see now that Blythe is just the ice princess, the queen is right here, hiding away in her castle.

"So nice to meet you, Mrs. Keaton." I reach out and shake her hand, which is a little awkward since she's still seated, sipping on a cup of tea. I turn to her husband, who did at least politely stand, towering over me with the same height of his son. "And you too, Mr. Keaton."

"Welcome to our home," he says after releasing my fingers. "Patrick speaks very highly of you." I sneak a peek at Patrick, who is smiling warmly in my direction. Maybe tonight won't be so bad. "Would you like a cocktail?"

I look around realizing he has a crystal scotch glass beside him, and another one waiting to be filled for Patrick. But somehow, alcohol just seems dangerous in this situation. I need all my wits about me. "Um, maybe just a glass of water, if that's all right?"

"Not a problem," he says and then nods to someone over my shoulder. I can't help but feel as though I've been transported to another century. These people have servants working for them.

"So, where did you grow up?" Mr. Keaton asks once we've all settled on the cushions. Patrick's arm is draped lightly across my shoulders, and I'm drawing comfort from the warm touch of his skin.

"In a small town in Pennsylvania, outside of Philadelphia," I respond. Let the interview begin.

"And what do your parents do?"

"My mom owns her own stationary store, and my father works in advertising," I murmur, waiting. But no snide remark from Blythe comes. No comment that my parents are divorced—something I'm sure the Keaton's would not approve of—or that the small town I come from is in the middle of farm country—something I'm sure they would find quaint but not acceptable.

Confused, I scrunch my eyebrows, glancing at Blythe. But she is sipping her cocktail, smiling politely in my direction. And I realize something when she meets my gaze—there are clock hands ticking in the center of her pupils. She's biding her time. I'm safe for a little while. But my stomach tightens in knots—when exactly is that countdown in her head going to hit zero?

"Your mother owns her own business?" Mr. Keaton nods approvingly.

"Yes," I say, jumping on the opportunity to impress while I still can. "The shop is sort of a cross between a design studio and a retail store. A lot of the cards we sell are from other merchants, but she does a lot of custom invitations for local events and weddings. I'm trying to help her expand, so I just recently put together a website for her to help reach a broader customer base."

Dang. That sounded pretty legitimate.

I sit up a little straighter.

"Very savvy of you," he comments. I grin, sipping my water.

But then a rumble vibrating against my thigh distracts me. Patrick shifts, reaching into his pocket, stealing the warmth of his body heat away and I'm left cold. He stands, signaling that he has to go with his fingers, pointing to the side.

The conference call.

I watch him disappear around the corner, veins turning to ice when I shift back around and catch Blythe's stare.

Time's up.

Her eyes practically blaze with excitement.

"So, Skylar, you work with Blythe at the newspaper?" Mr. Keaton asks.

I jump in before Blythe has time to comment. "I do. I'm also an assistant for the style section, and I write my own column, all about dating in the city in your twenties."

"How wonderful, your own column," he says. And I breathe easy for a moment. Mr. Keaton is actually very sweet—it's just the women in this family that have issues it seems.

"Which column?" Mrs. Keaton purrs from her teacup.

I swallow. Something in her tone unnerves me. The same prickly sweetness of her daughter. "Um, you probably haven't read it."

"Skylar, don't be so modest, of course she has. Everyone has," Blythe chimes in. I close my eyes, taking a moment to breathe.

Oh god.

Oh god.

"She writes it under a penname. Cooper Quinn?"

That's it. I'm done for.

But no bomb explodes. There's no screaming. No kicking me out. No reaction. I release the breath I was holding, exhaling slowly. The world hasn't ended. The earth is still intact. I open my eyes.

"Oh, Cooper Quinn?" Her mother pauses. And then she smiles. And for a second, I think—this cannot be happening. She reads my column? And approves? I almost want to point and laugh at Blythe—victory is so, so sweet. Her mom continues, and the sinking expression on Blythe's face is enough for me. "I recognize that name. I do read that column, all the ladies—"

Mrs. Keaton stops dead.

My heart follows, screeching to a halt. The elation in my chest evaporates as realization dawns, a flip switching in the depths of her hazel eyes, which are slowly narrowing to slits. Blythe's smug expression pierces like a knife.

"You write *that* column?" Mrs. Keaton asks.

I start to choke on my own breath, reaching for my glass of water, finding it painfully empty. Where are those servants when you actually need them?

"And, PK, is Patri..." She trails off into silence. Every word she's ever read in my column flickers in her gaze, every lewd detail she perhaps gossiped about with friends or read with shocked curiosity, devoured like a penny novel. Every little bit she once found entertaining is now turning utterly grotesque in her mind.

My face is turning beet red, I just know it. And Blythe is taking a mental picture by my side, grinning triumphantly. Mr. Keaton just looks confused. But I can't take my eyes off of the ever-rising eyebrows of Mrs. Keaton, the accusation in her glare, the utterly disapproving purse of her lips.

And I finally have an answer to my question about what could be worse than my own mother finding out I write a sex column. It's my boyfriend's mother finding out I write a sex column about her son.

I sit back in the chair, leaning into the cushion, trying to shrink—wondering if I can disappear if I just think hard enough.

But I don't.

Her eyes nail me in place.

I just bite my lip and sigh. This is going to be the longest dinner of my life.

Confession 19

*Patrick and I don't speak about his parents again. I mean, radio
silence. As the Christmas season passes, we get sugar-high on hot
chocolate, ice skate, go shopping, see a holiday show, have a wicked
snowball fight, but we don't speak a word about that night. And I
have no idea what that means.*

I haven't been alone with Ollie since the mistletoe incident—as
that moment will henceforth be known. Sure, I've seen him—I
mean, we live together. There's no way around that. But if he's
in the kitchen, I'm in the living room. If Bridget's not home,
I'm safe behind the closed door of my bedroom. And right
now, stepping through the front door of the McDonough
home for Christmas Eve dinner, I don't ever want to leave my
mother's side.

"Look at your hand!" Bridge calls as soon as we step
through the door.

I hold my wrist up, grinning. "No more cast, no more
splint! My mom and I went to the doctor this morning."

She runs a finger over my wilted skin. "It looks…"

"I know." I shake my head, flexing my stiff muscles.

The skin around my wrist is pasty white, like sickly, and the entire area is noticeably smaller than my other wrist. "It looks disgusting."

"No." She shakes her head, grabbing my other hand to pull me inside. "It looks like a Christmas miracle."

I lift an eyebrow, asking, "Did you get started on the eggnog a little early?"

Bridge pauses. "Maybe…"

But we've entered the kitchen before I can respond, and I'm immediately pulled into two enthusiastic embraces.

"Hi, Mr. and Mrs. McDonough. Merry Christmas," I murmur into the sweaters my face has been pressed into. Ollie remains on the other side of the room, idly stirring a pot on the stovetop. He glances in my direction, but I think he knows I don't want him to come any closer.

"It's so nice to have everyone together." Bridge's mom sighs, looking around with a goofy smiled plastered across her lips. "I don't think all six of us have been in a room together in years."

Four and a half years, if we're being exact. But who's counting?

My eyes drop away from Ollie and I lean into my mom's shoulder. The conversation turns to the multitude of Christmas cards taped to the fridge, half of which my mom designed for locals—McDonough family included. I listen politely, smiling, just taking comfort in my mom's presence. Or well, I was, until my eyes veered to the right and ran into Bridge's wide, imploring expression.

"What?" I mouth at her.

But Bridge doesn't say anything. She just opens her eyes wider. I sigh, stealing away from the nice warm spot on my mom's shoulder, and cross the kitchen to the kid's side. I settle into a spot next to Bridge, a little too close to Ollie, who seems suspiciously unaware of our presence.

"What?" I ask again.

"You're not the only one with news," she says, and then stops, eyes dancing. My lips twitch with anticipation. Bridge leans in, whispering, "I got a date for the New Year's Eve party."

"Who?"

"You know that guy I was telling you about from my gym?"

I raise my brows. "You mean the guy who can do one handed pull-ups and caught you drooling last week?"

"I was not drooling," she says, slapping my arm lightly. "That was a bead of sweat that just happened to start at the corner of my lips and make a painstakingly slow trip to the floor."

"Mm-hmm, sure it was."

"Anyway…" Bridge draws the last syllable out like it deserves its own sentence. "The gallery was closed this morning, but I decided to wait until Ollie got off work so I could come home with him. So, I had a few hours to spare and decided to test my luck at the gym. Low and behold, Mr. Hottie was there and right next to him was an open treadmill. So—"

"Let me guess, you did some stretching first?" I interject, trying to hide my grin.

Bridge bites her lip. "Light stretching, maybe."

"Did you wear that spaghetti strap shirt you claim is for working out but is really for showing an ample amount of cleavage?"

"Potentially..."

I can't help it, a little snicker squeaks out. "That's like the third date that shirt has landed for you."

"What?" She huffs. "Name the first two times."

I roll my eyes. "Bridge, come on. Freshman year, you found out when the lacrosse team had weight lifting training and went in booty shorts and that shirt."

She chews on her lip for a moment, and then grins. "Okay, but he was gorgeous. And an athlete. And we got into a lot of parties because of that little fling. What's the second time?"

"Do you really want me to say?"

"Please don't," Ollie mutters as he opens the oven, checking on the beef. Aha! So he is listening in. Sneak.

Bridge ignores him, waiting for my response. Oh well, she asked for it.

"Junior year, yoga on the quad?"

Immediately, a giggle fit bursts from her lips. "I totally forgot about that. I asked you to do yoga with me, and you showed up in gym shorts and a T-shirt, and then accidentally flashed the entire quad during downward facing dog. Classic."

"Yeah," I mutter, "and somehow you're still the one who ended up with a date."

Ollie snorts.

Bridge shrugs.

I roll my eyes.

All pretty standard reactions. And for a moment, I actually think maybe things can return to normal, someday at least. Maybe—

"Hey, Bridge," Ollie asks, looking over his shoulder while he stirs a pot of boiling potatoes, testing how soft they are. "Can you do me a favor and find the oven mitts? Mom bought new ones and left them in some shopping bag in the garage. I want to see the temperature on the meat. And I need to put the popovers in."

"Sure," she chirps, shooting me an apologetic look before she walks off.

And then I realize the one thing I didn't want to happen is happening.

I'm alone with Ollie.

I mean, not really because our parents are fifteen feet away and Bridge is fluttering around. But there's no one else in earshot. And I'm more afraid of his words than anything else.

"Um, I'll help," I quickly add, slipping from the stool I had propped myself onto.

"Wait, Skye," Ollie says, forgetting the stovetop to give me his full attention. "Come here for a second."

But I don't move.

He shakes his head. "Would you just get over here? I'm not going to bite."

"That's not what I'm worried about," I whisper, and then wince. Stupid.

Ollie's expression softens. "I'm not going to do that either."

"Good," I respond, even as my heart sinks just a little. Barely even anything. Except I notice it, and I don't really want to think about what it means. So I step next to him, leaning over the food, arm an inch away from his. And even with the heat of the steam and the food, I can pick out that special prickle of awareness, that little spark telling me Ollie is near.

"What's going on?" I ask, eyes stuck to the potatoes floating in the water, the vegetables steaming, the gravy brewing.

"Well, I told Bridge on the train ride here, and I just wanted to tell you myself rather than have you hear it from her."

At that, I do look up.

His shaggy black-brown hair is in disarray, curled from the steaming kitchen, tumbling over his forehead as he keeps his gaze concentrated on the food—concentrated down. I wonder if he doesn't want to look at me, or if it's that he can't. But I can look at him, and I do. I stare. His skin glistens from the moisture, making the contours of his face stand out even more than usual. Especially the rugged lines of his jaw, flexed and tense. I watch his hands, the authority with which they move, flipping and stirring, in complete command. And I know from experience that cooking isn't all those hands know how to do.

"What, Ollie?" I prod.

"It's nothing serious." He shrugs, still not meeting my eyes. "It's just—I'm moving out."

"What?" The word blurts out. I blink once, twice, in total shock.

He's moving out?

"I'm moving out," he repeats, almost as though he can read my thoughts.

And then he looks up.

Damn those eyes.

Those perfect, entrancing blue eyes.

I lose myself in them. And this time, my heart doesn't just sink a little. It plummets. Crashes to the ground.

"I just figured since it's almost the new year, I should let you and Bridge live with one of your friends and find my own place. I told her I would wait until you have someone new lined up. I don't want you two to get bogged down by the rent. But she said she has a friend she might be able to ask, so I just wanted you to be informed this time. I wouldn't want someone else to surprise you in the middle of a rant—I'm sure once was more than enough."

One corner of his lip lifts, a small grin, a secret one meant only for me.

But I can't process it. My mind is moving in slow motion. Surprise me in a rant? And then I remember, the virgin sex columnist confession—the first time I saw him in four years. He's just joking.

But my tongue feels heavy, unable to respond. My nerves are frozen. And it can only mean one thing. In my heart, I really don't want him to go. Because I know something scary—forgetting Oliver McDonough is impossible, but avoiding him is frighteningly easy. Before he surprised me in our kitchen, I hadn't seen him in four years. Even living together, I was able to barely speak to him for the past three weeks. If he moves out, there's a very real possibility that I won't see him again for months—that I won't see him again period. Is that what I want?

Staring into his turquoise eyes, my chest is thumping—no, no, no.

But remembering a different night, my head is screaming yes.

"Skye?" he asks.

I swallow, blink. One instant of dark, and the connection is broken, I look away—I seal my mind shut.

"Thanks for letting me know," I answer with a voice unrecognizable to my ears. For the first time ever, my tone sounds unaffected by his presence, by his words. It's shockingly light—the complete opposite of the turmoil churning my stomach into knots. "It was only a matter of time, right? You wouldn't want to live with your little sister and her best friend forever."

Ollie leans back. "Yeah, yeah I guess you're right."

"Where are you going to move?" I ask conversationally, words completely detached, as though someone else is speaking with my lips. "Closer to the restaurant?"

He looks at me for a moment, narrows his gaze, flinches just slightly. And then I lose him. His clear eyes return to the food. "I haven't really thought about it yet. Maybe."

"It'll probably make commuting easier."

"Yeah."

"Though midtown can be pretty expensive."

"That's true."

"Unless you're going to find another roommate."

"I probably will."

"Anyone from work?"

I wait for a short response, but it never comes. A moment of silence passes, and then he drops the wooden spoon on the stovetop, abandoning his meal, and runs his hand through his already disheveled hair. Like always, he only makes it look better, more wild, more untamable. "So you're okay with this?"

I really don't know what he expects. As always with Ollie, I have no clue what he wants from me. So I say what's safe, what's best for me. "Why wouldn't I be?"

He runs his hand through his hair again, teal eyes darkening, every bit of sparkle gone. "I don't know, Skye." He looks down, picks up the spoon, and gets back to dinner. "I really don't."

"Found it!" Bridget shouts, stomping into the kitchen with the fury of a hurricane about to hit the shore. I flinch, pulled immediately back to my surroundings. The bubble around Ollie and me bursts. "Mom, seriously, next time you go shopping and buy vital cooking supplies, you have to remember to bring the bag inside."

"The mitts!" Her mom winces, looking at the bright red oven mitts in Bridget's hand. "Is the roast okay?"

"It's fine, Mom." Ollie shrugs.

"What about the milk?" she asks.

Bridge just shakes her head, holding up a carton of milk with her other hand. "You smell it."

"I'm sure it's okay," Bridge's dad says, stepping forward to take the milk from his frustrated daughter's hand before she chucks it at him. "It's been below zero every day this week, the garage may as well be a refrigerator."

"Hey, kids, come take a look at this," my mom says, pulling our attention to the desk in the corner of the kitchen. She's holding out a frame. "Is this a new one, Claire? I don't remember seeing it last time I was here."

Mrs. McDonough nods. "I was going through the old albums last week and switched out some of the picture frames. Isn't that one just perfect? It's how I'll probably always think of the three of them."

Bridge gets there first. "Oh god," she snorts, but it's affectionate and warm.

Then she hands the photo to me. I take the frame in my hands, smoothing my fingers along the wood, flipping it so it's right side up. A half sigh, half laugh escapes my lips, just a puff of nearly soundless air.

Bridge and I are dressed in princess costumes—I'm Belle obviously, book nerd with dreams of traveling the world. And she's Cinderella—the rebel who sneaks out of the house, hijacks her way into a royal ball and lands the prince in the process. Total Bridge move. And behind our oblivious smiles is Ollie with a devilish grin, using his fingers to prop bunny ears behind our heads.

"Let me see," adult Ollie says, leaning over my shoulder, breath tickling my neck. I don't move for fear I might accidently touch him. And after a moment, he steps back. "I think I remember that. I'm pretty sure I pelleted you guys with my Nerf gun afterward, and then got sent to my room cause one hit Bridge in the eye."

"You did," Mrs. McDonough says, sneaking up behind us and slapping Ollie in the side of the head.

"Ow, Mom," he complains as he rubs the spot. "That was like fifteen years ago."

"And I smacked you then too," she teases. Then she wraps her arm around my shoulder, pulling me against her side. A place I've been many, many times. A place almost as familiar as the embrace of my own mother. "And poor Skylar, always stuck in the middle of my two ornery children."

"Please," Bridge chimes, "Skye was never stuck in the middle. She's always been on my side. The right side, obviously."

Her mom squeezes me tighter, holds for a moment, and then releases. I look around at the five familiar faces and know without a doubt that this is where I belong. In this kitchen, with these people, part of this family. And I can't do anything to mess that up. With one last fleeting glance at Ollie, I smile at Bridge. She's right. The only time I wasn't on her side was four and a half years ago, and you and I both know how great that turned out for me.

"Sorry, Ollie. Two against one," I say.

He looks at me. And for a moment, I expect to see the same expression on his face as the one he has in the photograph I'm holding in my hands. Devilish. Gleaming. Challenging. Filled with the barest sparkle of hope—the hint that he hasn't given up on me, that I haven't given up on him, or maybe that we haven't given up on each other, not yet.

I want to see it.

I'm terrified to see it.

But when I meet Ollie's turquoise eyes, the mischievous boy I used to love is gone. He's a man. Hardened. Distant. Someone I barely recognize.

Then he blinks.

The moment passes.

In a flash, the Ollie I know returns. He grins, gaze shifting to Bridge.

"You know what, sis?" he asks. She shrugs, raising her eyebrows with obvious attitude. "That's never stopped me before."

Out of nowhere he produces a spatula, pulls it back and releases. Everyone in the kitchen watches as the glob of mashed potatoes sails across the room, arching in slow motion, only to land with a splat on the center of Bridget's forehead.

We all freeze.

The cream mass holds steady for a moment and then slides, halting on the tip of Bridget's nose, drawing a trail of white residue down the center of her face before it falls. And falls. And falls. And—

Plop.

"Ollie!" Bridge screams.

He's already running. And now she's running. And because I'm so used to it, because it's second nature, because maybe I want to forget that look I saw on his face only a few moments ago, I'm running too. And it should feel just like old times, just like when we were kids. But it doesn't.

Something's changed.

Something I don't think I'll ever be able to undo.

Confession 20

I've never gotten a proper New Year's kiss—so lame, I know. My ex John and I were always apart on Christmas break. He with his family, me with mine. So I'm especially determined to make this New Year's count. In more ways than one.

I'm in a room full of people, yet somehow I feel totally and utterly alone. Isn't that just the most bizarre thing you've ever heard? I have my boyfriend and my best friend. What else could a girl need to help ring in the New Year with a bang?

On second thought, don't answer that.

You know too much.

"Let's dance," Bridge shouts over the music, pulling me from our safe spot in the booth Patrick reserved and dragging me into the wilds of the club.

We wiggle our way through tightly pressed bodies, only stopping when we find a small pocket of space in the crowd, just large enough for two. I move with the music, swaying my hips as best I can, lifting my arms in the air, trying to dislodge the uneasy feeling stiffening my muscles.

"Spill!" Bridge shouts, leaning close to my ear before spinning around.

I shrug. "What?"

"I've known you long enough to know when you're being silent because you have nothing to say, and when you're being silent because you're too afraid to speak." And then she squeezes her brows, face filling with concern. "Is it Patrick? Did you guys—"

"No," I interrupt before she can finish the thought.

But then her eyes widen and she latches onto my fingers, pulling me closer. Someone behind us whistles, a jerk expecting to get a show. But Bridge ignores the catcall, placing her lips almost against my ear, asking, "Is he pressuring you?"

"No!" I jerk back, shaking my head. "Not at all."

"Well, because I want you to know that if you're not ready, he can wait. And if he can't wait, he can be replaced."

I smile at the protectiveness in her tone. "Bridge, really, Patrick is great. I'm just a little tired, there's nothing going on that I can't tell you."

"Promise?" she asks, earnest, holding up her pinky finger.

I latch my pinky finger around hers, tightening the hold, binding the agreement. "Promise."

"Good," she says. And then adds, wiggling her eyebrows, "So, what do you think of my date?"

But before I can answer, the DJ's voice blasts over the music. "One minute until midnight, everyone. Let the countdown begin!" All the screens in the room flash from the view of Times Square to a blinking clock.

Sixty.

Fifty-nine.

Fifty-eight.

"Oh no!" I shout to Bridge. "Did you realize it was so close to midnight?"

"No!" she shouts back.

The booth where Patrick and gym-boy wait is all the way across the club, and it would take far more than a minute to get there.

Fifty-one.

Fifty.

"What should we do?" I ask.

Bridge is chewing on her lip looking around, shrugging. And I know what her silence means. There's nothing we can do. I've ruined yet another New Year's Eve.

Forty-four.

Forty-three.

I look around, eyes scanning the crowd. Maybe Patrick is on his way here. Maybe he'll surprise me. Maybe the night won't be ruined after I put so much hope on starting the new year the right way—as a new me.

Thirty.

Twenty-nine.

My eyes stop, narrowing, zeroing in on a boy turned away from me. His shaggy hair looks liquid black in the strobe lights. His head swivels enough to reveal cream skin illuminated blue then purple then pink. He's looking for someone, just like I am, scanning the crowd. He shifts a little farther.

His nose is familiar. His jaw is too.

Ollie?

Twenty.

Nineteen.

I take a step forward. Is that Ollie?

My heart pounds, louder to my ears than the music, thrumming with anticipation. Did he come for me? And I know the answer to that question is yes, because there's no other reason he would be here, searching the crowd. No other person he would want to find. My fingers tremble. My lips tingle. I want to kiss him at midnight.

I have a boyfriend.

I don't care.

Not when Ollie finally wants me.

Fifteen.

Fourteen.

Ollie turns. My heart stops. Sinks. There's an empty hole where it rested, a concave feeling in my chest. Hollow.

It's not Ollie.

I blink, shaking my head, taking in the face turned fully in my direction. The dark hooded eyes, the light of recognition for finding someone else in the crowd. The jaw, the nose, the lips, all nearly the same. But his eyes. His eyes are totally different.

Idiot. I step back. Of course it's not Ollie. He's never wanted me like that, not like I've wanted him.

Eleven.

And then the entire room pauses, shouting in unison, excitement palpable.

Ten.

Nine.

But I'm fading, disappearing in my own skin, shrinking away from the happiness piercing the room all around me. How could I be so stupid? After everything? Thinking Ollie would come after me—I'm delusional. And I need to get him out of my system, once and for all. I need this year to be different. I need this year to be more.

Six.

Five.

A hand grabs my fingers, twisting me around. And for a moment, I wonder if I was wrong. But it's Patrick. Smiling, wonderful, possibly in love with me, Patrick.

Four.

Three.

"You found me!" I shout.

He grins, honey eyes warm and meant only for me. "Of course."

Two.

I don't wait for midnight. I grab Patrick by the face, crashing his lips against mine, kissing him to make myself forget, to force myself to forget. The room erupts around us as the countdown ends. Noisemakers. Shouts. Fireworks echoing from the television screens overhead. And I know this is when I'm supposed to break away, to speak, to say something.

But I don't.

I wrap my hands around his neck, pressing against Patrick, deepening the kiss. Urgent. And he's the one who breaks away.

"Happy New Year," he whispers.

I breathe heavily into the silence, teetering on a precipice, not sure if I'm ready to fall. But it seems like no matter what I do, I'll be tumbling one way or another.

I meet Patrick's curious gaze with a hungry one all my own.

"Want to get out of here?" I murmur, and then I swallow the knot of panic back down.

His brows lift, surprised, but then he blinks and his whole face softens into a smile. "Yeah. Sure. Let's get out of here."

Half an hour later, he's slipping the key to his apartment into the lock and turning the knob. We don't wait until we're inside. Once the door is open, our lips are locked together.

Patrick kicks the door closed with his foot.

My jacket falls to the ground.

His coat follows.

Then his shirt.

Then my shoes.

And we're stumbling to his bedroom, leaving a trail behind. We stop against the door, him in his boxers, me in my bra and underwear. And I know once we're inside, those are the first things to go. Patrick's hands are exploring my skin. His lips leave a blazing fire down the side of my neck. Even in the heat of this moment, I close my eyes to see the vision of someone else pressing me against the wall, someone else holding me, someone else wanting me.

Turquoise eyes burn behind my lids.

I open, gazing into the hazel eyes before me in real life.

We're both breathing heavily.

We both know it's my move.

I reach back, fumbling with my fingers until they find the metal knob. I turn. The door creaks open behind me, sending a blast of cool air against my bare skin. A shiver shoots up my spine. Goose bumps rise along my arms.

Patrick still waits for my move.

I take a step back, tugging him forward. And he doesn't need any more motivation than that. He doesn't know I'm a virgin. I never felt comfortable enough to tell him. But on some level, he must know something. Because as soon as we cross the threshold, the power shifts and Patrick takes control.

We ease slowly onto his bed.

Smoothly.

There's no awkward movement. Patrick knows exactly what he's doing. Which is good, because I'm diving into unknown territory. And the closer I get to hitting the bottom, the more panicked I become. The heat beneath my skin shifts, constricting my breath. My heartbeat surges, pounding against my chest, painful. I grow dizzy, lightheaded, until I'm barely aware of what's happening around me.

But I press forward.

Every sigh that escapes my lips sounds of pleasure.

I have to do this.

I want to do this.

Patrick pauses above me, and I find his eyes. "Are you ready?" he asks.

Yes.

I want to say it.

One simple word. Yes.

Maybe if I do this, I can finally move on. It's the one thing I haven't tried. I close my eyes, Ollie's face appears. I open and it's Patrick. My eyes shift in rapid succession until the two images begin to blur.

I want to get him out of my head.

I need to.

So I open my lips, fully intending to say yes, but something else comes out instead.

"No."

Patrick recoils.

"I mean..." I shake my head, trying to recover. But my brain rebels. "No," I repeat and then I roll out from underneath him, putting my feet on the floor, grounding myself so I can try to think, can try to work this out in my head.

"What?" Patrick asks, confused. "What do you mean? What was all this tonight then?"

The bed shifts below me, and even though I don't turn around, I know he's fallen onto the mattress, energy zapped.

"I don't know," I say honestly. "I'm just not ready."

"What's the big deal?" he asks, and I can't help but release a soft puff of air, closing my eyes tight. Of course he doesn't understand. Why would he? "We've been together for weeks."

"I know," I murmur, "it's just..." But I don't know how to finish the sentence. I'm confused about the answer myself.

It's just that I'm a virgin? He'd understand that. He might be freaked out by it, but he would understand why it meant I wasn't ready. But somehow that doesn't feel like the truth, not quite.

It's just that I can't shake this crush on my best friend's brother? Yeah, because Patrick would really be okay with that excuse. And when I think about saying it, the words taste sour on my tongue. Because even though I'm stuck on Ollie, he doesn't feel like the real reason why I stopped, like the whole reason. There's something else, something I can't wrap my head around.

"What did your parents say about me?" I whisper instead. And I don't know where the words come from, but they sound right rolling over my lips.

"My parents?" he says, dumbfounded. "What does this have to do with my parents?"

I finally turn around, hugging the covers around myself, and fold my knees into my chest. I find his eyes, dark and tumultuous, no longer filled with sweet honey.

"Can you just answer?"

"Fine." He shrugs, exhaling an especially weighty breath before fixing his eyes up, resting on his pillow. "My dad thought you were very sweet with a good head on your shoulders."

"And your mom?" I bite my bottom lip, waiting for the inevitable.

Patrick flicks his gaze down from the ceiling. "Blythe was talking to her about your column."

I nod. I expected as much. "She doesn't approve?"

He doesn't say anything. He just lets his head fall first to one side, then the other, slowly.

265

"Did you tell her it's not true? That everything I write is an exaggeration?" And even though it would mean Blythe learned the truth, part of me wants him to say yes, part of me wants to hear that he fought for me, for us, that he tried to change her mind.

"No," he whispers. "I figured you had your reasons, it wasn't really my place to out you."

I lick my lips. He was respecting me. And I should be glad about that, but for some reason it just confirms a little feeling I had shoved deep down, one that's rapidly rising back to the surface.

He's prince charming.

I'm Cinderella.

And in the fairy tale, that's great. But in real life, we're from different worlds—ones that don't fit. I don't belong with his parents. I don't see myself ever calling their mansion on the Upper East Side home. Blythe will never feel like a sister to me. And as much as I like Patrick, it's not enough. Maybe if I loved him, maybe then things would be different. But I don't. And I never will.

With perfect clarity, I realize why I'm not ready. Why I said no. And maybe it has something to do with Ollie, but it's about so much more than him. It's about me. It always has been.

"I don't care what my parents think," Patrick says, sitting up, sensing the changing tide.

"I do," I murmur, and then I focus my eyes, finding his alert stare, "and you do too. It's only natural."

"So what are you saying?"

I've never done this before. My tongue feels heavy, my lips fat. I don't want to hurt him, but I can't pretend anymore. "I'm saying I don't see a future between us. And I wish I did, and I tried, but it just isn't there, and that's why I'm not ready. Why I'll never be ready." I pause, taking a deep breath. "I'm saying we're over."

I wait for his protest.

I wait for him to say something mean, to get back at me.

I wait for any sort of reaction.

But his silence speaks louder than any words could. It tells me that he's always known there was no future between us, that he's always seen the expiration date, that we were always just a temporary distraction to him.

The realization hurts more than I thought it would.

"I should go," I whisper. And then I ease off the bed, backtracking, picking up my discarded garments and tugging them back on as I follow the trail back to the door. I shrug into my coat, and then let my hand hover over the doorknob.

But I can't open it.

And I realize I'm waiting.

He needs to say something. Anything.

"Skylar?" Patrick calls and I drop my arm back down, chest constricting and opening at the same time.

I turn.

He leans against the wall, chest bare, elastic shorts hugging his hips, hands settled into his pockets. And part of me wants to take it all back, because he looks good and for a while he was mine. But there's no going back. And a bigger part of me needs to move forward.

I wonder what he'll say. Goodbye? It was fun while it lasted? Or maybe he'll curse at me, spill my secrets to the world, seek revenge. I'm used to messy endings. John and I broke up in a screaming battle—me blinking through tears as I shouted at him to get out, to go to his other girls, to leave me alone. And Ollie broke me in another way, not loud, but through an earth-shattering silence.

Yet Patrick's eyes are soft when he opens his mouth to speak. "I hope you find what you're looking for."

My lips shift into a small smile. "I hope you do too."

And it's enough.

It's the ending I was waiting for, the one I needed.

With Patrick still watching, I slip out the door and shut it behind me. The tears don't come until I make my way outside and realize how far away from home I am on the busiest night of the year. There are no cabs and the thought of the subway just makes me nauseous. So I hug my coat close and walk, unaware as snow starts to fall around me, white flakes speckling my clothes, my hair.

Maybe this was how my year was supposed to begin.

Alone.

The fresh start I've been seeking. But the idea just makes me colder. My tears freeze against my cheeks.

By the time I get home, I'm numb. Unaware of the world. So far within my own mind that reality seems like a distant memory. Which is why part of me thinks I might be hallucinating when I open my apartment door.

I blink, closing my eyes tight, opening. But the mirage is still there.

Rose petals decorate the floor.

Candles flicker warm and bright.

But I'm stuck on the other side by an invisible barrier, unable to step forward, because I can't tell if I'm walking into my dreams or into my nightmare.

Confession 21

Want to know the real reason I'm a virgin? Because I want to be. Maybe it's idealistic, but I've been waiting to be in love with someone who truly loves me back. So maybe my first confession shouldn't have been that I'm a twenty-two year old virgin. I mean, who cares? The real confession is that I'm a twenty-two year old who's never been in love. And to be honest, that's much more depressing to me.

"Hello?" I call through the door. My voice can pass the barrier but for some reason I can't. The roses. The candles. The romance. It just doesn't seem possible that it could be for me. I'm an intruder in someone else's happy ending.

"Bridge? Did you and your date come home?" I ask, raising my voice just slightly. But there's no response. Maybe they've already moved in to her room? Though I remember her telling me she likely wouldn't be coming home tonight.

I bite my lip.

My eyes shift to the left and then to the right, and I have this out-of-body moment where I wonder how strange I would look to my neighbors, standing outside my door with tear stains down my cheeks, too afraid to step into my own apartment.

And really, right now, all I want is my bed.

I take a deep breath.

Here goes nothing. I cross the threshold, heart rapid in my veins, but nothing happens. A few petals crush beneath my feet, but aside from the subtle crunch, all I hear is silence. Shutting the door behind me, I peer into the kitchen.

"Hello?"

Still nothing.

Taking a deep breath, I walk a little farther, hesitant, and enter the living room. My eyes find him immediately. Ollie. Asleep on the couch. And even though I want nothing more than to zap him from my brain, I can't stop how my heart swells watching him there with his feet resting on the arms of the sofa and his hand flung thoughtlessly over his head. The look on his face is completely peaceful, totally at ease, already soft features made more serene by the candlelight. But the longer I look at him, the more an irrational rage builds beneath my skin.

What in the hell is he doing here? Asleep on my couch? Surrounded by roses and candlelight? My heart tightens, wondering if he could have possibly been waiting for me. But then I remember the countdown, I remember midnight, I remember the sinking realization that Ollie did not come to find me, that I was an idiot for even thinking it. And I shove that little shred of hope into the farthest reaches of my mind.

Ollie did not do this for me. No matter what I might wish for, what—if I'm being honest—I've been wishing for since I was five, there's no way Ollie did all of this for me. It's not possible. And I have to stop believing it is.

Which just leaves one question, who did he do this for?

Hence, the rage. Which, I might add, is growing stronger by the second. My fists curl tighter the more I take the scene in. How dare he use my apartment to set up some romantic evening with a mystery date. I mean, the nerve! Sure, we never dated, but there's a history there that needs to be respected. And I mean, the candles everywhere. Hello? Fire hazard! And what a sneak to tell us he had to work when really he wanted us out of our own apartment. Well, sorry I broke up with my boyfriend and ruined your plans by coming home early, Ollie.

I bite my lip, holding back the urge to scream.

Really, I should wake him calmly, tug on his shoulder, nudge him alive. But before I realize what I'm doing, I'm filling up a cup of water at the sink and charging back into the living room, seeing red—and I don't just mean the rose petals.

"Ollie," I whisper furiously, just to be able to tell myself I tried to wake him up. In case I need justification for my actions a little while later, once I've calmed down and have started to obsessively relive the moment over and over again in my head, freaking out. And then I do what I really want to do, what maybe I've really wanted to do for four and a half years but never had the chance to.

I throw an entire cup of water on his face.

Bulls-eye.

"What the—" he spurts, jerking into a seated position, eyes practically popping out of his skull. Water drips off his eyebrows, making him blink rapidly as he wipes the droplets from his face. Without looking over, he asks, "Bridge, was that really necessary?"

I don't say anything.

I just wait with my hands on my hips.

"Okay," he says, running a hand through his somewhat soaked hair. "I—"

And then he finally decides to look up. All of his features freeze. The annoyance falls away, replaced with what I can only describe as shock, lips falling open, eyes widening. And then that somewhat devilish grin creeps across his face, the one that sort of made me fall for him in the first place. His eyes begin to shine bright as beacons, calling to me.

"It's you," he says.

I cross my arms, putting up the best guard I can. "Of course it's me, I happen to live here in case you forgot."

The smile deepens, grows more mischievous. "You're late."

"What are you talking about?" I ask, shaking my head. "I'm early and clearly I've interrupted something, but I hope you realize how easily you could have burned our entire apartment building to the ground. I mean really, falling asleep when there are what, a hundred candles in the room?"

But the more I speak, the less authoritative my voice becomes. Because Ollie is still looking at me with that look, with his eyes blazing and glittering in the candlelight, and despite my conviction, the tune of my heartbeat changes subtly.

Ollie stands. "I got tired of waiting."

I take a step back as he takes a step forward. "I'm sorry if you got stood up or something, but I've had a long night and I'm tired."

I start to turn, to run, to flee, but his fingers land on my arm and even the barest touch is enough to stop me dead.

"I didn't get stood up," he says calmly. "Like I said, you're late. But you're here now."

Thud.

Thud.

Thud.

My heart pounds—fear or anticipation, I'm not sure what. But I can't concentrate on anything besides the fact that Ollie is still touching me, and I haven't moved out of his reach yet.

My gaze slowly lifts. "What does that mean?"

"It means I wasn't waiting here for some girl," Ollie whispers, tracing a line of fire up my arm. I find I'm not breathing anymore. I'm hanging on his every word instead. Ollie licks his lips, taking a deep breath. "I was waiting here for you."

"Why?" The word tumbles from my lips, made almost entirely of air. A quiet gasp of disbelief.

Ollie lifts his brows, shaking his head just slightly. "Such a typical Skye response. Why do you think?"

But another question is the exact opposite of what I needed to hear, what I wanted to hear. It's another riddle, another game. And even with the roses, and with the candles, and with that passionate look in his eyes, I don't believe this can really be happening. I don't believe him.

I step away, breaking contact. I breathe in cool air, trying to organize my frantic thoughts.

Ollie knows he made a mistake. "Skye?"

But I shake my head. "No, why tonight? Why this? How did you even know I'd be home? How'd you know it wouldn't be Bridge walking through that door instead? Or no one?"

"I didn't," he urges, stepping forward. But I need to think clearly. I need to not be touching him. Ollie stops, dropping his hand and furrowing his brows, confidence shrinking before my eyes. "I didn't know you'd come home. I didn't know if I would be waiting here all night for nothing. But I hoped. Which is why I did all this. I decided to let fate play its hand. If you came home, I'd try one last time to make you see. And if you didn't, it's a new year and I'd let you go. But here you are, you came home. To me. Fate."

Neither one of us moves.

I'm made immobile by incomprehension.

"One last time to make me see what?" I whisper, eyes looking at the candles, at the roses, at my coat crumpled on the floor. Everywhere and anywhere but him.

Ollie takes both of my hands in his. They're small and delicate compared to his callused chef's palms. A heat gathers beneath my skin, warm, a rising tide. My eyes travel to the spot, thinking how perfectly our fingers seem to fit together, as though made to hold onto one another.

And then I finally look up. Right into those turquoise eyes that have a way of undoing me, of making me melt, of shattering all the convictions that so closely guard my fragile heart.

"Isn't it obvious, Skye?" he murmurs. "To make you see how much I love you."

I inhale sharply, releasing a slow breath. Part of me wants to rip my hands away and hide. Part of me wants to wrap them around his neck and never let go. I'm torn down the middle, frozen. But now that the words are out there, I can't ignore them. I can't misinterpret them. I can't pretend they don't exist.

"Since when?" I whisper.

He holds me tighter. "Since I let you walk out my door four and a half years ago."

And with that, I do break away.

I thought I'd buried it, but the pain is still raw, and I'm not strong enough to sit there and take it. And if we're going to finally talk about that night after so long, I can't hold his hands and pretend that everything is okay.

"Ollie…" I challenge, trailing off, not sure what I want to say, to ask.

"Skye," he challenges right back, daring me.

My chest expands, swelling with all the unsaid words I've kept inside for the past four years, all the bitter remarks I ached to scream, all the vengeful accusations I've wanted to yell, all the nasty and hurtful things I've only said out loud in my dreams. But there's something else beneath all of that pain, something I told myself time and time again that I would never admit, not to him, not to anyone. But there it is, pushing past everything else, bringing a confession rather than an accusation to my lips.

"You broke my heart," I whisper.

"Skye." He sighs.

"No." I shake my head. It's my turn to speak. "You say you're in love with me? You say you've known ever since that night? Then how could you do that to me? How could you have been so cold, to not even speak to me, to let me walk out your door in complete silence while you listened to me cry? I don't think you even understand what was so horrible about that night, what made me need to never see you again. It wasn't the rejection. I was prepared for the rejection, I went in there expecting you to turn me down. No, the part that broke me was those few moments when I thought you loved me too. To have that little hope I always tried to ignore actually come true, and then to have it ripped away without so much as a sorry, without so much as a goodbye. Before that night, I never imagined you could hurt me so much. And ever since, it's the only thing I expect you to do."

Ollie steps back as though punched.

I stand firm. Because I meant every word and he had to hear them.

"I hated myself for hurting you," he says, still keeping his distance, vulnerable across the candlelight and the silence. "But you have to understand where I was coming from. Before that night in my room, I never once thought of you that way. You were my little sister's best friend, one of my closest friends. I never allowed myself to cross that line, not ever. And then you were there in my room, beautiful in the moonlight, like some sort of vision from my dreams, and something shifted. You touched me and sparks burned my skin, heat that had never been there before. And then you looked up at me, so honest, and told me you loved me. And I did the only thing I wanted to do in that instant, I kissed you. And it felt so right, I never wanted to stop."

I swallow the tightness in my throat. "Then why did you?"

Ollie shakes his head, laughing darkly, little bitter exhales. "Because, Skye, what was I supposed to do? You were leaving to start college the next day. I was leaving to go back to California, hundreds of miles away. We were in completely different places in life and I thought if I just stopped it, everything would go back to normal, that we would both forget. Only that's not what happened. I went to California and I couldn't stop thinking about you. I couldn't escape the memory of that kiss. And I went home for Christmas that year wondering if maybe you thought the same thing, if maybe it was worth trying. But you never visited the house. You never came over for dinner, never came in to see my parents. Bridget always met you out somewhere. And I realized I got exactly what I wanted. You forgot about the kiss. But you forgot something else too. You forgot about me."

"I never forgot," I whisper, voice raw. How could he think I forgot? For four years, I tried everything I could to push Ollie from my mind. And for four years, I've been able to think of nothing else, no one else. Even when I was with John, it was Oliver who burned in the back of my mind.

Ollie steps closer, still not touching me, but my awareness of him feels like a soft caress, stirring every part of me, zapping my every nerve to life. Our bodies are only an inch apart and palpable energy electrifies the small space. Still though, I make no move to close it.

"Me neither," he says, and his voice brushes warm against my cheek, pulling me closer. "Which is why I came to New York when a job became available. I wanted to see you. And I never meant to show up so unannounced, but when you came in that day, speaking to me like nothing had ever changed, I knew you thought I was Bridge but I didn't care. For a moment, I got an idea of what we could be. But I didn't know if you felt the same way. And I waited, sending you signals, trying to read the look in your eyes. But I couldn't. And then I kissed you, and you ran away, which was a pretty obvious sign that I should bow out. But I couldn't do that either. So that brings us to tonight, to right now."

Ollie brushes his fingers across my cheek, trailing them around my neck, back into my hair. I look up, swallowing as my eyes meet his smoldering gaze, but the words are still trapped beneath my tongue. A shy smile plays on his lips.

"I'm in love with you, Skylar Quinn," he whispers, leaning down so our foreheads touch and our lips rest a tantalizing inch apart. "And I couldn't give up without making sure you knew exactly how I felt. I'm in love with you. Now it's up to you to decide what happens next."

I can't breathe. Can't think.

Oliver McDonough is in love with me.

I've waited my entire life to hear those words. And still, after so much time, I have no idea what to say.

So I don't speak.

I lean up and kiss him instead.

And just like four and a half years ago, the fire sparking between us flares to an inferno in an instant. Ollie kisses me back and before I know what's happening, I'm in too deep. My hands slip into his hair. His arms hug me tight, lifting me onto my toes. We're both hungry after waiting so long.

But there's something else. Something wrong. A prickly sensation in my chest that even the flames won't burn out.

I try to ignore it. I want to. But I can't.

And really, I've been ignoring my gut for too long already.

I break away, ripping myself free of Ollie's embrace, turning my back on him, breathing heavily as I bend over my stomach, eyes on the ground, trying to fight the dizzy spell threatening to overwhelm me. And I realize my eyes have started to burn.

All of my dreams are coming true.

So why am I crying?

"Skye?" Ollie's voice is deep and dark.

But I can't look at him.

"Skye, what's wrong? What happened?" And the vulnerability in his tone just brings me back to the moment four years ago when I asked him nearly the same thing.

"I don't know," I whisper, voice trembling. My entire body is shaking. "This is all happening too fast."

He puts a hand on my arm, but I don't spin around. "We can take things slow, Skye. I don't care about that."

And with those softly spoken words, I do turn. I meet his confused gaze. "Not that," I murmur, shaking my head. "This. Us. It's happening too fast. I was in love with you for most of my life, and then I spent four years trying to stop being in love with you. And now here you are, telling me all the things I always wanted to hear, and it's happening too fast. I just—I'm just..."

I shake my head, trailing off, unsure.

"You're just what?" Ollie asks, stepping back. And I can't help but notice how cloudy his teal eyes have become, how dark, how lonely.

"I'm waiting for the ball to drop," I admit quietly.

He recoils. "What the hell does that mean?"

I take a deep breath. What do I mean? Why am I doing this—do I really want to break my own heart? But as much as I want to reach up and kiss him and make this knot in my throat disappear, I don't think I can. "It means," I say slowly, only understanding the words once I speak them aloud. They're not coming from my thoughts—they're coming straight from my soul. Brutally honest. I try again. "It means that this happened four years ago. I thought I was about to get everything I ever wanted, and then just as quickly, it was all gone and I was left empty. Even though you're saying all of these things, I'm just waiting for something to happen that will take them all away. I'm not sure if I believe that you and me are possible. We're more like a dream, and eventually I'll have to wake up and realize I never had you in the first place."

Ollie's face is stone, not moving as I speak. His brows twitch once and I wonder what he's hiding from me. "So you're saying you don't even want to try?"

I shake my head, because hearing those words from him sends a splintering crack down the center of my heart. "No, I don't know what I'm saying. I just, I feel like I can get my heart broken now. Or we can try and then when it all falls apart, it'll just be that much harder for me to put myself back together again."

He steps closer, touching the tip of my chin with his fingers, urging me to look up. "But what if we try and we make it. What then? We both get everything we ever wanted."

But I don't say anything.

I don't know what to say, because I've been hurt by Ollie before in a way I never dreamed possible. And I don't know if I can see past that, past the pain.

He drops his hand and steps back, squinting. "Do you trust me, Skye?"

"Ollie…" I trail off, looking away, self-conscious.

"It's an easy question, do you trust me?"

But it's not easy. Not really. I trust him with my life. I trust him to protect me, to keep me safe. I trust him as a friend. I trust him to want what's best for me, to care about me. I trust him in so many ways, in every way but one. But for the purposes of this conversation, there's only one way that really matters.

Do I trust him with my heart?

"No," I whisper.

For a moment, I think he doesn't hear me and I can't say it again. But a shudder passes through his body, a pulse of utter defeat, and he sags. I can't look up from the floor as he stares at me, waiting for something more, for something else. But I don't give it to him. After a few moments of quiet, he slips past me. Each step echoes in my ears, louder than the last.

But I'm stuck, immobile. The creak of the apartment door slipping open sounds as loud as lightning, but it's the click of it shutting closed that hits my heart like thunder, booming, impenetrable, rumbling on and on without end.

And then it passes, leaving me totally and utterly empty, swept away in the winds and unsure where I've been stranded.

All I'm left with is one single thought.

One question.

Is this how Ollie felt four and a half years ago when I was the one walking away?

Confession 22

I can finally admit it. I'm in love with Oliver McDonough. I never stopped loving Oliver McDonough. And it terrifies me, more than I think I ever realized. But there's one thing that scares me more, one thing that sends a horrifying chill to my core. And it's the idea that I might regret this moment for the rest of my life, that I'll look back and forever wonder what if.

I'm on my knees and I'm not sure how I got here or when or how much time has passed since Ollie left the apartment. It feels like hours. But I can't imagine it's been more than a minute. And the longer I stare into the candle flames flickering around me, the more I wonder just what the hell I'm doing.

Ollie said he loves me.

And even though I didn't say it out loud, I know I love him. I've known it for a while. I never stopped loving him.

So again, I repeat, what the hell am I doing?

I stand, taking another look at the rose petals scattered along the floor, the candles delicately placed all around the room. I remember Ollie, who fell asleep on the couch waiting with blind faith for someone who might never come. And maybe it's the romance decorating the room around me, or maybe it's the fact that I finally said all the things I'd waited so long to say, or maybe it's just the fact that I know if I don't do something now I'll never have the chance again, but I think of Ollie and I let go of the fear.

I dive off the cliff.

I free fall.

And though I just said I didn't trust him with my heart, everything changes in an instant. Because I've finally admitted the truth to myself. I'm finally being honest. Deep down, I believe in him. In us. Part of me always has, the part that never stopped hoping. The part that's always been falling, that's always been waiting and trusting that Ollie will be there to catch me.

"Ollie," I whisper.

Then I turn to the door. I scream.

"Ollie!"

And then I run.

No shoes. No coat. No purse. Nothing.

There's no time to waste and my head can only think of one thing—finding him. So I race out the door, into the empty hallway, and I fly as fast as I can to the elevator.

"Ollie!" I shout again once the doors open to the lobby, but he's not here.

So I rip open the front door, ignoring the cold, ignoring the ice that shoots through my stockings and into my toes as my feet fly over frozen pavement. It's snowing and it's January and I'm wearing a short sequin dress, tights, and nothing else—but I really don't care. Frostbite be damned. I'm in love.

I'm not afraid anymore. And you know what? A little cold is worth it if it means at the end of the night, Ollie might be the one to keep me warm.

"Ollie!" I yell into the vast open sky.

And then I see a figure pause at the end of the street and I know it's him.

"Ollie," I say again, softer this time, more a sigh of relief, a push to keep going.

But when I close the distance, when I'm a foot away, I stop and stare at his back, unsure of what to say. He hasn't turned around. He's waiting.

My whole body is shivering. My teeth chatter and I hug my arms around my midsection, trying to hold in a little shred of heat. So I totally blame the cold for what I say next, for the slight stall, and don't at all blame any lingering doubts or fears clogging my throat. "I broke up with Patrick tonight."

Silence.

Flurries fall in front of my face, like the tick of a clock reminding me that time is indeed still trudging forward.

"When?" Ollie asks, still not looking around, still facing the opposite direction.

"Before I came home, after the New Year's party. We went back to his apartment, and I thought something else was going to happen, but then I broke up with him instead, surprising us both I think."

"Why?" he says, even quieter this time.

I lick my lips, breathing, watching the puffs of air flutter white before my lips, before evaporating into the black night. "I wasn't in love with him."

Ollie still doesn't move.

But I can't say this to the back of his wool coat. I need to see him. I need to look him in the eyes to know he hears me. So I reach out, slipping my fingers into his, and at my touch, he finally turns around, hope a fire in his crystal eyes.

"I love you, Ollie." His fingers tighten, but that's the only move he makes. So I do the only thing I know how to do when my nerves are at an uncontrollable level—I babble. "I love you, Ollie, and I'm sorry, so sorry I didn't say it before. Because obviously I love you, I never stopped loving you, even when I hated you. And believe me, I did hate you for a while there. But, I mean, let's not focus on that. Because you, me, we have another chance now, and I really don't think we should give it up. Not over a little thing like my being insanely stupid and not telling you this five minutes ago, because I'm here now, in below zero temperatures I might add, telling you I believe in us and I trust you and I want to give us a chance. We need to. Or, I don't know, we'll both—"

"Skye?" he says.

"Yeah?" I look up from the spot my eyes have found in the center of his chest to see Ollie is grinning widely, silently laughing with his eyes.

"Stop talking." And then he takes my cheeks in both hands and kisses me. His lips are soft, almost hesitant. This is unknown territory for us, an honest space we've never been before. And I kiss him back, just as gentle, just as slow, exploring this new sensation gathering beneath my skin. For the first time with Ollie, our kisses don't feel desperate or urgent, they feel tantalizingly untouched by time.

And though I don't want to stop, my toes are growing a little numb and I'm so cold that it's getting hard to move my lips without feeling somewhat like a fish.

"Ollie," I whisper.

"Hmm," he sighs against my mouth.

"I'm not wearing shoes," I murmur and he breaks away, eyes wide as they focus on the ground. "And, I'm sort of not wearing a coat either."

Ollie just shakes his head, lifting the corner of his lip. "So this is what I signed up for?"

I shrug, biting back a smile. "Guess so."

And before I can move, Ollie sweeps me quite literally off my feet, lifting me effortlessly into his arms. And you know what? It's not too shabby of a place to be. I curl into his chest as he walks us back inside. I don't even protest when he makes no move to put me down as we make our way into the elevator. Because his chest is warm and his muscles are firm beneath me, and my hands are too busy tracing lines across his chest, up his neck, across his face. I can't concentrate on anything else.

He doesn't put me down until we're back in the warmth of the apartment. We don't speak. Ollie slips his coat to the ground, and then his lips are back on mine and I don't want to think about anything else.

But because I'm crazy, obviously that doesn't happen. A nagging sensation paws at the back of my mind and I can't help but notice how precariously close his coat landed to a candle. It isn't long before visions of a fire fill my brain, and really, that's the last thing I want to be thinking about right now.

Ollie stops moving. "Skye?" he groans.

"I'm good, I'm good." I shake my head.

He pulls back, eyebrows raised. "What?"

I bite my lip. "Nothing, it's just…" My eyes flick to the coat. He follows, expression growing more amused. "It's just, it's close to the flames and really the candles are a fire hazard and—"

Ollie puts his finger over my lips. "You're probably the only girl in the world who doesn't find this romantic."

"I do," I mutter against his skin, voice muffled. "It's super romantic. It's just super dangerous too."

He shakes his head. "That's just part of why I love you."

And then he steps away, circling the room to blow out each and every candle in the space. The space grows darker around me until only a sliver of silvery light remains— moonlight trickling in from the window. Somehow, it seems even more romantic to me.

"Anything else on your mind?" he whispers, stepping closer.

I shake my head, pursing my lips.

"Are the rose petals a tripping hazard?"

"No," I murmur.

"Is the room too hot?"

"No…"

"Too cold?"

"No…"

"Are you at all hungry?"

And now I know he's just completely making fun of me. So I don't give him the satisfaction of a response. I just reach out, grab a fistful of his shirt, and tug. It's a pretty effective way of getting him to shut up, and I smile against his lips, knowing this is probably the first time of many that I'll use the move against him.

But really, we're both winners here.

And the longer the kiss lasts, the more my mind finally shuts off. The passion that's always burned between us is still there, but for the first time, I don't feel swept away and out of control. I ride it. And all that does is make the fire beneath my skin flare hotter.

Ollie's lips slip from mine, kissing their way across my cheek, down my neck. His fingers trail the path of my spine, slipping lower and lower, pausing at my hips to hold me closer, and then sinking to the edge of my dress. Mine slip beneath the folds of his T-shirt, finding the smooth skin of his abdomen, tracing the contours of his muscles, enjoying the way they constrict as I feel my way up his chest.

Both of our breaths turn ragged. But we don't speed up, if anything we just move slower, enjoying the fact that we have all the time in the world. Our hands explore first, then our lips. Ollie sighs and whispers my name. His love is a physical force, washing over me, cocooning me. And I realize, I've spent my entire life waiting. I don't want to wait any longer.

He senses the change. An electric snap heats the air around us. Suddenly his hands grip my waist, lifting me, and my legs wrap around him. And we're moving, but I don't break the kiss to see where. Because I know. And there's no part of my heart or my body that has the will or the desire to say no.

Confession 23

Okay, so…you probably already guessed it, but, well—eek!—I'm not a virgin anymore. And you know what? The wait was totally worth it. Definitely. Sigh. Ollie is all mine. Please excuse me while I go melt into a puddle on the floor…

Soft yellow light is just starting to seep through Ollie's window, casting a soft glow across the bed. I trace the lines of his chest, watching the shadow of my hand flutter over his skin, marveling at how our bodies mold together. We're like two puzzle pieces that had to get ripped apart before we could see how perfectly we fit together. I almost want to pinch myself to make sure I'm not dreaming, but I know I'm not, because you know, you actually have to go to sleep to be dreaming.

And well, Ollie and I had better things to do than sleep. Trust me.

"What are you thinking?" he whispers.

I glance up, finding his twinkling turquoise eyes, still a little unable to believe they're shining for me. "Nothing."

He just looks at me pointedly. "You know, Skye, that might have worked with other guys you've dated but I've known you long enough to know there's always something going on inside your head. Spill."

Hmm, it would probably be easier to say what's not going on inside my head, because right now my thoughts are zipping from one extreme to the other. We've got visions of a white picket fence and children playing in the front yard on one side. And on the other, the look of rage that will cross Bridge's face as soon as she finds out. Throw in the fact that I'm now a sex columnist with a sex life—which you think would be a good thing, but really it just makes everything I'll be writing more real somehow, less like pretend fiction and more like, oh god what does everyone think about me?—and you've got a small idea of the turmoil stirring my brain.

"I could always guess..." Ollie suggests.

"True," I comment lightly, "but what if you guess something that's not on my mind, and then you put it there, and it's all your fault when I fall into hysterics."

Ollie frowns. "Good point."

"Let's just lie here in peace while we still can, okay?"

But before Ollie can answer, a knock shatters the silence of the morning. Someone's at the door. Someone—

"Oh my god." I sit up, hugging the sheet to my chest, searching for something to throw over my shoulders.

Ollie watches me with a grin. "Here we go..."

But I'm ignoring him. I've already moved on to the rambling portion of the morning. "Oh my god, what if that's Bridge? What if she forgot her keys and needs me to open the door? What will she think about the roses, and oh crap, the candles everywhere? What are we going to tell her? Oh my god, she's going to freak out."

"*She's* going to freak out?" he mutters. And then he opens the drawer next to his bed, handing me a T-shirt. I shrug it on and stand. But then—

"I can't wear this," I shriek, ripping it off. "She'll know it's yours and then she'll ask why I'm wearing it and then she'll see the flowers and the candles. You, you have to go out and clean them up now. You put them there."

"I'm glad to see we're going to handle this like adults," he teases, pulling the shirt he gave me over his torso instead.

"You're right… you're right," I mutter. Breathe, just breathe. "If I'm not calm, she'll know something's up."

"Would that be the worst thing in the world? We can't exactly hide from my sister, your best friend, forever."

"Of course not, it's just, we don't even know what we are yet. And as soon as we tell Bridge, she'll either want us to break up or get married, no in-betweens. We're not ready for that yet."

He clicks his tongue, thinking, and then gives in. "You're right," he says with a sigh. And then the knock sounds again, harder this time. He grabs me by the shoulders, staring at me, forcing me to calm down. "You, go put on some of your own clothes. I'll go clean the living room. And then I'll open the door. You stay in your room until you hear us talking and pretend to just be waking up. Deal?"

He holds out his hand and I shake it, already feeling better now that we have a plan. "Deal."

And then we split. I race to my room, trying to slow down the heart palpitations while I pull on sweatpants and a baggy T-shirt—nothing sexy or romantic in the slightest. And then I wait by my door, listening as the knock comes again. Ollie's feet shuffle over the wood floor, racing back and forth, until finally, I hear the door open.

I wait for Bridget's voice.

Only it never comes.

"Who the hell are you?" Ollie snaps.

My heart stops.

I rip open my bedroom door and jump into the living room, racing for the door. Only halfway there, I see who's waiting on the other side of the threshold. I halt dead in my tracks. Because I know who the hell it is. And really, it's the last person I ever expected to see.

"Hey, Skye," he says, shrugging with an awkward smile.

My mouth falls open, releasing one shocked word on its way down. "John?"

Thank you for reading!

**Don't miss Confessions of an Undercover Girlfriend!
(Confessions #2)**

So, I'm no longer a virgin sex columnist—thank you, Ollie—
but if I thought that was going to make my life easier, boy was
I wrong! John is back in town determined to win my
forgiveness. Blythe is more ready than ever to take me down.
Bridget is totally onto the new twinkle in my eye. And, well,
Ollie is just as distractingly delicious as usual.

So, naturally, I have a few more confessions to make.

Confession #1: I came up with what I thought would be the
perfect plan to keep my relationship with Ollie a secret—
pretend to get back together with John!

Confession #2: It backfired. A lot.

About The Author

Bestselling author Kaitlyn Davis writes young adult fantasy novels under the name Kaitlyn Davis and contemporary romance novels under the name Kay Marie.

Always blessed with an overactive imagination, Kaitlyn has been writing ever since she picked up her first crayon and is overjoyed to share her work with the world. When she's not daydreaming, typing stories, or getting lost in fictional worlds, Kaitlyn can be found indulging in some puppy videos, watching a little too much television, or spending time with her family.

Connect with the Author Online:

Website: KaitlynDavisBooks.com
Facebook: Facebook.com/KaitlynDavisBooks
Twitter: @DavisKaitlyn
Tumblr: KaitlynDavisBooks.tumblr.com
Wattpad: Wattpad.com/KaitlynDavisBooks
Goodreads: Goodreads.com/Kay_Marie

CPSIA information can be obtained
at www.ICGtesting.com
Printed in the USA
LVHW02s0043280618
582155LV00010B/249/P